A Song Of Methuselah:

THE BOOK OF

SOFIA

VOLUME 1

PETER BEALE

To my children

"Who may tell the tale of the old man?"

—Samuel Beckett

OVERTURE

45.4158° N, 141.6732° E HOKKAIDO, JAPAN

The monastery is built above a rocky promontory on the northernmost tip *of Japan. It has been there for over one thousand years. It is a place of solitude and hardship. Access is difficult, visitors rare. None of the monks, not even the oldest, have any idea when or how the old man arrived. Only the fish know. The jellyfish, turritopsis dohrnii, are always in the water waiting for him. They are said to be immortal, capable of an endless cycle from their birth as a bottom-living polyp in the parent hydroid colony, to their liberation to swim free in plankton, growing in size from a tiny medusa of 1 mm with eight tentacles to an adult measuring 4.5 mm with 80 or 90 tentacles, which, on reaching sexual maturity, eat other jellyfish species, but exposed to stress, attacked or sick, can revert to being a polyp again. Over and over, forever. They hover there, in the cold waters of the Sea of Okhotsk which lap the old man's rock, sometimes just one or two widely separated, sometimes in a curtain with their tentacles drifting in the current like lace in a breeze, more and more, as the freezing waters warmed, in large blooms, so many they were difficult to swim through and he got stung often, so often he developed an immunity to them. They also taught him how to drift, his body vertically suspended under the sea, moving to the same subtle currents as the jellyfish with scarcely a movement of his fingers to alter course, rising to the surface to breathe every five minutes or so, the sea now more familiar to him then the monk's cell he so rarely visits.*

In the Book it is said he lived 969 years, and his father 365 years and his grandson 950 years. Remember them? Methuselah? Enoch? Noah? Noah who found favour with God for he alone was righteous among the people of his day? Who remembers their names now? Lost in the mist of time and the myths of history. Does it even matter as the Sun warms our planet?

He slowly expels air from his lungs; each bubble rising to the surface encapsulates a thought.

Do the polyps have thoughts? Can they remember? Distant lives, distant events? Memories. There are no blueprints for memories. As ancient neurons fire across a synapse and in his visual cortex he sees blue. Cornflower blue eyes, a gap-tooth smile. And in his head hears a voice. A child's voice, saying, I am glad you are my friend.

PRELUDE

Three seconds.

Three seconds of a bright sunny morning in July. Temperature 23°C. Sea calm, no wind. An unimpeded view from the clifftop along the north-east coast of Sicily as she fell 50 metres down to the granite ledge.

Death is instantaneous according to the coroner's report.

The Investigating Magistrate looks down the cliff. Knowing he must answer a question.

Did she fall? An accident. Did she jump? Suicide. Or was she pushed? Murder.

If he is honest it frightens him.

What frightens him more is he knows the answer.

What frightens him the most is the answer will get him killed.

"Now, on the record," said Chief Justice Bombelli, the Investigating Magistrate, "I have here a heavily redacted copy of another autopsy you made two years ago in 1971 on the death of a young female. It is signed and dated by you." The Magistrate, face blank, voice neutral, looked at the coroner. "Please confirm your signature and that this is your report."

For a moment the coroner hesitated.

"Yes or no?"

Reluctantly the coroner said, "Yes."

"Speak up, please. The stenographer needs to hear you. Thank you." The Magistrate opened the report. "You identified the deceased, I quote, as a 'white, Caucasian female, 17 years old, weight 54 Kgs, height 1m75cms.' Correct?"

"Yes."

"You performed an autopsy on the deceased. Correct?"

"Yes."

"Your report is remarkably detailed. I am impressed by such professionalism."

The coroner shrugged aside the compliment. "It is what we do," he said.

"You have calculated it would take 3 seconds and that the velocity on impact of a body falling unimpeded onto a granite ledge from 50 metres would be circa 112 kilometres per hour and that death would be instantaneous. Correct?"

"Yes."

"You are sure?"

"Yes. The velocity on impact ruptured all the internal organs. It would be worse than getting hit by a car going that fast."

"You state that the ilium, ischium and pubis of the acetabulum on the left outer surface of the hip bone was shattered by the impact, with multiple complex fractures. Correct?"

"Yes."

"You detail concomitant spinal injuries, significant thoracolumbar fractures, disc herniation, compressed and bursting vertebrae, injury to the osseous pelvic ring and the thorax and chain fractures of the left leg, ankle and foot consistent with a high velocity fall. Correct?"

"Yes."

"Further, you detail multiple open fractures in the left forearm, distal radius and ulna and severe compound fractures of the skull with lacerations tearing the epidermis and the meninges and depressed bone fragments in the brain. You write that the body position at impact is crucial and posit that in this case the victim landed at an oblique angle on her left side. Correct?"

"Yes."

"A blood sample was taken for toxicological examination for drugs or alcohol concentrations. None was found. And there was no sign of menstruation. Correct?

"Yes."

"In your professional opinion was there any evidence to suggest foul play?"

"None."

"I see." The Magistrate makes a note. "Now, under Cause of Death you have written 'Suicide'. Correct?"

"Yes."

"How did you ascertain that she committed suicide?"

"Her body was found on that ledge half way down the cliff."

"Found by whom? By you?"

"No."

"Did you see the body on the ledge?"

"No."

"Did you see a photograph of the body on the ledge?"

"No."

"A drawing, a sketch, a diagram?"

"No."

"And yet you concluded she committed suicide? Why?"

"How else to explain how she got there?"

"She could have fallen?"

"It is possible. Unlikely but possible. Apparently she habitually climbed up and down that cliff face."

"Where did you first see the body?"

"In the morgue."

"Did you receive the body in the morgue?"

"No."

"Who did?"

"My assistant."

"Is this your modus operandi? Your assistant always receives the cadavers brought in?"

"If I am not available, yes."

"He took these photographs?" The Magistrate extracted a sheaf of photographs from the report he held in his hand and spread them across the desk. In stark anatomical detail they showed the severely mutilated body of a naked young female.

The coroner barely glanced at the pictures, shrugged and said, "Yes."

"Following his usual routine?"

"Yes."

"These are all his photographs?"

"Yes."

"Why are there no pictures of her clothed?"

"The cadaver was delivered to the morgue nude."

"By whom?"

"An old man in a van driven by Rizzo the innkeeper and a couple of carabiniere - so I am told. I was not there. I did not interview them."

"Who did?"

"My assistant."

"I see. Was it your assistant who supplied you with her name and her age?"

"Yes. I mean no. He got them from the report made by the carabiniere."

"Which of these pictures were taken before your assistant washed the corpse?"

Silence.

"I have taken the liberty of having certain details in several of these photographs enlarged. I draw your attention to this picture. How do you explain the grab marks and bruising on the inner surface of the victim's upper arms?"

Silence.

"In this picture of the victim's right hand how do you explain the torn fingernails?"

Silence.

"Why is there no mention made in your otherwise exceptionally detailed report of either one of these injuries?"

Silence.

"Did you or your assistant examine the vaginal tract of the victim all of whose internal organs were ruptured by hitting a granite ledge at 112 kilometres an hour?"

Silence.

"If not, how did you ascertain there was no sign of menstruation?"

Silence.

The Magistrate made a note, looked up at the coroner, said, "I am waiting?"

Silence.

The Magistrate made another note. "Who concluded she committed suicide, you or your assistant?"

Silence.

The Magistrate sat back, steepled his fingers, and looked at the coroner. "One way or the other you will answer my questions. In the privacy of this room or in open court. Your choice?"

Silence. A long drawn out silence. Finally . . .

"If I were you," the Magistrate said, "I would be fearful the moment Angelo Lividiani realises the implications of your silence. I am sure he will find out you were here being questioned by me. Good day to you, Signore. Thank you for coming."

SVILUPPO

Sicily, 1973

In the heat of the day, the old man walked through the bead curtain in the doorway of Vittorio Rizzo's small bar, paused for a moment to accustom his eyes to the incongruous darkness of the place, went up to the bar, ordered a café 'ristretto', drank it, paid and left to go the few metres down the narrow street to Ciccio Guglielmo's general supply store, where, since this worthy was in Rizzo's along with most of the adult male population of our village, it was his wife, Mirella, who sold the stranger two 25-kilo sacks of cement, which he picked up, one in each hand, much as if they were filled with feathers, thanked her and walked back, past the bar, out of the village, into the baking countryside. In a silk shirt. Nothing caused more comment. It was beautiful, coloured ivory, no collar, buttoned with three buttons at the wrist and throat. To look at this shirt, and the unaffected elegance it bestowed on the man wearing it, made us immediately and acutely aware of how poor we were, our village, our clothes, our customs, ourselves.

Over the ten-odd years before the murders, once or twice a week, we would see the old man in his silk shirt, his long hair sun-bleached white, held in place by a bandana, walking into the village, having a coffee, picking up building supplies, walking out. Always on foot, his boots covered in dust, never a sign of sweat staining the perfection of the floating silk which most obviously covered a very strong body to carry what he did with so little effort. We speculated who he was and where he could possibly live, but since he never spoke, other than the few words necessary to order his coffee and such things as he needed from Guglielmo's, we were left to wonder. It wasn't until the shepherd, Pietro Paoli, in for a drink and gossip, as was his seasonal habit, his sheep and goats filling the street with their stench and droppings, told us he regularly saw the old man walking far out in the hills, occasionally stopping at the spring on Batistero's farm, heading for the coast. But there was nothing there. Just cliffs. Not even access to the sea, which is why the developers and speculators had left that part of the island alone. And it was at least fifteen kilometres away; a thirty kilometre round-trip on foot – in our heat! It made you think.

To most people an island in the Mediterranean is a small place inhabited by a few locals who are overwhelmed by hoards of summer tourists whom they righteously exploit. But an island as big as Switzerland? With the population of Finland or Norway? Sicily is that – and more. Much more. For a start we are older. Our civilization predates the Scandinavians by thousands of years and the Helvetians by -! What does it matter? We have a saying that when the Swiss are civilised the Mafia will speak. Well, that is not quite fair. We refer to them, the foreigners, as the people from the north – 'dal nord' – and to the older generation of Sicilians, enfolding in their genetic makeup centuries of conquests layered one on top of another, who remember that Italy as a unified country is scarcely 100 years old, this would include anywhere north of Rome. So the old man was always 'il vecchio venuto dal nord'. It was reckoned to his credit that he kept his mouth shut, particularly about himself. We are close, you see, a tight-mouthed race even when we are curious. So this man, who was not really old when we first saw him, became old over the years, but to us he was 'il vecchio' from the beginning, which gave him substance somehow, a gravitas not normally accorded a stranger, leave alone 'un forestiero'. Then, of course, he saw what he should not have seen, which changed everything between us. Forever.

CHAPTER ONE

G.I.P. (Giudici per le Indagini Preliminari). The acronym is on a sign that hangs on the door of one of the two rooms of the old schoolhouse. A guard, with a submachine gun, sits outside the door at all times that the Investigating Magistrate is inside conducting his enquiry from behind the schoolteacher's desk. The witness sits in front of him on a worn wooden bench. The interrogation will be long, difficult and complete.

INVESTIGATING MAGISTRATE: So, let us continue . . . You have read your statement to date?

WITNESS: I have.

I.M.: Is it accurate?

W: It is what I recall. Sofia's . . .

I.M. We will come to that. I wish to understand the death of her parents.

W: Murder. There was a half-baked inquest held back then; must be at least nine, ten years ago. Surely you have a transcript?

I.M.: To be accurate it was eleven years ago. Humour me, okay? I have to cross-check every word of every witness. Just initial each page, please, and give them to the stenographer.

W: Why? Can't it wait till the end?

I.M.: We are in Sicily, you know. See all these files? It is how I run my business. At least this way you will have signed as you go along. Like an instalment plan. Then, if anything happens, I will not have wasted my time.

W: Are you trying to frighten me?

I.M.: No. I credit you with more intelligence. It would be a stupid man who was not afraid.

W: Are you?

I.M.: Of course. All the time. I take precautions; it is why I am alive. It is also why I again ask you to have sandwiches, whatever, sent up here for your lunch instead of going to that place, Rizzo's.

W: It is not possible.

I.M.: Why take the risk?

W: As they say, that is for me to know and for you to find out.

I.M.: Very well. But just to be clear, you will do nothing on your own. This is a matter for the law. Now let me see . . . It is July, 1962, and you were walking from your home in the watchtower, or however you describe it, to the village . . . continue.

W: I had been walking maybe an hour, six kilometres, seven, and I was just approaching Batistero's farm - there's a right-of-way through the middle – and it was hot, middle-of-summer hot, and I was thirsty. I had come to an arrangement with them over the years where I could get a drink of water at their well.

I.M.: This is the well with the mysterious sweet spring water that has now dried up?

W: Yes. There was nothing mysterious about it. Quite the contrary, it was delicious. Anyway, the well was in the shadow of an outbuilding where he kept his machinery and –

I.M.: Batistero?

W: Yes, Batistero. As I came up the track around the building, I could hear voices, angry voices, arguing about something. I saw –

I.M.: I want you to be very accurate now.

W: I am trying to be.

I.M.: You round the corner of the outbuilding and you see what . . . immediately?

W: I clear the corner of the building and I see a group of people in front of the well.

I.M.: A group? What does that mean? Describe exactly what you see in the moment, not with hindsight.

W: I see three men in suits, with their backs to me, one of them in a wheelchair, facing the Batisteros, who stand together.

I.M.: The man and his wife?

W: Yes. Adelmo Batistero has his arms folded across his chest. He looks furious. Giuseppina Batistero, who is taller than her husband, stands close to him, their shoulders touching. Her little girl is holding her hand.

I.M.: Name?

W: Sofia.

I.M.: Sofia . . . yes. Yes. Just so. Now, can you say what they are doing?

W: They are staring at the man in the wheelchair who is pointing at them.

I.M.: What do they do when they see you?

W: Nobody sees me, only the little girl, and she is looking straight at me and me at her when the man in the wheelchair gives an order.

I.M.: Can you recall what he says?

W: I remember exactly: He said: 'You realise I have come here, personally, twice. I have warned you, but you insist on being stubborn which will get us nowhere. My offer is generous, your refusal unacceptable.' Then, in the same sharp tone, 'Ucciderli!'

I.M.: 'Kill them!'

The Magistrate is shocked.

W: Yes. There is the blast of shotguns. The Batisteros are blown off their feet – the parents, that is, because the little girl and I are still staring at each other. For a fraction she glances at her hand which had held her mother's, then to where her parents' bodies lie, then screams, and screaming runs to me and hides behind my legs. I can feel her trembling.

I.M.: How many guns?

W: How many? I don't know.

I.M.: You see them shoot the Batisteros and you don't know?

W: No. You said to be accurate. At the exact moment of the shots I was looking at the girl. I didn't even notice the men had guns. Then, between her screams and running toward me, I saw them well enough because they were pointed at me. Two! They had two of those sawn-off shotguns, luparas I think they're called, aimed by the men standing behind the man in the wheelchair. They tracked the girl as she ran to me.

I.M.: Keep it in the present tense; I see it better. She runs to you. Why don't they shoot her as she runs?

W: A child? Are you mad?

I.M.: Even so . . . Now, the man in the wheelchair – what is he doing?

W: He has turned – sorry – he turns his chair without me noticing. He faces me.

I.M.: How far away?

W: Maybe five metres, nothing, his face is quite unemotional. His eyes show no surprise seeing me there. He says, 'Signore, posso fare un dolce suggerimento: per favour, stand away from the girl.

I.M.: Un dolce suggerimento?

W: Yes, like that, quite softly. 'A sweet suggestion.' And then, 'please'.

I.M.: Weird. And you say?

W: Well, it's more what I think I say because I'm not sure what comes out. I say something like, 'what difference can it make?' And he says, 'Certo, it is not your lucky day'. And he opens his mouth and his two men wait to shoot at his command when the little girl . . .

I.M.: Yes?

W: Sofia steps out from behind the safety of my legs . . .

I.M.: What!

W: Yes. She holds out her hand, palm first, to stop them, like this. And she says, 'No!'

I.M.: No! Extraordinary!

W: She is still trembling. I can see it and so can they, but the way she defies them is complete. Seemingly, she is totally unafraid. There is a moment, an eternity. The man in the wheelchair finally nods, says, 'Basta!'. Then to me, 'You understand your responsibility?' Then, to his men, 'Andiamo!' The two gunmen seem surprised, they hesitate, then lower their weapons, push him away to a car I have not noticed before. From the car he looks back at us, and from us to the bodies bleeding in the dust beside the well, then back to us again. With his thumb and forefinger he makes a gesture of sealing tape across his mouth. Then the men put him and the wheelchair into the car and they drove off.

I.M.: What make?

W: I don't understand?

I.M.: What make of car?

W: A black one.

PAUSE. The Magistrate shakes his head. He makes a note.

I.M.: A black one? I see. How long does all this take?

W: I don't know. Three, maybe four minutes.

I.M.: What do you do?

W: I am trembling. I can feel the adrenalin pouring through my body. I shake so badly I have to kneel in the dirt. The child is crying. It is as if we have to comfort each other. I hold her thin body in my arms and she wraps hers around my neck. Paoli, the shepherd, finds us like this. He heard the shots up in the hills where he grazes his sheep and came down to help us.

I.M.: Did you call the police?

W: That's a laugh. Of course we did. They didn't show up for three days and by then we had buried the parents.

I.M.: Without a benediction?

W: What could a priest do? Make the smell go away? Anyway, the Batisteros had no time for the church. They were old-fashioned Communists. We wrapped them in shrouds and buried them by the spring. It's what they would have wanted. When we were done Paoli made that same sign of sealing his mouth with tape. I understood . . .

I.M.: What?

W: How clever it was. I was trapped into silence because of the girl. There was nothing I could tell the cops without endangering her. The Batisteros were dug up again during the inquest, a charge of manslaughter by persons unknown was found and then we had to re-bury them. In proper coffins this time. The whole thing was gruesome and left me feeling guilty. Still do.

I.M.: And the girl through all this?

W: She never left my side.

I.M.: How old was she then?

W: Sofia? Eight, I think.

I.M.: Now – this is important – did you recognize the men?

W: Then? No.

I.M.: But you knew who they were?

W: I do now. That pig's sicari, Lividiani and his hired killers.

CHAPTER TWO

I am determined to tell the truth in this matter. I had a front row seat to a drama that unfolded slowly over twenty years. I came to know the actors well; in my own way I played a small part. I am the schoolteacher – no, let us say, I was the schoolteacher. Twenty-eight years ago the war ended and our country has still not recovered. In our small community we're down to one hundred eighty inhabitants, mostly elderly, from an original population of over twelve hundred, with all the young blood leached away to the cities, the Continent and America, to such an extent that the school shut its doors for lack of students and the Church for lack of a congregation, obliging us to share a priest with three neighbouring villages (and all he does is officiate at the evermore frequent funerals which are the mesura that orchestrates the sad, slow melody of our life). Very few of us have work. Real work that is, not what we invent to fill the day, to kill the hours between drinks. Of course, I speak of the men.

Men who were formerly road-builders, masons, stone-cutters, roofers, plasterers, carpenters, farmers, bakers, brewers; men who could build a house or a bridge; plant a crop and harvest it; grow grain and bake their own bread; who could tend vines and make wine and the barrels to put it in; clear a field, divert water, erect un-cemented stone walls which would stand for centuries, so perfectly were they dressed; artisans, apprenticed from their earliest youth to an endless line of fathers, whose distilled knowledge was their only inheritance, a bitter treasure destined to die with them for a lack of heirs. Real men, born to labour. So they may be pardoned for swallowing their extra glass of cheap rosso da Rizzo, in a commune of vanished dreams and shared delusion.

Women? What of them? After their primary function, they do what they have always done: cook, clean, wash, mend, iron, complain. They certainly do not come into Rizzo's. A fact Don Angelo chose to ignore the day he dropped off his wife and two small children while he attended to business in the village. Although the man was a cripple and had a genuine difficulty getting about in his wheelchair, nothing of importance happened in our village without it being his affair, which, of necessity, required his personal attendance. Certainly, as a man of respect, like most of his peers he could have obliged those in trade with him to travel to Nicolazzo, a distance of 40 kilometres, where, from an undistinguished fortified compound, comprising a manor house and two other buildings, that dominated one side of a sleepy piazza – whose other three sides were reputedly occupied by relatives or retainers of the Family – he ruled without pity over his fief. Maybe he moved about to give the lie to his handicap, or to pre-empt the thought that his lack of mobility was in any way a weakness – who knows. Suffice it, that as poor as we were in our village, we had to have certain basic supplies, and, whatever these may be – nails, alcohol, medicine, cement, toilet paper, the list was endless – they came from him . . . had to come from him, as was made clear to those hard-heads who thought they could avoid paying him his pizzo, his protection money, who tried to circumvent him, whose trucks mysteriously caught fire, whose bank loans could not be renewed, whose material lives hit a wall. Directly or indirectly, he controlled us and affected a despotic interest in our welfare, which in turn dictated his well-being and gave meaning to his acceptance of the honorific title, Zu, uncle. Zu Angelo. Who gave a party every Easter we had to attend, obliging us to dress in our best clothes to bow before his generosity and eat the sumptuous food we could never afford on our own. The uncle from whom the poorest of the poor could get a loan - at a hundred percent interest per annum when it could have been a hundred and twenty.

Ironically, it was our ever-declining population that drove him into a frenzy, and lent a paranoid undertone to all his meetings, laced with the suspicion that dropping demand was part of a conspiracy to impoverish him. And, since he could do nothing about it, perversely this gave us some comfort, although none of us were brave enough to voice the thought.

What we did discuss, endlessly once we had seen her, was his beautiful wife. How or why any woman with such a divine, gentle face, always slightly hidden behind a short veil, would or could give herself to a confirmed psychopath, leave alone mate with a cripple, incited the wildest speculation. Added to which her sensuous body, just hinted at in the modest black dresses she favoured, was a lubricious spice in our frustrated imaginings. To say nothing of her legs, which were impossible to hide, and to which one's eyes, unbidden, were drawn, particularly when her bodyguards looked away.

They were always there, the two of them. Surly peasants from Don Angelo's natal village who got out of her car almost before it stopped, checked the street in the usual way, which had something both menacing and comical about it, yanked open the bead curtain to make sure nothing had changed in the bar, then rather graciously opened the door to the rear compartment and helped this lovely woman step out of the vehicle with her two children, a boy and a girl, always dressed as if for Sunday, their shoes shining and their hair coiffed to a ridiculous perfection.

This small group then waited while her car pulled forward and Don Angelo's took its place. From the open rear window the children learned what their father would do to them if they did not behave, which was followed by a curious entertainment, his wife being obliged to contort herself uncomfortably to put her head through the same open window to be kissed, affording us onlookers an admirable view of her no less admirable posterior. It was embarrassing and humiliating, but then maybe it was meant to be, stamping, as it did, his possession of her on all of us pretending not to look. It didn't seem to bother her though, and, standing straight again, she would not enter the bar until he had driven off.

Coincidence, that jester in human affairs, played a hand the first time this lady and her two children visited Rizzo's. They had hardly sat down and ordered, through one of the bodyguards, she, a coffee, the children, ice cream, (and I surreptitiously tracing in my mind the perfection of her mouth), when the bead curtain rustled and there stood the old man in his silk shirt.

In the heartbeat it took the bodyguards to recover from their surprise, he was at the bar, with a quick nod to Rizzo polishing glasses and a glance around the room. If he noticed anything different he gave no sign.

'Un caffè - ristretto,' he said.

CHAPTER THREE

WITNESS: I don't really remember the first time I saw her, just that one day she was there, in Rizzo's, with her children. I had no idea who she was, nor did I immediately connect her with the bodyguards. They were my concern, though I tried not to show it, since, of course, I recognized them, as they did me.

INVESTIGATING MAGISTRATE: From Batistero's?

W: Yes. The gunmen, now older, but the same two. They were propped against the far wall. It was also obvious that others in the bar knew something. But what? Since nothing happened, I drank my coffee, paid and left. Nobody said a word. It . . .

I.M.: What were you going to say?

W: Well, it seemed disloyal to Sofia not to do something to avenge her parents after so many years. I felt guilty about my silence, still do for that matter, as I said.

I.M.: What could you do? Omerta.

W: That's the point, whatever I did, if anything happened to me, she would be alone again.

I.M.: And by then she was . . . ?

W: Fifteen, nearly sixteen.

I.M.: You were in effect her father.

W: In effect? I wouldn't say –

I.M.: If you look after a child from eight to sixteen you can legitimately claim some kinship. After all, you adopted her. I must tell you, this is an aspect of the case that troubles me. Didn't she have relatives?

W: None willing to take her in.

I.M.: The authorities then, a home, an orphanage . . . ?

W: Why be obtuse? They'd put the word out. Nobody would come near her.

I.M.: Well, wasn't it awkward? I am curious. How did you manage, day-to-day? It must have been difficult for you.

W: What has that to do with your enquiry?

I.M.: You are right. It is an unforgivable intrusion. I apologise. Let's move on. You give your date and place of birth as 1896, in Hawaii, on the island of Molokai.

W: Yes.

I.M.: Doesn't that make you an American?

W: No. Hawaii was a republic then. My mother was on a ship out of San Francisco, bound for China. I was premature. The captain thought it wise to have help. What has this . . .

I.M.: Please, be patient. Her name?

W: Ilse Bélanopeç.

I.M.: Nationality?

W: Swiss-Hungarian.

I.M.: Which?

W: Both. Her mother was Swiss, her father, Hungarian.

I.M.: I see. And your father?

W: . . . Unknown.

I.M.: You hesitate?

W: It gets complicated. My mother was pregnant when she got on that boat, alone but for her other children, two girls and a boy. We were all very different. Forty years ago, in the '30s, when I had a short career writing in the movie industry in California, a man came up to me on the set - this was on a ranch in Santa Barbara - and asked after my mother by name. He was a native Indian, a Crow, an old stuntman of legendary reputation. We talked briefly and I enquired how he knew my mother. To which he just smiled, and then, unexpectedly, said: 'I am glad you have her eyes.'

I.M.: You mean . . .

W: I don't know. He left the crew when we finished the shoot and I never saw him again. I guess it's as the Jews say, only the mother is known.

I.M.: That is extraordinary. Did you ask her who he was?

W: I couldn't. She died before the War.

I.M.: But . . . oh, you mean World War 1?

W: Yes.

I.M.: I am sorry.

W: For death? It comes to us all. Isn't that why we're here?

I.M.: Unfortunately. So what happened to you and your siblings after your mother passed away?

W: She died in China where she had followed Qiu Jin, a revolutionary she had met in a martial arts school in Japan who went around dressed as a man, part of Sun Yat-sen's Tongmenghui. Qiu Jin was beheaded. No one knows exactly how my mother died. We were shipped back to Europe by the Austrian consul and split up, entrusted to different relatives. I ended up on the estate of a great-uncle in Schleswig-Holstein in a place called Bad Oldesloe and he turfed me out as quickly as he could to a boarding-school for orphans in Saffron Walden in England. I never saw my brother or my sisters again. With the tens of millions who died in the war or were killed by the Spanish flu they simply disappeared along with the rest of my family. I... I don't like talking about it.

I.M.: Santo cielo! . . . and then to look after a child. How did you know what to do? Were you married before? Did you have children?

W: Once. In Africa. I don't want to talk about that either.

I.M.: Che complicato!

+

Of course it was complicato, bloody complicato. Who said life had to be simple? Yet he was right to be curious. A seed is always planted innocently. Stating the facts changes nothing, though they might beg understanding. A man takes in a child, a girl. What was familiar becomes awkward. A simple habit, taking a pee in the garden after dinner while checking the weather by the night sky before turning in, is suddenly a furtive business. I swam naked, dived for the rocks naked, lived naked. Suddenly clothes, clean clothes, tangled hair, brushed teeth, proper meals at proper times, assumed an enormous importance — self-inflicted, because there was none to say otherwise. You just do it. Become responsible despite the nagging notion that the course of your life has been changed. And that you might be inadequate. Somehow you feel better. Of course you are culpable. How could you possibly replace a mother and father? Or remotely imagine that a small child would grow into a beautiful young woman.

✝

I.M.: Continuiamo . . ? Go back to meeting Lividiani's wife.

W: Sorry. I had been working very hard for several years attempting to rebuild the watchtower, and the routine, walking from the coast to the village for supplies, was haphazard, depending on what I needed to continue. I never brought Sofia with me, but left her things to do, always making sure that Paoli saw me on the path in, we having agreed that he would watch over her in my absence. So what happened next was an accident, literally in fact. I came into Rizzo's one day and Don Angelo's wife and children were there again. By this time I had seen them on several occasions and knew who they were and had made the connection between them and the bodyguards. I was at the bar drinking my coffee when I became aware that something was not right. The usually quiet children were squabbling, the girl teasing her brother over some toy that belonged to him and that she held just out of his reach across the table where they were sitting on either side of their mother. She seemed distracted and not inclined to intervene, apart from asking them to be good, which, for once, they ignored. As the quarrel escalated a palpable fear infested the bar. It had the effect of unnerving the bodyguards. They were hesitant, exchanging glances and almost embarrassed at what was happening in public on their watch. The boy chose this moment to lunge for his toy and in the process knocked over his sister's hot chocolate which went everywhere. The effect would have been entertaining if not for what followed. Reacting out of all proportion to such a simple accident, the bodyguards bellowed, charged at the children, one hitting the boy hard enough to knock him off his chair. The children were hysterical, their mother terrified, the habitués of Rizzo's, frozen. And I, God's fool, choose this moment to open my mouth.

I.M.: What did you say?

W: Come here, children. I have a story for you.

It was the way he said it, quietly, a peculiar timbre to his voice, his Italian foreign, but exactly right for a storyteller. And what was pandemonium a moment before, became calm. While Rizzo cleaned up the mess, the old man went to a vacant table, the children following. When he sat down, the boy climbed on his knee as if he had always done that and the girl pulled a chair close.

"You are not burnt?" the old man said.

"No," she said.

"What is your name?

"Allegra." She looked at her brother. " He's Guido."

"I see. Now let me clean your dress and then we will start."

From his pocket he took a silk handkerchief and wiped chocolate from where it had splashed her.

"That's better," he said, and glanced across to her mother, still seated at the other table. What transpired between them is impossible to know. Some say it is pheromones, an alchemy of invisible molecules hanging in the air, transmitting their scented messages to those who would receive them. Who can tell? Whatever it was, all in that room sensed it and were terribly afraid for them. It would be the duty of the bodyguards to recount, in every minute detail, what had happened and Don Angelo's revenge for this affront to his respect would be appropriately ferocious. But not today, not now.

Now, the old man said: "C'era una volta . . . "

CHAPTER FOUR

"*O*nce upon a time, far in the North, there was a small, rocky island connected to the mainland by a single, rickety bridge, overlooked by an old, old castle, at the foot of which was a village. Very few people lived there anymore. The rain came down endlessly, moss grew on the rooftops, weird ferns pushed out of the soggy ground. It was a time for toads and leeches.*

A strange couple inhabited the castle, he, scarcely taller than his pet monkey which followed him everywhere in case he got lost, she, a wobbling jelly of good intentions. Lord and Lady of all the land they could see, which, in truth, was not much, it had been their custom to travel when they were young because they were curious and wanted to learn about the world. But, instead of buying souvenirs to remind them of all the exotic places they had been, they collected animals and birds and fish and insects. This was not something they intended to do , it just happened, the way things will. Her Ladyship would be un-packing their luggage in Dar-es-Salaam, and a centipede with a missing leg would fall out of his Lordship's colonial shorts. 'Oh, look,' she would cry, 'the poor wee thing is limping. Quick, find a matchbox and a lettuce leaf!' Everything would stop until the centipede was safely in its new house.

In the same way they had found a pair of striped kittens abandoned under their bungalow in Bangalore and put them in a shoebox. They fed them with milk from a goat with one blue eye and one green eye who'd been found eating the rug in their car while they were having a picnic on the beach in the Bay of Bengal. Since the goat refused to leave the car, they brought it along and found it had many uses apart from its appetite to eat whatever it saw. It rode in the backseat and made an excellent babysitter for the kittens who were always trying to crawl out of the shoebox to explore any open door or window. Gently taking them by the neck in its mouth, the goat would put them back in their box. Its patience was exemplary and only came to an end some weeks later when the kittens had grown so much that it was discovered they weren't kittens at all, but tigers. This created something of a fuss on the boat home, as the other passengers refused to eat in the dining room with this odd couple and their animals. The Captain thought this was nonsense and made sure they sat at his table throughout the voyage.

Over the years a great variety of creatures ended up living in the castle. Macaws, parakeets and cockatoos flew screeching in the rafters, disturbing families of bats trying to sleep; cobras, pythons, vipers and rattlesnakes huddled under the ancient, pinging radiators in an effort to keep warm and out of the draughts whistling under the doors; the knitted cobwebs of all the many spiders grew so thick in places it seemed they held the walls of the castle together instead of the other way around. Great Danes, Irish wolfhounds, German shepherds, Hungarian pulis, Mexican Chihuahuas, Irish setters, Welsh corgis, Rhodesian ridgebacks, French poodles, Chinese chows, plus a few mongrels, were sprawled on chairs, beds, carpets, sofas, under the grand piano in the ballroom downstairs, and behind the harpsichord in the library upstairs, getting in the way of servants and kicking up a tremendous din at mealtimes. In comparison, the porcupines and hedgehogs, the lonely armadillo, the lizards and geckos, the giant Komodo dragons, and an assortment of bugs and beetles, were quiet, going about their business of trying to eat without getting eaten.

On this particular day, his Lordship had gone down to the beach and was hopping from rock to rock, hoping the sun would come out so he could catch a rainbow in his butterfly net. He was peering up at the clouds through his very thick eyeglasses when he distinctly heard a baby's cry. Startled, he looked at his monkey, only to find his monkey looking quizzically at him.

'Did you hear that?' his Lordship said.

The monkey nodded.

'Wherever could it be?'

The monkey shrugged, and then they heard the baby cry again. This time it did not stop.

"It wanted its Mummy," the little girl said.

"Exactly," said the old man.

"Go on," said the little boy.

'So they looked everywhere and finally, caught in the rocks where the waves had pushed it, they found a coracle, which is a sort of small, round boat made like a basket, and, wrapped in a blanket in it, a baby girl, with one big blue eye in the middle of her forehead. They stared at her and she stopped crying to stare at them. Then she smiled a beautiful smile and held out her arms to be picked up. Bending down to do that, his Lordship saw a note pinned to the baby's blanket. On the note was written: 'They wouldn't let me keep her.'

Tears came to his Lordship's eyes and blurred his glasses, so it fell to the monkey to pick up the baby. His fur tickled her nose so she giggled. 'Wonderful,' said his Lordship, and later he was to repeat this to his wife while she cradled the baby in her arms, gazing down into that lovely blue eye.

'It was wonderful,' he said. 'As if the sun itself was shining in her face. That fat bumblebee of yours came to have a look and it must have told half the island before we could get back across the beach. Such a reception, my dear! They all peered into the basket, the dogs trying to lick her, the birds singing their best songs, that damn goat eating the note. What shall we do?'

'Whatever do you mean?' said his Lady.

'About the baby?' he said.

'We'll adopt her,' she said. 'She'll be very happy here.'

'What a love you are,' he said, giving his wife a kiss. 'I knew you'd say that. Now, what about a name?'

'Shhh,' said his wife, as the baby closed her eye. 'She's falling asleep. Anyway, you've already named her.'

'I have?'

'Wonderful. She's Wonderful,' she said.

CHAPTER FIVE

ere he stopped. With his particular gravitas he explained to the children that someone was waiting for him to come home and that they would continue the story another day. He put the boy down from his knee, shook hands with him, bent and kissed the girl's cheek, and left after a glance at the mother to whom he nodded an acknowledgement. Of exactly what was debated by us at length, but she certainly followed him out with her eyes until her children ran to her full of comments and questions about the strange story they had just heard. Which, curiously, were much the same as our own, because we had all listened and subsequently retold the story to those unlucky ones who were not in Rizzo's that day, to such effect that the story began a life of its own, and, as each chapter was added by way of these chance meetings in the bar between the old man, the woman and her children, we couldn't help wondering how far he would get before Don Angelo wrote 'finis.'

I am a pedantic sort. Not for nothing was I a schoolteacher, trying to give form to language being used by our children as if it were chewing gum and they were talking with their mouths full. Generations of inbreeding didn't help and if you went far enough back we were all interrelated, which threw up the odd moron but also some original specimens. I recall one of them, an untidy brute, Bugugnani, the son of our postmaster, idly wasting time gazing out of the classroom window instead of applying himself to proving the theorem about the line A – B passing through the point C. When I called on him to stop dreaming, he cheekily replied that he had finished. "That's impossible," I said, and to teach him a lesson, ordered him to bring his paper to my desk, which he did, while his comrades smirked in anticipation of his downfall. The meaningless gobbledygook he had scribbled was much as I suspected, but his conclusion was masterful: ' . . . if the line A – B does not pass through the point C, it is not far off!' Today he is a dentist in Montreal.

Which leads me to my point: you cannot know what goes on in the mind of another, however intimately you think you know them. The memory of my late wife arrives, un-invited, God bless her, who was in the habit of projecting Marcello Mastroianni into what I innocently thought was a private passion between us when we were making love. I only found out long after her death in the confession of my neighbour, that bastardo, Pizzuta, who was once our mayor, when, on his own deathbed, he told the priest to make sure to tell me he could make my wife come without recourse to the famous movie star. Think of all the treachery involved here. Quite apart from her infidelity, she told him a secret she wouldn't admit to me, her own husband. He put horns on me, relished the fact for years, and, knowing the priest for the blabbermouth he was, saved up this juicy item to the last in the sure knowledge that he was going somewhere I could not get at him. The sanctimonious wretch must have enjoyed the thought that the priest's absolution was salvaging his soul for something he'd indulged in for years. During school hours, if you please. Nice touch that – he insisted the priest give me this detail. I pretended it was a lot of rot made up by the jealous faggot, but, given that she'd seen every Mastroianni picture at least six times, there was no way he could have known of her fantasy without having been told by her in the privacy of lust.

Well, they're dead and I'm here. Time has healed the pain, though small boys still make horns with their hands behind my back when they think I won't see them. And it makes me wonder what private fantasy the Mafioso's wife entertained when she thought of il vecchio in his silk shirt.

CHAPTER SIX

INVESTIGATING MAGISTRATE: Is it your feeling Angelo Lividiani knew you were telling his children a story?

WITNESS: Of course. Why not? His men heard every word. Everything was reported back to him. Even out at the tower he had us watched, done discreetly mark you, but there was no way it could be hidden. Paoli would warn me when he saw strangers and I am sure he told them what we were doing.

I.M.: Still it is strange he did not stop you?

W: Telling a story? Why speculate? Somewhere it suited him, obviously.

I.M.: This went on for . . . ?

W: A year or so, until . . .

I.M.: In all that time did you ever speak to Signora Lividiani?

W: Never once.

I.M.: You understand, I am looking for motive.

W: To justify murder?

I.M.: More to explain it.

W: What has any of this to do with Sofia?

I.M.: I am getting there. You have said you never took her with you when you went for supplies; understandable when she was a small child, but as she grew older . . . ?

W: She badgered me to come along. We almost had fights about it, particularly when I told her I was telling the children the story about

Wonderful which she thought belonged to her. She was almost in tears. How can you tell them my story, she said, you wrote it for me. Stories are like paintings or music, I told her, once created they exist to be shared. You should be happy the children love your story. Then why can't I meet them, she said. How do you explain to a child the morbid evasiveness of a community which wanted nothing to do with her after what had happened to her parents in a culture where being nosy might get you in trouble? I was trying to shield her. With hindsight it was stupid of me.

+

It was the day of her sixteenth birthday. A day that would change everything. Our lives had a routine based on the labour involved in restoring the watchtower. When I was on my own and undertook this task as a way of burying the unmitigated memories of the war, the routine was deliberately such that it soon obliterated any need to observe holidays, feast days, or any other special occasion. Never mind days, I rarely knew the month I was in. I lived like a naked savage, with no neighbours, no timetable, no allegiance to anyone, no obligations.

The date the tower was built, or how long it stood guarding the coast, is not known exactly. Constructed of stone, round in plan, two-stories high, its function was to serve as a place from which to detect danger, whether from marauders or pirates or an invading enemy force, and give early warning to the villages and towns inland by the lighting of a fire on the roof, the smoke and flames of which could be seen for many miles. There was a succession of these towers built on prominent locations and their effectiveness is mentioned by Caesar himself when Proconsul in Sicily, at which time he already called them 'venerable'. To a Roman nothing was 'venerable' unless it had stood at least a thousand years, so a conservative guess would suggest they were built circa 1500 BC. For centuries before that the fires were lit directly on the ground, as can be seen at sites where multiple layers of ash have been excavated under the foundations of ruined towers, confirming both the efficacy of the system and the intelligence of those communities using it.

My tower was destroyed by one in a series of earthquakes which followed the eruption of Mt. Etna in 693BC., leaving nothing but part of the ground floor intact, tumbling the rest of the massive dressed stones, some weighing more than a ton, down the shattered cliff face into the sea 80 metres below, where you could see them, lying piled in a jumbled field of debris covered in coral and seaweeds, on those days when the water was calm.

The strategic usefulness of the place found an odd attestation when an anti-aircraft battery was temporarily stationed there in 1943, part of Montgomery's Anglo-Canadian force advancing up the east coast, bogged down by the determined opposition of the outgunned Italian defenders, outnumbered five to one, fighting a desperate delaying action against the invading Allies. I first saw it when our truck driver stopped to cadge a cigarette off a mate he knew in the ack-ack crew. We were on our way from Syracuse to Catania with a load of special ordinance we needed to blow up a road or a bridge or a railway line, I can't remember, we blew up so much stuff back then, and we all got out to stretch our legs and enjoy the view. It was Bojidar Kaloyan, our Bulgarian killer, masquerading as an interrogation specialist, who correctly identified the site for what it was, having previously seen intact watchtowers here and there on islands in the Mediterranean basin. He is dead, like so many others, horrendously killed in a futile attempt not to betray his friends, his exquisite musician's hands squashed to pulp in a metal vice and then chopped off. I know I suppress these memories, along with the equally horrific stories of what we did in our sabotage-and-demo squad, but after getting demobbed in '47, when the show was over, dumped in London with the Thames frozen and pea-soup fog you could cut with a knife and rationing of everything from hot water to margarine, I needed a bolt-hole in which to hide and forget and I remembered this place.

In the early '50s , the provincial government was more than happy to sell a few hectares, a small grove of olive trees on a hill and a useless ruin to a madman in the middle of the devastation that had overwhelmed their country.

From the start, I decided to do everything myself, convinced of the therapeutic value of blind labour. I thought of myself as hardened by war, in body if not in mind, but grossly misjudged what was involved. The goal was to rebuild the tower with the same stones with which it had originally been constructed. In hindsight this was completely idiotic, but given my then mindset, consistent with the monkish penance I felt I had to make for having destroyed so much. I had the vague notion I could complete the project in five years; in the event it took fifteen. Just clearing the site took a year of backbreaking work, ironically involving the same skill-sets I had been taught in the army

I lived in the open, with a groundsheet stretched over a line tied between two trees as the only shelter more from the sun than from bad weather. There was a sweetness to the very morning air, when the waning moon and the morning star conspired to make each new dawn an event of such lightness one could forget the heavy hand of history on Sicily. The distant smell of rosemary, thyme and lavender; the buzz of honeybees awakening; of the dew being gratefully savoured by goats in far-off fields, who knew, as I learned, that twenty minutes after the sun came over the horizon it's implacable heat would parch grass even in the darkest shade. Half-an-hour into each morning's work got rid of the romance.

While clearing the site it became obvious that five distinct challenges had to be overcome if the tower was to be re-built. First, the foundations would have to be reset on bedrock that had itself been shattered by those long-ago earthquakes; second, a device needed to be invented to bring up the stone from the seabed; third, the stone had to be freed from the accumulated debris of centuries under the sea and some efficient way found to work for lengthy periods 5 to 10 metres underwater; fourth, the actual design of the tower, identifying each stone and how each stone fitted; fifth, building the tower.

Finally, burning off an overgrowth of scrub and thorny bushes revealed that even when cleared, the site was not large. The original builders had quarried the stone on the spot, the local pinkish granite being well-suited to their purpose. Adze marks could still be seen in the rock face from which the stone had been hewn, and gave me goosebumps when I cleaned them out, so close did I feel to those ancient stonemasons. In the quarrying they had cleverly created the level space on which to build, and of this perhaps a third had fallen into the sea, but enough was left to deduce an original platform measuring 18 metres by 12. On this, the semi-circle that remained of the tower's foundations projected out to a building having an inner diameter of some 6 metres, with walls up to two metres thick. That part of the ground floor wall still standing was shoulder-high in most places, but for an opening for a doorway, with stone jambs and lintel intact, by which it was possible to guess an original ceiling height of about 2 metres, low by modern standards, but maybe people were shorter then. Assuming 2 metres clear per floor, plus the thickness of the floors themselves and the stone roof, each was approximately 1 meter, the building had an overall height of 6 metres, with a parapet wall enclosing the roof. It was immensely strong and obviously designed to last forever. Nature decreed otherwise.

At irregular breaks for lunch or tea, I would fool around trying to puzzle out solutions to problems that kept popping up – how to support the floor and roof loads for instance, how to belay the rope ladders I needed to get up and down the cliff, how to improve the latrine and septic tank and what to grow in the leach field, how to maximise fresh water from the solar powered desalination plant I'd rigged up backed by a small electrical generator. If I couldn't find a solution I would set the problem aside, convinced that over time I would acquire the necessary skills to overcome any difficulty.

Sofia became part of my life in the summer of '62, by which time I'd been working on the tower for nearly ten years. The foundations and ground floor were complete, as was the staircase to the first floor. Where it had taken three months to get the first stone up, it now took as many days. Although the site must have looked a shambles, the tower had an obvious identity, but it was Sofia's first words on seeing it, when I carried her there on that terrible day, which changed everything - "è questa la mia nuova casa?" she said. Is that my new home?

Similarly, when it was nearly finished, which took five more years, and we'd been living in it for a further two, on the day of her sixteenth birthday when Paoli and his son came over for the occasion to ask her a question and it was her answer that again changed everything. As she unwrapped the present I had made her, a simple ring of braided copper and platinum wire which she immediately wore on the second finger of her left hand, she smiled at me and said, "What will you do if I say yes?"

A whole world lived between those two questions.

+

INVESTIGATING MAGISTRATE: Off the record. It is a fascinating story you tell, but it's getting late. My wife asked me to invite you to dinner. She's an excellent cook.

WITNESS: Is that wise? I thought you were meant to be impartial?

I.M.: Who cares? I'm hungry. We live nearby. My car is armour-plated and I have a police escort. So, yes or no?

W: 'When last seen, the State's witness was observed dining in the home of the Investigating Magistrate!'

I.M.: That sounds about right.

W: They'll have a field day at the Giornale.
I.M.: Fuck 'em. I'm going to tell her you're coming.

CHAPTER SEVEN

ignora Bombelli was not just a good cook, she was a great inquisitor. As soon as they stepped in the house she shouted from the kitchen to come in because she was not quite ready. In the steam and smell of the place, simultaneously being kissed by her husband, stirring a sauce and handing the old man a heady glass of Nero d'Avola red, she took command of the interrogation as of right.

"You unfortunate man," she said. "Sit there. Make yourself comfortable. You won't mind dining in the kitchen? I didn't think so. I am Sicilian. I told this poor excuse of a husband, bring him here, let him see that Sicily is not all made of swine, like that Lividiani. Una merda. It is unspeakable what he does, may God curse his name. My heart goes out to you. Did you love her? Of course! How could it be otherwise? I am told she was of such beauty it was like seeing a miracle. Here, try this." On a wooden platter was an array of thinly sliced salami, cacciatore and soppressata. "If I talk too much, tell me to stop."

Her husband laughed. "Good luck," he said.

"What do you know, Bombelli? Women intuit things. It comes from the gut, not your vaunted objectivity. Put a man and a girl together, what's going to happen? The Gods decide."

"Don't listen to her," Bombelli said.

"Don't listen to him," his wife retorted. "He's uncomfortable talking about sex and cannot remotely imagine what takes place in the mind of a 16-year old girl. You are how old, Signore?"

"Old old," the old man said.

"At least sixty?"

"In my seventies, what does it matter?"

"Madonna! Ha, Bombelli, beware I will leave you for this titan. Take your shirt off, please."

"Here in the kitchen?"

"Well, I'm not taking you up to the bedroom with my husband watching!"

"Let him at least finish his pasta," said her husband, laughing harder.

"Is it always like this?" said the old man.

"With her, always."

"Please, indulge me," said Signora Bombelli. "I need to confirm something."

To his own amusement the old man acquiesced, put his glass of wine down, unbuttoned the cuffs and collar of his shirt, took it off and when the inspection was finished, put it back on again.

"I am told you have fought in many wars but you have few wounds," said Signora Bombelli.

"Luck," the old man shrugged.

"I would be frightened to be badly wounded. Were you frightened?"

"Sometimes."

"What did you do afterwards?"

"After combat? Sleep. Dream. Try to avoid nightmares."

"No, after the war."

"It was almost a superstition not to think about that - in case you didn't make it." The old man found to his surprise that he was enjoying the exchange with Signora Bombelli and when she offered to refill his glass he had not been aware it was empty. "Thank you," he said. "The one time I was seriously wounded and ended up in hospital, an Aussie sergeant in the bed next to mine asked me the same question. He'd lost a foot and was practising using crutches. He said to me you know what you're going to do when the band stops playing, they give you a medal for putting on a jolly good show and kick you out onto a garbage heap of unemployed yobos? Nobody really gives a fuck about you, me or any of the mental retards in here. Let me give you a tip, nick every piece of gear you can lay your hands on - bullets, guns, bombs, a tank if you can find one, whatever's out there. Good money in it. So I teamed up with him and became a thief. We were good at it too. He had found and requisitioned an abandoned warehouse where we stashed the stuff and by the time I was demobbed 18 months later we had enough war surplus gear to equip a battalion and some very dodgy customers willing to pay cash and not ask any questions. It's how I got the money together to buy the tower."

"And in between?"

"Sorry?"

"Between the First and Second World Wars? What did you do?"

"Knocked about. I had few skills other than what I was taught in the army. I had no wish to go back to England where it was almost impossible for an unskilled man to get a job in 1919 so when I got out of hospital -"

"Again?"

The old man smiled, rubbing the back of his left shoulder. "I doubt anyone other than the generals got through the First World War without getting wounded. After Verdun I was treated in France so I stayed in France, in Paris, which, in '18, had been bombed and shelled by long-range cannons the Germans called Paris-Geschütz which terrified the city but compared to the trenches was paradise for a recovering soldier. Somehow I was immune to the Spanish flu which was decimating the population and I thought that would help me find work."

The old man's face was a mask. He shrugged and stopped talking. Signora Bombelli reached out a hand in sympathy to cover the old man's where it lay on the table next to his once-again empty glass.

"I am sorry." she said.

"You cannot help asking yourself why me? Why am I still alive . . . I don't know why. The past makes me sad. It marked me and used to bother me. Now -" the old man shrugged again. "It is not something I like to discuss."

"And in Paris?"

"I was a student. I lived cheap in a broken-down atelier where Eiffel housed the workmen who built his tower. I still remember the address, 49

Rue Boissonade on the edge of Boulevard Raspail in Montparnasse. The place was a rat's warren -" the old man hesitated . . .

"Go on," said Signora Bombelli.

"Let the man eat," said her husband.

"Zitto!" Signora Bombelli shushed him. "Continuare," she told the old man.

"To get in you had to go through a small metal door in a red-brick wall covered in soot and ivy, walk through a garden of dead plants and weeds and try and get past Madame Lucette, the concierge - you really want to hear all this old stuff?"

"Yes," said Senora Bombelli, leaning forward. "Every detail. Leave nothing out."

+

Chère Madame Lucette. The thin-lipped spiteful face behind lace curtains, plucked eyebrows raised in mute question: Who are you? What do you want? Where have you been? But under the purple toque with the zircon brooch hiding her thinning grey-dyed-black hair was an inquisitive mind living vicariously through the lives and misfortunes of the multitude flowing in and out of the refuge she oversaw. For all the zeal with which she nailed backsliders whose long-overdue rent she was supposed to collect was a woman with a soft heart broken once by the loss of the only man she had known whom she impulsively married at the outbreak of war and who managed to get himself killed in the enemy's opening salvo 'en me laissant veuve et vierge'. She supplemented her meagre widow's pension and miserable concierge salary with occasional modelling down the street at the Académie de la Grand Chaumière where everyone from Bourdelle to Zadkine took pleasure in limning her slim rotundity and putting fin to her long-preserved virginity. She started my career in art by feeding me - 'Tu es beau mais trop maigre.' - insisting I share the stew she had been cooking on her stove until, suitably fattened up, I could join her in modelling at the Académie for a few francs a day. This led to other jobs. Nobody had any money then, we lived like cockroaches scrounging whatever we could, so between poses I swept the floors in the studios, cleaned paint brushes in buckets of turpentine, stretched un-gessoed canvas on frames, ground various minerals to mix with gypsum, chalk, linseed oil and egg white to make paint, until the day an English artist, Walter Sickert, overseeing a class, said 'Don't just sit there, have a go.' He took me under his wing and just like that I became a painter. 'Loosen your mind, boy,' he said, 'and loosen your wrist.' It took some years for me to understand what he was getting at but I slowly developed a style of my own. Madame Lucette was thrilled. "You know they say he is a suspected murderer in London. Jacques le Ripper. Only kills prostitutes. I don't believe it, mais, qui sait, derrière lui il y a quand même des cadavres."

She relished gossip the way a gourmand looks forward to a good meal and when we had our own little murder - 'Pauvre Mademoiselle Fifine, 5eme étage gauche - a limited actress, but that should not get you killed. She was pregnant, I'm told. Va savoir!' - the juicy details coming out every time you walked past her lodge. "Monsieur Pyotr, a moment. The police came back. I told them it was dark that night, a storm brewing, the Quartier empty of tourists, no footsteps in the gallery, but I know what I saw, believe me, there is no mistake. Through the palisade I could see in the Passage a woman drinking in the bistro and a man buying wine from Legrand. It was going to pour but that didn't stop M. du Pont turning up on his bicycle with a new painting for Mme. Celeste, the owner of the dry cleaners. They pretend to be just good friends but I know they are having an affair. I saw some photos he left on the counter there, supposedly of his holiday in August, walking on a beach hand-in-hand with a woman and I saw them together in the Louvre and on the deck of a bateau-mouche going under the Pont Neuf. 'Good friends', my eye. She's married, you know? He's a nice man, takes her to Igor's restaurant, where she falls asleep. He's so boring. Igor buys pictures from M. du Pont, so I'm sure he knows. He likes nudes. He has that daughter that lives in New York with a man she hates but cannot leave. Stupid, right? Anyway, what I wanted to say was the other day, Sunday, when it started snowing, our landlord, M. le Comte, lives across the street in his mansion with that jealous wife of his and their newborn baby, on his way to Mass, spots the young man he suspects of being in love with his wife strolling along with another woman! Pretty enough, I suppose. He tells his coachman to follow the boy and report back. They go into Willi's Wine Bar to meet some friends, a rough lot. They look like refugees from the Balkans, I can always tell, hiding behind their beards. And more women. God knows where they find them . . . you can guess, I'm sure."

Signora Bombelli was laughing so hard tears were squeezing out of her eyes.

"Shall I go on?" said the old man.

"Yes, of course, go on, go on."

"The cops are questioning everybody who knew her," said Madame Lucette. "I'm sure they'll get to you. Of course nobody saw a thing and all the newspapers tell different versions of the same story after they ask the voiturier and even the waiters from La Rotonde and Le Select for their opinion. Upstairs Mlle. Fifine's flat is immaculate; I know, since I clean it. But it cannot be re-let because it is now the scene of a crime and the cops have found photographs suggesting there might be a woman involved. M. Weill, 1st Floor right, says, no, find the person driving the Peugeot with the Belgian number plates. A man in a blue hat was seen getting out of it in the storm. Grandmaster Ivanov, who's since disappeared, while moving a pawn in the room next door, thinks he heard a scream which the Chinese couple on the 3rd floor confirm. All her leading men are questioned . . . good looking lot . . . but not murderers. They even question Fifine's brother, beat him up, he knows something the cops say. Who's he protecting? I could have told them. I know what went on behind those lace curtains. What will M. le Comte say when they find his fingerprints on the teacup I left unwashed in her kitchen. 'Ridiculous!' M. le Comte said. 'I was with my wife.' Even their baby didn't believe that."

After so many months of silence, in the warmth and conviviality of the kitchen, he found himself talking on and on, encouraged by the empathy he saw in the face of his listeners. It was only walking home afterwards that he wondered if he had not said too much.

+

About Sofia. It was filtered at first because he had never discussed his own feelings with anyone. Not even in his own mind with himself. Never acknowledged the panic he felt which came and went when he realised his responsibility in caring for the child. His reactions, almost impossible to express, leave alone put into actual words. You see two people murdered and end up holding their child in your arms? Of course it was difficult, beyond difficult, something unimaginable. In a way it was like being back in the front lines. Before every mission the doctors drilled into us that for anybody seriously hurt the first 24 hours were critical. The victim would almost always be in shock, traumatic shock if they were injured, emotional shock even if there were no physical symptoms. Lie them down, keep them warm. No food, no water. Check no racing heartbeat, no clammy skin, no cold hands, cold feet, dizziness, rapid pulse, shallow breathing, enlarged pupils, nausea or loss of consciousness - until the medics gave the all-clear and everything went back to normal. So I did all that. But what can be deemed normal in the case of a child who sees her parents assassinated? Does the brain shut down? Everything happened so fast I was in shock, never mind the child. I couldn't put her down. No, to be accurate, she wouldn't let me put her down once we got to the tower, her 'new home'. Left on her own, even for a moment, she crouched on the ground, chin on her knees, arms wrapped around her legs, looking at the floor, whimpering. So I carried her everywhere wrapped in a blanket. I tried but I could not find the words to get through to her. How did she accept what had happened? I have no idea, her pain impossible to imagine. Death vomited on her. The shocking blast of the guns robbed her of the reassurance of her mother's hand, the warmth of her fingers twined in hers - instantly gone. Nothing. Her own small hand, impossibly empty. Her mother - gone. Forever. Gone. All her life she had been part of a triangle, mother-father-daughter, anchored by the familiar geometry of place, their farm. The familiarity of having a mother who woke you up for breakfast and made sure that you were dressed properly for the day. Gone. Of seeing your father out in the field turning to wave to you from where you were watching him through your bedroom window, father knowing you were there watching, you knowing he would turn and wave. The beck and call of domestic habit. Gone. Your toys lined up in an order only you knew, the one-eyed teddy bear unable to go to sleep if it didn't have the grimy long-eared rabbit in its arms. Gone. The door that was there where it had always been. The windows, there. The light that came in just so and the shadows that moved in their pre-ordained way across your room. Disturbed by nothing more than the slow change of the seasons. Order. Your chair at the table, papa's chair to the left of you, your mama's chair across from you. Without looking, your bare feet know the texture of the mat next to your bed. Gone. All gone. Uprooted and replanted in less than a day, an instant orphan to all that was familiar. To begin again. A new life with a stranger in a strange place. 'Is that my new home?' she said, slipping on a new reality like a new jumper, the freakishness of her situation - our situation - only becoming apparent ghost-like, a photographic image in a chemical bath slowly emerging into focus.

What was strange, even bizarre, seen from the outside was an arrangement seen from the inside, from our side, that was natural because it couldn't have been otherwise. We clung to each other. We had to. Make-do with each other because that's all we had. Life moving forward however haphazardly. For weeks she was almost mute, turned inwards. All she said was 'devo fare la pipi' when she needed to go to the toilet. Both there and not there.

I felt useless. Fortunately, sleep saved us. Sharing the warmth we generated wrapped together in the blanket, we slept for most of the first two days under my tented groundsheet. I doubt if she weighed 20 kilos, her breathing was so light she hardly moved. It was only when the wind got up and made the groundsheet flap that I knew I could not just lie there. Various things had to be secured on the cliff face to prevent damage. But as I went to untangle myself her eyes opened and she held out her arms to be picked up. 'I have to go down the cliff to the sea,' I said. 'Go back to sleep.' 'No,' she said, 'Portami con te' - take me with you. So I made a sling for her across my back and like a baby monkey clinging to its mother she went up and down the rope ladders with me. Then she wanted to try on her own and in no time she was scaling the cliff as if born to the task, infinitely more agile than I could ever be. Which is when I found out she couldn't swim. She would crouch on a rock watching me dive. 'How do you breathe under the water?' she said. 'You don't. You hold your breath,' I said. 'Come in. I'll show you.'

She was always ready to learn and she was brave, very brave as long I was near her. I taught her to float, then to dog paddle and then swim. 'You have to open your eyes under the water,' I told her, 'like a fish and if you keep them open you can see the fish and you'll see them looking at you.' By chance the first time she did it she actually saw a grouper and was so excited she wanted to tell me about it that she opened her mouth and swallowed half the sea and came up spluttering. I would challenge her to swim from this rock to that, the distance nothing, maybe two or three metres. You could see her looking, judging the distance, hesitating, looking at me, letting go of my hand, grabbing it back again and then finally making up her mind and thrashing madly to the other side looking back victoriously and saying 'Did you see me? Did you see me?' - each time coming out of the sea freshly minted. It was the echo of my own lost childhood and I wondered if all fathers felt as proud as I did when your child does something new. So doing things was therapeutic. Learning new things was a step out of the darkness she was locked into.

Food helped. It was not important to me. On my own I had eaten whatever I happened to have only when I was hungry. But now suddenly I had to plan ahead and buy what I could not grow to always have the necessary ingredients to make regular meals for us. So whether store-bought or dug up I made it a point to ask for her help peeling potatoes or washing carrots or making a salad. Soon she was a dab hand behind our stove and would laugh at my clumsy efforts and say, 'Guarda. Let me do it. Mama showed me how.' After the nightmare of those first few months, after we had grown accustomed to each other and she felt safe, there was a gradual thawing out as much on my part as on hers as we took on specific roles and mutually helped each other, and I began to see a future for us after the chaos, a strange clarity and a palpable sense of solidarity.

Every evening we would make a campfire with bits of wood - not easy to find in an arid landscape. I would sit on the ground cross-legged staring into the flames and Sofia did the same, sitting on my lap when she was small, her back snuggled against my chest, my arms around her. We saw things in the flames, images gone before you could name them, but the more you looked the more you saw or thought you saw. "There's a bear," Sofia would say. "No, it's a donkey - oh, now it's a dwarf, see?" Once she thought she saw her father. "There's Papa," she said. These evening campfires were as much board meeting as church confessional where we discussed the most prosaic things and the most intimate. Out of the blue one evening she said, "Would you have preferred to have a son?"

Paoli had two dogs, mongrels, better shepherds than he was, and they both instinctively seemed to know that when I had to go to the village for supplies one or the other stayed to guard Sofia. She had an affinity and trust in animals and those two dogs formed an unquestioning bond with her which helped I think more than anything I could do to bring her out of the desperate misery in which she must have found herself. They would play tirelessly with her and often if I was late coming home I would find her asleep curled up with one of them. It naturally followed that she started running the hills with the shepherd and his boy, carrying a long stick and imitating the cries and whistles they used to herd the flock.

Word seeped out of course with all kinds of rude speculation about what had happened and who had murdered her parents which I suppose is why the priest came to call one day. He felt it his duty to enquire why she no longer came to Sunday school and asked anxiously about her soul. He spoke to me as if she was not there listening to our conversation. I could see her looking around, searching, and she finally said, 'Where is it?'

'It cannot be seen, my child,' he said. 'It is the essence of you, that invisible part that is aware, that knows you are living, existing through your feelings and interpretation of the world around you, knowing who you are and that you are, independent of your body.'

'Can I touch it?' she said.

'No,' he said, 'but it is there.'

When he left Sofia said, 'I didn't know I had one. If it can't be seen and can't be touched how do we know it's there?'

'It's a belief that humans have a soul. That there is a 'real' other you,' I said, knowing I was out of my depth. 'Mostly religious, which we use to explain what cannot be explained, that something is beautiful, something is wonderful, something is mysterious. It's the 'something' inside you that unconsciously you know is there. But it cannot be proved.'

Sofia frowned. 'If I have one, do you have one?' she said.

'No,' I said. 'I don't believe any of that. I think it's all part of a fairytale we humans have conjured up out of our ignorance . . . ' and fear of death I was about to add but stopped the word getting out of my mouth.

It was years before we could even refer to that awful day and because she wouldn't talk about it I couldn't talk about it. The breakthrough came when reading one of my books she came across the word evil and for a long time just looked at it and then looked at me and said what is evil? It was too easy to say the opposite of good. We were reading Shakespeare - 'the evil that men do lives after them' - taking turns trying on different voices for the different characters. I had glided over the meaning but she stopped me. 'No,' she said, 'what is it, evil?'

I was hopeless at subterfuge and spoke to her as an adult. 'Good and evil are each a concept that people have invented. Good and evil do not exist in the natural world. No tree or flower is good or evil and the same goes for animals and insects and birds and fish and thunder and lightning and the sky and the clouds and the earth and the sea, the dark and the light, night and day. Nothing is good or evil. We humans invented these concepts as a way of understanding ourselves and explaining the unknown. It is not easy to explain our fear of what we don't know. Why do we do what we do to one another? You are kind to *someone, you love someone, and it is considered good. You don't like them and wish them harm is considered bad. You knowingly and maliciously hurt them is evil. That we are capable of evil makes us afraid. The one certainty in the great unknown is what will happen to all of us and we fear it and fear those who would inflict it on us - death.'*

There. I'd said it. The word lay between us. After an infinity of time, Sofia nodded.

'It is what they did to Mama and Papa. Evil.'

✝

Later that night, in the confines of their bed, staring into the familiar darkness, his wife's head on his shoulder, Bombelli said: "How did you know?"

"The silk shirt."

"I don't understand?"

"The man is an ox. His body has been broken many times and yet each time it is stronger. Those shoulders . . . he looks like the Masai warriors in your National Geographic. But he is hiding from his past, from what was done by him and taken from him and even though they are healed, the scars, physical and emotional, always remind him . . . so he covers them in silk, the softest, lightest thing he can think of. I would like to have seen the rest of him."

"I will recite that in our divorce."

"It doesn't seem possible he's fought in both World Wars – is it true?

"From what I have been able to piece together he is the sole survivor of a very large family from central Europe and ended up in a British boarding school for orphaned children. When Britain and Germany declared war on each other he was considered to be an enemy alien and aged just 17 sent back to his uncle in Prussia who immediately enlisted him in his own regiment for military service in the Kaiser's army."

"So he has an uncle."

"Not for long. He was killed in the same engagement in which the old man shot his English schoolmate."

"Now I don't understand."

"Neither do I. Remember he's not under investigation for any crime. This is all background information. Apparently, unknown to him, this boy who was almost his twin and with whom he shared a desk in class had also been called up, but by the British, and he was serving in the British lines when the German advance at Verdun overran the Allied trenches. In the heat of battle, he found he had killed his boyhood friend. And gets a medal he didn't deserve. It's marked him more profoundly than he lets on, I think."

"Santo cielo!"

"There's more. And this part is really confusing. He takes his friend's place, effectively switching sides, and because he is wounded becomes a British war hero and, as if to redeem himself for what he did in the First World War, fights for Britain in the Second. You didn't believe him when he said he had no other skills, did you?

Silence.

"And now this," Signora Bombelli eventually said. "My God, the lives of others . . . she must have loved him. Pity the poor man. He has to live with what he's lost. He must have been devastated."

"Still is I imagine."

"I wonder how he got into writing for the cinema?"

"I'll ask him."

"You will invite him to come again, amore, won't you? Such stories! I really want to know who killed Mademoiselle Fifine." She rolled onto her side, putting an arm across her husband. "More importantly - did she, Sofia, ever have a boyfriend? "

"Perhaps you should not have mentioned her?"

"I meant no harm. I'm sure he knew that. He seemed relieved to talk about her."

Much later her husband said: "Are you sleeping?"

"No. I am thinking Lividiani must have been, must still be, terrified, if for one moment he thought his wife had ideas about such a man."

"The schoolmaster made the same comment. That's what worries me . . . maybe I shouldn't have let him go home alone in the dark."

And much later still, her husband said: "What are you thinking of now?"

"His hands," she said.

CHAPTER EIGHT

"I only have two hands – I need your help," I said.

"Tell me what to do," said Sofia.

"See those wooden pegs? When I pull on this rope it runs over these wheels, called pulleys. Those ones, with teeth, are called gears. I've drilled holes through them, here and here, so when the holes in two different gears line up opposite each other, if you push a peg through when I tell you, it will lock the gears and the rope won't slip through the pulleys and let the rock fall back in the sea."

"I think I'm too little to reach up there."

"Not if you stand on a chair."

"We don't have a chair."

"Then we'll make one."

"Show me how," said Sofia.

+

She never said no, never once. She was endlessly curious; physically brave; frightened only of the dark and the invading nightmares. What had happened to her haunted the night. She would wake me up screaming, shivering in my arms, reliving the horror, whimpering, thrashing around, calling out to her parents, sobbing. Sobbing sometimes for hours. God alone knows what images played out in her head. As I said I was at a loss, out of my depth. I had no words to comfort her. Just held her. All through those first days and weeks and months. It was unbearable. Her grief exhausted, she would look up at me, her face pale, her mouth pulled back in a rictus. "I'm sorry," she would whisper. "I'm sorry." Close her eyes and at last, sleep.

I had made her a small bed on a pallet next to mine under the tented groundsheet, yet she rarely slept in it, rather using it as her doll's bed. A faded, raggedy doll, a gift from me when she was three. She called it Lorenzita, the only thing she wanted me to bring away from the Batistero farm when I had gone there to get her clothes - the farm which legally was now hers, to which she refused to return until it was too late. She spoke to the doll all the time, as if there were three of us living under our tent, and she would lean out of my bed to kiss its eyes goodnight, then say her prayers out loud, which she did each evening before going to sleep. I had to watch and if I didn't, because I was busy, she would lie quietly awake until I came to sit beside her and hold her hands.

"Dear God," she said. "Look after Mama and Papa. Keep them near you. Make them better. Tell them I am trying to be a good girl and Lorenzita is a good girl too. I am helping my friend build our house. I am very lucky to have him. He teaches me new things every day. Bless him and guide him and keep him safe from danger. Bless and protect Pietro and his family and all his goats and sheep. And also his dogs. Bless me too and look over us all until the morning. I am going to sleep now so tell Mama I remember how she used to kiss my eyelids and that I do the same for Lorenzita and that I love her and Papa and will never forget them and they mustn't forget me. I ask this in Thy name, who taught us to say: 'Our Father, who art in heaven . . . '"

She was usually asleep before she got to the end and then I would kiss her eyelids and hoped she wouldn't open them to see me crying. Although I had known her from birth and seen her often at her farm she was naturally shy as a child and she didn't know what to call me so I was her 'friend' and every now and then, when we were working, I would catch her looking at me, and she would say it like that: "I am glad you are my friend." Her prayers had bits and pieces of rhetoric she'd picked up from the priest or at her old communion classes, but really she was on first-name terms with God. What sounded quaint in someone so young, was no less meaningful spoken in her small voice, and her blessings were a comfort to me who had stopped believing long, long ago. For years though I failed her as I had no magic formula which could explain away her nightmares, and she would clutch on to me, gripping my hands, saying over and over: "Non lasciarmi andare! Non lasciarmi mai - Don't let me go! Don't ever leave me!".

INVESTIGATING MAGISTRATE: You look distressed. Shall we stop?

WITNESS: What is the point of dredging this up? We all know who's guilty.

I.M.: Knowing it and proving it are two different things. If you are willing to testify in court they will claim we have no right because of the statute of limitations, ten years have passed, you said nothing at the time of the inquest, blah, blah, blah. In court they are formidable. I know of a Mafioso, witnessed by an entire village killing his victim in the main square, and in court nobody saw so much as a stray dog that day. Omerta. The rule of collective amnesia. A way of life that dictates each man solve his own problems and woe betide the man who tries to interfere. Clichés maybe, but as true today as in the past. The law must be implacable. I must build my case like a mosaic, each little piece carrying its share of the truth, until, locked together, they present a picture of such irrefutable clarity as to convince the most prejudiced mind. Bear with me, please. I want to go back to something you said a moment ago; two things in fact. You say the child prayed, yet her parents were communists?

W: Yes. So?

I.M.: Strange contradiction, wouldn't you think, sending her to the church, to the priests?

W: Maybe, but they did it . . . perhaps so she could be with other children. Where are you going with this?

I.M.: I don't like contradictions. Never mind. Now, Signorina, read from where he said 'the farm was legally hers . . . '

STENOGRAPHER (from the record): ' . . . the farm which legally was now hers, to which she refused to return until it was too late . . . '

I.M.: Thank you. What did you mean by 'until it was too late.'?

W: Somehow Lividiani acquired her farm and all the land.

I.M.: He claims he went before the Communal Tribunal who had foreclosed on the property for delinquent taxes, and that on the date of the foreclosure sale he legitimately bought the property by paying the past due taxes. He further claims that all the proper notices were posted, the deed notarised and he is being unfairly criticised – his word is 'victimised' – for doing what anyone could have done if they had bothered to go to court. Why do you laugh?

W: The whole thing was rigged. The 'notizia' is in some obscure legal journal in print so fine you'd need a magnifying glass to read it even if you knew where to look. Nobody else shows up in court. There's not a single other bid and he gets it for the price of the property taxes! In less than a year after he's murdered the Batisteros he ends up owning all their land. Talk about adding insult to injury. It's pathetic.

I.M.: But perfectly legitimate. We have checked. Everything that should have been recorded, was recorded. The Tribunal even sent out repeated reminders to the farm regarding the taxes, served a lien, including a final reminder threatening condemnation if the taxes were not paid. We have copies of every document.

W: Don't you get it, her parents were murdered! She's seen them killed and buried. You think an 8-year old thinks 'oops, must remember the property taxes – wonder if they sent me the bill? Better nip up to the farm, step over my parents' grave, see that I don't get dispossessed.' She's an orphan who could hardly read a nursery rhyme leave alone a legal document. The courts should have been protecting her, not conniving in a charade to defraud her out of her inheritance. Everyone knows Lividiani wanted that spring.

I.M.: Ah, yes. The mysterious spring again – motive for murder. Why would he want it? He controls the water around here anyway.

W: But isn't that the point, to have it all? Nothing short of a monopoly seems to satisfy these bastards.

CHAPTER NINE

In the silence of the lunchtime break in the empty schoolroom ringed by shelves loaded with files, a long-ago smell of used chalk still lingering on the stagnant air, an untouched plate of food and glass of wine sits on the table in front of the Magistrate. He doodles on a sheet of paper, lost in thought . . .

He was right, of course. It started with the roads, then the electricity, the gasoline, war surplus, construction, organised labour, whatever they thought essential. They'd always controlled alcohol and prostitution, every kind of protection racket, food distribution, the fishing fleets and thereby, indirectly, tobacco smuggling, tomb robbing and even hiring out the seats in nearly all Sicilian churches, but there was a limit to how much could be made in a poor country from such trade. Drugs were for the big shots, the pezzo da novanta in Palermo, who spent their time blowing each other up in their cars. It was a stroke of genius to see a source of profit in the white dusty dirt roads, la strada bianca, bleached ribbons stitching together the sun-blasted countryside; immense profits from supplying rocks, gravel, asphalt, cement from their own pits and quarries; endless profits in their repair; and a corrupt and willing partner in the provincial government with its hand out to Rome. The sweetness of such graft! Listen how it is called here: 'fari vagnari u pizzu' - wetting the beak! Such an image! Plus the refinements! The refinement in sealed bids! The unbeatable offer! The two cheques in one envelope, both signed, one for a paltry 10,000 Lire, the other blank, to be filled in later with the appropriate amount. How many contractors, developers, entrepreneurs from the Continent must turn away in disgust on learning: 'Scusi, Signore, but you have been over-bid by

10,000 Lire, alas! Better luck next time.' Luck, mi culo. The cuteness of these rackets! I know; they know I know; and they know I can't prove a thing.

How long can this go on? A long time; forever. From the end of the 1ˢᵗ World War the modern infrastructure of Sicily is slowly built up, through the rise of the Fascisti, Mussolini's dictatorship, the rise and fall of the Nazis, the Allied invasion, the munificent bounty of the Marshall Plan, the endless games of musical chairs being played by the successive governments in Rome ever hungry for re-election – and linking all of it, the Mafia, 'putting the island through their wine-press.' We estimate their take just from Palermo at over 100 million dollars a year and for the whole island at maybe 10 times more.

Nothing better illustrates their remorseless consolidation of power than the control of public works, and nothing is allowed to impede this happening, least of all the law – la sonnambula. In fact, in all but name, they are the law. I should know. Too often, in chambers, a Judge has said: 'Your zeal is admirable, Bombelli, but you should let it sleep. Sempre un po' di discrezione. It will do wonders for your career.' Or the Colonel of the Carabinieri, over what was supposed to be the camaraderie of a drink in Palermo at the Birreria Italia, filled, as usual, with Mafioso talking shop, who cautioned: 'Piano, Signor Magistrato. I observe in you a man of conscience. Bene. But learn the rules first, eh? Why put a light on what's best left in the dark? Proceed, yes, but proceed cautiously . . . it is the way to avoid accidents. Piano, piano, no?' And even in church, in the confessional no less, the priest whispers: 'A word of advice, my son, learn to bend. Go with the wind; the reed, not the oak.' Followed by the slightest shrug of the shoulders, that gesture that intimates an insider's knowledge of the futility of charging against windmills. So I can't say I haven't been warned.

Water, in a parched land, is an obvious commodity to be controlled; its scarcity a prop for price, perfect for wetting the beak. Better not to build a dam; let the winter rivers spill into the sea so long as you possess every ancient conduit, every spring, every cistern, ditch and lake. But it never amounts to much financially until the curious vogue for mineral water takes off. That appeals to the pigs. Bottling what has always been free, stick a fancy label on, add a 'Professore's' analysis of the supposed benefits of the mineral contents, mark it up a few hundred percent over cost – a perfect business for La Famiglia. Better still if there is no competition. So, first buy up all the delivery trucks, then all the bottling plants, finally all the natural springs; a remorseless, economical strangulation right up the food chain. As for those who refused to understand, who chose not to sell . . . of course it was motive enough for murder, as if that were ever needed . . . particularly for a sociopath like Lividiani. Files a metre long detail what is known of the man's suspected criminal activities. The medical assessment alone fills a bloated volume. Bombelli has read it so many times seeking to understand the man that he almost knows it by heart. Contracting polio while still a child, the only son of the Cosa Nostra capo of Nicolazzo, he was raised as a man of honour who, despite his malady, was entitled to 'rispetto', something he made sure he got when he succeeded his father when that worthy was sent to prison where he died. Half the checklist of traits related to sociopathy clearly applied to him, from his superficial charm, impulsivity, enormous sense of self worth, manipulative behaviour, callous lack of empathy, remorse or any sign of guilt towards his victims, sexual promiscuity seeking no emotional context and criminal versatility. Conversely, baffling in its contradictions, the man rarely lied, was a responsible leader making realistic long-term goals and plans on how to achieve them, and had no juvenile delinquency record staining his reputation. The choreography of his movements, given the handicap of his confinement to a wheelchair, were well documented and he made no attempt to hide. He claimed he was just a businessman . . .

A discreet cough from the stenographer standing in the doorway to the schoolroom brings the Magistrate out of his reverie.

"The old gentleman is here, Signor Magistrato," she says. "Shall I ask him in?"

"Yes," the Magistrate says. He looks down at the sheet of paper under his hand. On it is written one word: *timeline?*

CHAPTER TEN

INVESTIGATING MAGISTRATE: How was lunch?

WITNESS: The usual. I see you didn't touch yours.

I.M.: Not hungry . . . tell me, do they ask you what goes on here?

W: Who?

I.M.: In Rizzo's.

W: No, we just nod.

I.M.: After all these years?

W: We have nothing to say – nothing in common. Anyway, as I get older, I find I need others less. I'm becoming a savage. It suits me. I'm easily bored by what passes for conversation these days. It's just the same cud chewed over and over. They probably gossip behind my back, maybe even plant a knife or two. Who cares? You know Bukowski's line, 'you get so alone at times it just makes sense'? That's me. Shall we continue?

I.M.: By all means, let us continue. But before we do, I must emphasise that however trivial my questions may appear to you, they all have a purpose. If we ever get to trial you will face a battery of the finest defence lawyers this friend of the friends can buy – and since they have more money than God, believe me they will be the best. They will attack you to discredit your testimony. It will not be pleasant. In many ways you are an inconvenient witness for me. A foreigner, no local family, no connections that might cause trouble, no history, no name, nothing that might become embarrassing to them if it came to the notice of the press. A single man. A convenient target. From the most innocuous questions – where and how did you get a resident's visa; what money do you live on; where did it come from; have you paid your taxes on it? – they will proceed to more devious ones – did you have a proper building permit? By whose authority did the child live with you? Why did you agree to caring for a vulnerable young girl? Did she attend school? Was she chaperoned . . . you understand? They will hint at pedophilia, maybe even try to make that a motive. I will object of course, but even if their questions are overruled, they will plant seeds of doubt in the jury, who will be made up of local people ever-ready to believe the worst in a foreigner and naturally scared of the consequences of finding against la Famiglia. I want to impress on you that our only chance to beat these people is if I know everything, so I can anticipate and pre-empt any line of questioning they dream up.

W: If we ever get to trial . . . ?

I.M.: Yes, well, let me worry about that? Signorina, what did I do with my piece of paper?

STENOGRAPHER: This one, Magistrato?

I.M.: Thank you. Now, I am attempting to make a timeline of events. Okay? Before landing in Sicily where were you stationed?

W: North Africa.

I.M.: Where?

W: Classified.

I.M.: What do you mean?

W: It means I cannot tell you. It is classified information. Secret.

I.M.: The War finished thirty years ago . . .

W: Yes, and secrets are still secret. I suggest we leave it there if you ever want to get done.

I.M.: This is not satisfactory.

W: Probably not.

I.M.: You arrived in Sicily with the British Army in 1943. You are, by then, nearly fifty.

W: No, actually, forty-seven.

I.M.: Correction, forty-seven. Still, rather old to be a soldier, non?

W: I had certain talents.

I.M.: These were . . . ?

W: Classified.

I.M.: Where did you land?

W: Classified.

I.M.: You keep saying that. In court -

W: I will repeat it.

I.M.: It is exactly what I was alluding to earlier. Their lawyers will jump on this, they'll have a field day.

W: So, strike it from the record. None of this has anything to do with your investigation.

I.M.: Perhaps in this instant you are right. Signorina, strike everything onwards from his date of birth.

STENOGRAPHER: Si, Signor Magistrato.

I.M.: Maybe we should call it a day? I like to get home while it is still light. May I offer you a ride?

W: No, thank you.

I.M.: Are you sure? It will be dark long before you get back.

W: Stop worrying, I'm used to it. Like this I get a chance to take my thoughts for a walk.

I.M.: But I do worry – anything could happen out there.

W: Like what? You think a few thugs will succeed where the entire German army couldn't catch me?

I.M.: You weren't alone then.

W: You'd be surprised. Same time tomorrow?

I.M.: Please reconsider. It would be foolish to underestimate these people.

W: Have faith, Signore. Did I not say I had certain talents? I bid you good evening. Please give my regards to your charming wife.

✝

"And that is all you have on the tape?"

The hard eyes belie the quiet voice. Not for the first time the stenographer wonders if she made the right decision. "Si, Signor Lividiani, I assure you I did not switch it off until they had left. The official

59

transcription stops where the Magistrato wanted, but I have brought you everything they said as we agreed. You may compare your copy with the original if you wish."

"No. It is good work, well done. You must continue – being vigilant, of course; they must never suspect you."

"Thank you, Signore. My mother . . . ?"

"I have kept our bargain. Your mother has been moved to a private room with a view over the city, with the best medical care. She told me to tell you how grateful she is. She looks forward to seeing you on your day off and asks that you remember to bring her new shawl. Yes? Bene. So, thank you for coming. I apologise for not getting up. My man will show you out."

Dismissed, the stenographer turns to leave, hesitates, stops, turns back to face the Mafioso. She is trembling.

"Is there something else?" Don Angelo's voice is barely audible.

"I don't know how to say this, Signor Lividiani. The – "

"Say it!"

"The–"

"Spit it out, woman! I don't have all day."

"The old man . . . his eyes . . . when he said he had certain talents, his eyes truly frightened me."

"What rubbish! Why should you be frightened?"

"No, no, Signore. Not for me. It is for you that I am frightened!"

CHAPTER ELEVEN

As I told the Magistrate, one day I arrived at Rizzo's later than was my custom, overslept, must be age, and immediately noticed that Lividiani's wife was there at her usual table and the old man at his, with her two children engrossed in the story he was telling them. It looked like he'd hurt his right arm in an accident, with a heavily blood-stained bandage down to his wrist, over which he had left the silk cuff of his shirt undone. But his voice was the same. It took me a moment to realise what was different - there were no bodyguards.

✝

"Thunder rumbled through the dark clouds, louder and louder," the old man said. *"Then, CRACK!, a tremendous bolt of lightning slashed across the sky, lit up the laboratory and made Wonderful jump."*

"Was she scared?" said the little girl.

"No, she's six by now," said the old man. "How old are you?"

"Nearly seven."

"I'm sure you're not scared of lightning."

"Yes, she is," said the little boy. "She hides under the covers in a storm."

"I do not!"

"Oh yes, you do!"

"So do I," said the old man. "Much safer. But Wonderful cannot hide because she is conducting an experiment. Watched by all the bugs and a

61

white rat with its broken tail in a splint, she stands on a stool carefully pouring water from a pipette into a centrifuge."

"What's that?" said the boy.

"Do you have an electric mixer in the kitchen at home?" said the old man. "It's similar."

"Shh, go on," said the girl, frowning at her brother.

"'Distilled water,' Wonderful says. '70%.' She empties the pipette to the last drop. Then, from a series of beakers, boxes and bowls lined up across the workbench in front of her, she adds to the water, after carefully weighing each item on an atomic scale, a long list of chemicals and minerals which she names as she goes along.

'Carbon: 18% . . . Azote: 14% . . . Phosphorous: 2% . . . Potassium: 1% . . . Sulphur: 0.5% . . . Sodium: 0.5% . . . Chlorine 0.4% . . . Calcium . . . Calcium?' Wonderful looks puzzled, searches the workbench, when, out of the corner of her eye, she just catches sight of one of the Chows diving under a table, a bone in its mouth.

'Wrinkles!' she says. 'Bring that back! How's this going to work if I don't put in the right ingredients?'"

"What's she making?" said the little boy.

"Stop interrupting!" said his sister.

"Wonderful shrugs," said the old man. "She consults a recipe, takes up a soup spoon, and suits her actions to her words: 'Now a heaped spoon of magnesium . . . and one of copper . . . now fluor . . . manganese . . . iodine . . . nickel . . . brome . . . and silicum . . . there.' She gives everything a careful stir, puts down her spoon. 'Let's see — what else? . . . a pinch of cobalt . . . aluminium . . . molybdenum . . . vanadium . . . lead' (she drops in a lead soldier) . . . 'tin' (in goes an old tin can) . . . titanium . . . and borium. That's it . . . ? Hmmm . . .'"

Frowning, she wipes her hands on her apron, jumps down from the stool, approaches the table under which Wrinkles is hiding. Wrinkles growls. Wonderful growls back, gets down on her hands and knees, dives under the draped tablecloth and presently emerges with the bone. In triumph she marches back to the workbench, climbs on her stool, takes up a grater and grates bone dust onto the pan of the atomic scale while Wrinkles barks at her from behind the tablecloth. 'There, calcium: 2%,' says Wonderful. She raps what's left of the bone against the grater, then pours the dust from the pan into the centrifuge, closes the lid, winds up a large alarm clock and sets the time. Checking that all the pets are at a safe distance, she puts her hand on a switch to start the centrifuge. 'Stand by! Here we go!' she says.

She throws the switch, there is an instant surge, a banging and clattering, then a smooth turbine-like whine. Wonderful watches the clock anxiously, as behind her the door to the laboratory opens and in comes the monkey followed by his Lordship. He is scarcely taller than Wonderful on her stool, so he has to stand on his toes to kiss the top of her head and is about to say something when Wonderful puts her finger to her lips, SHHH!, and they all wait in suspense for the alarm to go off. Finally it does and the centrifuge is switched off, they all lean forward as Wonderful lifts the lid and—"

+

And, as in a cheap melodrama, two of Lividiani's hoods choose this moment to come into the bar, hard men we had never seen before. Everything stopped, even the flies that had got past the bead curtain. The men surveyed us, saw the old man, went to him, said something too low for me to catch, but I clearly heard his answer: "Be so good as to inform him that I am telling his children a story. As soon as it is finished I will be at his disposal."

They didn't like that. I thought he would be hauled off, but something in his demeanour stopped them. One went out to report while the other positioned himself beside the door. To no one in particular, the old man said:

"Trust a thug to spoil the punchline."

It is curious how a simple phrase can take on a life of its own. This one was not just adopted by the village to highlight an interruption, but in the re-telling of every detail of the tragedy, it gained currency across the island, a priest even weaving it into one of his sermons, the one about Jesus urging his disciples to turn the other cheek.

I noticed it also made Lividiani's wife hide a smile and I venture to say enhanced il vecchio's reputation, standing up to la Famiglia. We started speaking of him possessively, with the beginning of affection, and, dare I say, respect. Besides, we all wanted to know what was in that centrifuge.

✝

"When Wonderful takes off the lid," the old man said, "inside was some awful-looking, greeny-grey gloop. In disgust, she dumps a spoonful of the stuff on a plate, glares at it and then at her recipe. Wonderful's eye begins to fill with a tear, her lower lip quivers, she looks at his Lordship, then back at the recipe. He follows her glance to where, next to a picture of man, he reads:

The chemical composition of a Human, homo sapiens, is 70%

distilled water, 18% carbon, 4% azote, 2% phosphorous . . . .

He stops reading, picks Wonderful up into his arms, hugs her tight, unable to speak.

'I only wanted to make someone to play with,' she says.

Now it's his Lordship who has tears in his eyes.

'My wonderful wee lass,' he says. 'Try, try, try again. I'm sure good God himself didna get it right first go round!'

As if in answer, a terrific clap of thunder shakes the castle, followed by more lightning and rain dashing at the windows. His Lordship has to shout above the din: 'But ye have a right to ask yerself what the Auld Bugger's up to, muckin' up the weather like this?'"

CHAPTER TWELVE

INVESTIGATING MAGISTRATE: Previously you said Angelo Lividiani knew you were telling his children a story and that for some reason it suited him?

WITNESS: Yes. I told you his men reported every word.

I.M.: So what did he want when you were interrupted?

W: I've no idea. He was in his car parked in front of the bar. He wanted to look at me, he said, then he laughed and had himself driven away.

I.M.: You are joking.

W: Do I look like I'm joking?

I.M.: You were telling his children fairy stories? Then he wants to look at you? I can't make the connection. I'm trying to nail this piece of shit for murder. Are you mad or am I?

W: The man's a psychopath. The children are innocent.

I.M.: They always are. But you, of all people, should know how urgent this is. I only have - never mind. To business - have you seen the newspaper today?

W: I never read them here.

I.M.: Really? Maybe this will interest you though . . .

La Stampa, *Messina, June 17, 1973.*

Two men were found dead in an Alfa Romeo sedan on the road between Catania and Acireale. Their vehicle overturned and caught fire. The bodies have not been identified. It is estimated the accident occurred after 20.00 hours in the evening on October 16. Any person having information who could assist the police is asked to call 96.81.88.

All calls will be treated in the strictest confidence.

W: So what?

I.M.: Isn't that the road you walk?

W: Sometimes, yes.

I.M.: And you saw nothing?

W: No.

I.M.: Leaving here when you did last evening would put you approximately at that location if you walked at a steady pace.

W: Meaning?

I.M.: I'm getting there. It would have been dark by then. The road is straight for at least two kilometres at the location of this so-called accident. There are no brake marks, no skid marks. Yet the vehicle rolls over and catches fire. Curious, no?

W: What can I know? Maybe they were driving too fast.

I.M.: Maybe they had stopped.

W: Make your point.

I.M.: Maybe they were waiting there, on the side of the road,

for someone to come along. You.

W: What is this nonsense? How would they know . . .

I.M.: We know who they were.

W: That's not what it says here.

I.M.: We don't necessarily tell the press everything. Sometimes we let someone else tell us what we already know. It's like fishing. Catch a little fish, hang it over the side of the boat, see if you can't get a bigger fish to bite. You know who came swimming up ever so discreetly to nibble at my bait? A very big fish, from Palermo. Discreetly, mark you, through an intermediary, the mayor of Mussomeli. Two of his villagers had gone missing, did I know anything? What could I know? Nothing, except the coincidence of that also being Lividiani's birthplace, where he recruits all his foot soldiers.

W: And . . ?

I.M.: It bothers me. A straight road. A lonely man walking at night, perhaps trapped suddenly in the headlights of a car he doesn't see – yet the car and its occupants are demolished? I was wondering about the special 'talents' you claim you have?

W: You think I'm a magician who can flip a car over?

I.M.: I don't know and I am bothered by what I don't know. I am even more bothered by the thought of who else does not know. If those men were sent there to intercept you someone sent them. That someone must be asking himself a very big question today. They are dead and you are alive. How come?

W: I had no idea magistrates were given to wild speculation.

I.M.: It's our stock-in-trade. Understand, I don't care about two petty crooks burning up, but I care about my only real witness. The stakes in this game have gone up dramatically if they are attacking you directly. Even more if this is your answer.

(Stenographer's note: the Magistrate points at the newspaper article. The Witness shakes his head.)

W: It's not. I wasn't there.

✝

He's lying. Chiaro. What actually happened? That's what I'd love to know. Unseeing, the Magistrate stared out of the speeding car's window. *Also what prompted Lividiani to send his two men. Why now? Is he scared? And if he is, that makes him much more dangerous. Much more. Means I must be careful. Concentrate, or the old man will end up down a mineshaft and I'll have shit. Maybe that's it, Lividiani knows he's gone too far. His own people disapprove? Cosa Nostra doesn't need this publicity and he has to clean up? No. He could have done that anytime. No? It's . . . It's personal! Must be. Between him and the old man? The law's a sideshow. I'm a sideshow. But getting closer. He'd have a fit if he knew how close. Lamb, she'd said, agnello con polenta, the way I like. Delizioso. Then coffee and a cigar . . . bed. I wish. Still, two hours should take care of the notes. Midnight, that's okay. I should call the coroner. Ask him to be especially careful. If they're not too badly burned, can he tell if it really was the fire that killed them. Because that Alfa was not moving when it happened. Only thing, how can one man put a car on its roof? Doesn't make sense. Not if you're seventy-five. What am I saying, not even at twenty-five, no matter how strong you are -*

"Fanculo!" his driver said as they swerved. "Scuzi, Magistrato. That asshole should get his donkey off the highway."

Typical. What a country. Put the fucking belt on, what's the matter with me? I never follow my own advice to others. That's how easy it would be, carabinieri or no carabinieri. I should have a tank. What a laugh. At least you could ignore traffic jams, roll over whoever's in front. Shit, I forgot the wine. She told me. I'll say . . .

"We are being followed, Signor Magistrato . . . Three cars back, a dark blue Alfa," his driver said.

"Don't they ever buy anything else?"

"I don't know, Signor." He flicked on his radio. Immediately one of the four motorcycle escorts came on.

"Si?"

"Blue Alfa, three back."

"Got him."

"Call for backup. Don't do anything dumb."

They accelerated. In a precise, well-practised manoeuvre, the two Polizia Stradale in front switched on their sirens, broke out of the traffic pattern and streaked ahead, followed by the Magistrate's car, while the two cops behind slowed down, forcing the following traffic to a crawl.

"Do you ever get bored?" said the Magistrate.

His driver shrugged, glanced at the speedometer as it touched 180 kilometres, then up into the rear-view mirror to meet the Magistrate's eyes. What a cool bastard, he thought, he's actually enjoying this.

+

"Policemen and crooks are two sides of the same coin. Neither thinks the law applies to them," his wife said, just before he turned out the light.

"What gives you that idea?"

"It's a game you play, one side breaking the rules, the other enforcing them. But both sides are certain the rules are only for ordinary people to keep."

"Am I included?"

"Maybe. Perhaps not personally; you're too good a man. But what you represent, yes, it's part of the apparatus. The way it is, one side couldn't exist if the other wasn't there, like good and evil. If society were perfect you'd be out of a job and so would Lividiani."

"This is what you think about in your kitchen?"

"It's not a joke, Bombelli. You think I didn't see how excited you were about your stupid car chase. What sort of life is this where I sit waiting every evening with my heart in my mouth dreading a telephone call and you – stop smiling! – you come home to tell me how clever your chauffeur is! I hate it! I hate it! I don't want you dead."

"Please, cara mia," the Magistrate reached for his wife to shelter her in his arms, " . . . amore, please control yourself. You are my life. I am here. Nothing will happen. You must not worry. I'm sorry if I bring the job into our house. I'm truly sorry. Don't cry."

"I can't help it, I'm frightened," his wife said. "I couldn't live without you."

"What can I do?" he said. "I am tied to this thing."

Fear is pervasive, numbing thought and action. Late into the night, the Magistrate lay awake in the bed that had always been his haven, holding to him what was most precious in life, his confidant, his champion, the source of his strength, unable to comprehend why she had so suddenly broken. He knew by her breathing she was not sleeping either and feared, as nothing else, the enormous, growing, silence between them. Her weight on his shoulder, normally so light, seemed also to grow with each passing moment, and he ached with his effort not to move and disturb her. He could feel his blood thudding and, for a moment, panicked, he felt his heart strain. Yet the words he wanted to say died stillborn on his tongue, and only made the silence louder.

CHAPTER THIRTEEN

WITNESS: You do not look well.

INVESTIGATING MAGISTRATE: Rough night. My wife, she . . . well, she worries for my safety. W: I see. Is there –

I.M.: No, nothing. It is not your concern. I should not have mentioned it. She has always been strong; she'll get over it. We should –

W: Something happened?

I.M.: Nothing important. Let's get back to the timeline. You were born, let me see, in Hawaii and came here in '43 with the British, then again in '52, when you bought that ruin, and you've been here ever since.

W: Not all the time, no.

I.M.: Oh?

W: Well, the girl had to know something of the world. Before she was eleven we were making regular trips to the mainland and later all over Europe. She took to it like a fish to water.

I.M.: Wasn't that difficult?

W: Difficult?

I.M.: I mean she was scarcely cosmopolitan I imagine, more a peasant?

W: So? I'm not a barbarian. I felt it important to get her out of here. As much as I could teach her, there were still things she had to see and hear and experience for herself. When I was young, before the Great War, it was fairly common in our milieu to have tutors, particularly if you travelled a lot. It never did me any harm, quite the contrary, so whether here or abroad, wherever we went, I made sure Sofia had a tutor, preferably one with children she could play with, as it troubled me that she had practically no friends her own age. She could read a bit when she first came to me but had never really had access to books. The minute she saw mine it was like a revelation. She was after me to read to her in every spare moment we had every single day and, whatever the subject, she would try a few paragraphs herself. My books reflected my interests and had to do with history, biographies, political science, art, structural engineering, psychology, with a few plays and poems, not exactly stuff suitable for kids. Plus my weakness, Westerns, which she loved, going around in the bushes as an Indian or practising a fast draw as a gunslinger.

I.M.: Westerns? You?

W: You may smile. But once she got the hang of it, she devoured the books. She got hooked of all things on Freud and Jung, loved the idea of the id, the ego, and the superego, and went about charting her conscious, preconscious and unconscious thoughts and behaviour in a journal she kept. Dante was her lodestone - 'l'amor che move il sole e l'altre stelle.' In a way she grew into the different characters that engaged or enchanted her, which she would transpose from one book to another and you could hear her talking to herself as Emma Woodhouse playing with Tom Sawyer and Huckleberry Finn as if they were real people she knew. And anything to do with Sicily captivated her, followed by the questions, endless, endless questions, about Carthaginians, Phoenicians, Greeks, Arabs, Byzantines, anybody and everybody who ever set foot on the island . . . is any of this important? I could go on for hours about her.

I.M.: It's all important. Every detail. Every scrap of information helps me, allows me to put together an image of her, of what went on in her life. I have to understand her to understand what happened. Please go on.

W: One day she read Walter Scott's account of Waterloo and insisted I take her there to see the battlefield. She could not believe that in the space of half a day 48,000 men died in those small fields and gentle hills. As on that fateful day in June, 1815, it was pissing with rain when we got there. From the farmhouse which is still there at Hougoumont she played Kim's game reciting the allied regiments facing the French to the delight of the Duke of Wellington. *"The Scots Greys, the King's Dragoons, the Royal Horse , the Life Guards, the Hussars, the Coldstream Guards, the Royal Welch . . . "* on and on, and the ominous cry *"La Garde recule. Sauve qui peut!"* strange in her small girl's voice. *"How can the French revere Napoleon when what he did killed so many young Frenchmen?"* she said. And when she saw King Vidor's version of War and Peace at the Pagode she sat through all three and a half hours completely mesmerised and walked about for a week afterwards acting Audrey Hepburn playing Natasha. She was bewitched by the movies -

I.M.: So is my wife.

W: - never having been to one with her parents, and she loved seeing films in the old cinemas, sitting on the edge of the ratty seats with her half-forgotten ice cream melting in her hand while she stared at the screen. We saw 'The Lavender Hill Mob' at the Everyman in Hampstead, 'Il Notte di Cabiria' in the Sacher in Rome and when she found out Frank Capra was Sicilian and that I had met him in Hollywood and that he had won Oscars for 'It Happened One Night', 'Mr. Smith Goes To Washington' and 'You Can't Take It With You' she drove me crazy until we had seen all three multiple times in the revivals put on at regular intervals in the Teatro in Catania.

+

One Saturday, coming out of the Cinema Teatro, Sofia said, "I didn't know Clark Gable had such big ears. Did you know him?"

"No. I met him a couple of times but I didn't really know him. He was just starting out back then. I'll tell you an odd thing. I was born five years before him and he died five years after you were born. Only fifty-nine. After five wives."

"Is that what killed him? The number 5, or having five wives?"

"Very funny. He had a heart attack from a blood clot in a vein. Too much booze."

We were walking down Via Filippo Corridoni on our way to a late dinner at La Paglia in the fish market. Even late the streets were crowded and you would have to be blind not to notice the way men looked at Sofia. She hooked her hand to my offered elbow. Fifteen, already 172 centimetres in her bare feet, her mane of blonde hair tumbling down her back to the hem of a turquoise miniskirt and those endless tanned legs. A boy on a

Ducati revved the engine of his bike, grinned at her and shouted, "Dimentica il nonno!" as we went by. Forget Grandpa, bloody cheek. I felt her hand tighten on my arm as a chorus of whistles followed us down the street and another boy called out "Che bomba!" and yet another "Bel culo!" and suddenly we were surrounded by gaping faces, illicit fingers groping and hands making rude signs of fornication. Sofia flinched and I could feel the adrenaline surging in my bloodstream in response to the danger. Nobody noticed a black Alfa sedan silently parting the crowd. A window went down. Something was said to the boy on the bike. He went white. Killed the engine on his machine. Sat stock still in shock while his mates scattered.

The car came level with us and from the dark interior a quiet voice said, "Excuse them, Signore, they are just being boys. You will not be troubled again." The window went up. The car drove off.

"Who was that?" said Sofia.

Lividiani.

++++

I.M.: Dio mio!

W: Wherever we went we were under a kind of discreet surveillance I think. There was always someone around who didn't quite fit. We would be in an art gallery or a museum and out of the corner of your eye you'd see a man patently not there for the art, looking without looking if you know what I mean. I never let on to Sofia what I suspected. She loved painting, one of the few things she tried but was not very good at, despite haunting all the museums and galleries we came across. Her hero was Antonello da Messina whose work was in almost every church and cathedral on the island and provided more heavenly inspiration to her than any boring sermon. I'd once thought I could be an artist and carried around sketchbooks and a box of watercolours to maintain the illusion. So of course she did that and copied whatever caught her fancy, usually some detail like an owl or a rabbit in the background of a lurid crucifixion.

One day I was doodling and Sofia propped her elbows on my desk to watch.

"What's that," she said, "it looks like a face?"

"It is a face -- the moon's face."

"How's that?"

"I'll show you. First you have to recite a nursery rhyme in German: 'Punkt, punkt' - with my pencil I made two dots - 'komma' - I made a line straight down between the dots - 'strich' - I drew a hyphen below the line - 'Fertig ist das Mondgesicht' - I drew a circle around the lot.

"These are eyes," I said, pointing at the dots.

"And that's the nose and that's the mouth. And the circle is the moon! Let me try!" She grabbed the pencil and turning the paper over, suited her action to her words while muttering -

"Punkt, Punkt, Komma, Strich:

fertig ist das Mondgesicht."

She frowned at her work. "Mine's different to yours."

"That's the fun of the thing. They're all different."

She tried again and again. Each time was different. She was delighted and soon had a gallery of moon-faces, smiling, sad, cross-eyed, puzzled, grim, happy, grumpy, and even a mad one with long hair held back by a bandana. "That's you," she said.

She was like blotting paper the way she absorbed everything. Same with writing. In my mother's day, it was her rule that we learn to speak the language of whatever country we were in, and to make sure we did she would label each object in every room of the house or apartment or hotel in which we were living with their local name and a translation underneath, which we were expected to repeat and memorise in short order. So again, I did that with Sofia. It was our favourite entertainment. Wherever we arrived she would race ahead with her glue and bits of paper, sticking them onto everything, every surface, then writing, say, 'tavolo' – 'table', 'la porta' – 'the door', and so on, you understand, cheering herself if she knew the correct translation, looking at me expectantly, her eyebrows raised up under her fringe, if she needed help. In hotels it drove the maids crazy cleaning up the mess, but by fourteen she already spoke four languages fluently and had a working knowledge of two more. Plus Latin, of course, and some classical Greek, picked up from a poor scholar at the Vatican, glad to make some pocket money teaching *(laughs)*. He really fell for her and would blush whenever she caught him looking at her.

I.M.: What an extraordinary child. It's hard to believe.

W: Believe it. I don't make this stuff up. It was hard *not* to look at her. All that work on the tower, diving in and out of the water for hours, hauling rocks, running up and down the cliff face on our rope ladders, totally transformed her physically. As she grew older she grew taller until she was nearly as tall as me. She had the body of a gymnast with the strength of a blacksmith. I am sure it had the same therapeutic value hard work had on me, stopping her more morbid thoughts about her parents. Her curiosity was unbound. She had a verve, a wit, rare in a child. She made poems out of book titles. Danced to tunes she heard in her head. Her independence was magical. One day in Paris, at Lipp, I was about to order the wine and she said 'May I do it this time?', and proceeded to order what I thought was completely wrong for our lunch. When I hinted that perhaps something else would be more appropriate, she was on to me in a flash. 'Let me make my own mistakes!' she said. She was just twelve.

I.M.: You allowed her wine?

W: Of course. We shared everything. She would have her half glass of Bordeaux, pour some water in to make rosé, and offer a toast. You had to lock eyes. You could not look away until you'd had the first sip or you'ld have bad sex for seven years.

I.M.: Esci di qui! She said that?

W: And a lot more besides, God knows. On our trips she was forever picking up stuff talking to porters and taxi drivers, maids and waiters, questioning them about their jobs, their children, their wives, husbands, boyfriends, whatever came along, including an entire dictionary of swear words. We were staying in the Crillon once and having breakfast downstairs engrossed in the Herald Tribune, a habit she copied from me, when three men walked by, obviously Americans from the Embassy next door. One of them hesitated, stopped, then came over to our table. "Well, damned if it isn't the elusive Pimpernel, Major Hart himself. We thought you were dead."

The man had been a colonel, one of Patton's intelligence protéges in the North-African campaign, a nasty piece of work then and no doubt worse now. I hadn't seen him in over twenty years and couldn't remember his name, which he saw straight away. 'Wilberforce,' he said, 'mind if I sit down?' - and went to pull out a chair. Before I could open my mouth, Sofia said, 'We do mind. You have not been invited to sit at our table.' 'No kidding?' he said. 'Get used to it, Missy, I've invited myself.' 'My name is not Missy,' she said. 'My father and I are having a private breakfast. Please leave or -' 'Or what? Hart, is this kid really your daughter? Where'd she learn her manners?' 'Mais il est con ou quoi?' she said, and then raised her voice, 'Monsieur Taittinger, please ask this gentleman to leave our table!' Sitting across the room was a dapper figure, the owner of the hotel, enjoying his own breakfast while going over some bills. 'Mademoiselle . . . ?' he started to say, but got no further when Wilberforce said, 'Did she just call me an asshole?'

'No,' said Sofia, 'asshole is trou de cul. I called you a cunt.'

I.M.: What!

W: It created a nice diplomatic incident, but I'll say this for old Taittinger, he backed Sofia and threw the bugger out. She learned the word from Marcel Pagnol's myna bird.

I.M.: Wait! You mean the writer, Marcel Pagnol? La Femme du Boulanger? That Pagnol?

W: Yes. He was trying to sell his estate in the hills behind Cagnes-sur-Mer and we went up there to have a look. His head gardener showed us around. Sofia wandered off and ended up in the billiard room watching Pagnol playing against his myna which he had taught certain choice phrases. Every time he missed a canon the bird would flap its wings, hopping up and down, saying 'Il est con, Marcel, il est con.' Then the bird would show him how it should be done, skipping on its little black legs across the baize of the vast pool table, lining up the white cue ball by ducking from side to side in order to see the red, pushing the ball with the back of its beak and running after it to make sure it hit the target. It had Sofia falling about laughing, particularly when Pagnol told her the bird's name was also Marcel. The billiard table was so big Sofia asked how it got into a room with such small doors and windows and Pagnol told her some coolies carried it up the hill on their heads, chopping down the surrounding trees to build the house around the table. Sofia could see the myna bird watching her digest this information, shaking its head from side to side. The message was clear: 'Non!' "Je crois qu'il me prend pour une conne," she said to the bird, her grammar faultless. Pagnol was delighted. He autographed a set of his famous books and gave them to her. "Vous avez la chance, Monsieur," he said to me, "d'avoir une fille pareil. Je serais ravi de l'échanger contre la domaine." I was tempted but Sofia was glaring at me.

I.M.: My God! Look, please, we must proceed slowly. Her parents were killed in '62.

W: Murdered.

I.M.: Per favore – alright, murdered. She's eight at the time, you said. So she was born in . . ?

STENOGRAPHER: 1954, Magistrato.

I.M.: Grazie, '54. And at eleven years old, in '65, you began travelling regularly around Europe with her. How?

W: Boat, train, car, plane, the usual – what do you mean, how?

I.M.: Didn't she need a passport?

W: Of course. I got her one.

I.M.: In what name?

W: I . . . Where are you taking this?

I.M.: Answer the question, please.

W: My name! I'd adopted her by then as you know. It's all in the original statement I made. Look it up.

I.M.: Signorina?

STENOGRAPHER: Si, Signore. A moment, please. I have it here . . . yes: 'By way of special dispensation, at the Questura, the registry office in Palermo, the child, Sofia Batistero, aged 11 years, an orphan, was given in adoption on May 18, 1965 to me, her guardian.'

I.M.: Let me see that . . .

W: This is an outrage! I must protest your . . .

I.M.: Bear with me, sir. Were there any witnesses in Palermo?

W: Witnesses? What for? She didn't have a family; in fact she had nobody, as I've already told you. As far as I could gather the State was damn glad to have someone take her off their hands, and even then it took forever.

You can't imagine the paperwork. Finally the village priest came with me, since it had been his idea in the first place, we filled out more papers, a few weeks later they called us back, I signed some things, he countersigned, and that was it. I suppose that made him a witness.

I.M.: Did you get a copy of what you signed?

W: Certainly. How do you think I got the passport?

I.M.: Do you remember the name of the priest?

W: Father Mazotto, Maziolo, something like that. Why?

I.M.: In case we need to corroborate your statement.

W: Well, he won't be much good. He died four years ago.

I.M.: How?

W: I haven't a clue. Old age. Illness. How do people die? Or is that a stupid question in Sicily? Look, all I know is that he's dead.

I.M.: Then we have a problem.

W: Why on earth . . .

I.M.: Previously I told you all my questions have a purpose. The problem we have is that in Palermo there is no record at the Questura of the adoption of Sofia Batistero. Niente. Nothing at all. And before you ask the obvious, we very carefully checked to make sure their records had not been tampered with, altered, effaced, or in any way faked.

W: Hold on. Ten minutes ago you're expressing surprise at me taking her to Europe with a passport, then this pretence that you didn't know what was in my original statement, and now, suddenly, you've already checked with Palermo? Am I an idiot? Is this some sort of farce? I still have the passport and the copy of the documents they gave me. You want to see them? Say so. I'll show them to you.

I.M.: I believe you, but I must ask these questions.

W: So what are you implying? I invented them? They're forgeries? Or . . .

I.M.: Please do not get upset.

W: No. I have every right to be upset. You are questioning me as if I were the criminal instead of a man whose life has been torn apart by murderous vermin who complacently carry on with their lives in the certain knowledge that there is nothing you can . . .

I.M.: Stop! Signorina, off the record . . . Come, Signore, let us get some air. We will walk together.

+

The Magistrate and the old man walk out of the schoolhouse and down the street toward the church in the centre of the village, followed by the carabiniere with the submachine gun. The church is disproportionately large for such a small village and its crumbling yellow stucco façade tells its own story of neglect. The street is narrow, heavily shadowed, and, where it meets the church, flows around it like a rock in a riverbed, to continue on the far side, out of town. The shutters on the houses are closed against the sun. There is no traffic at this time of day. Nothing moves except a few chickens scratching in the dust and a dog that lethargically picks itself up out of their way and then flops back down again once they have passed. The men walk slowly, their hands behind their backs. They do not talk until the village is left far behind.

"Let us sit for a moment," the Magistrate says. In the poor shade of a bedraggled tree beside the road the two men sit on the ground, resting their backs against the tree trunk. The carabiniere moves off some distance out of hearing, to another tree, un-slings his gun, sits, yawns, stretches out and is soon asleep. Slowly the heat of the day settles around them and the susurration of insects becomes the only sound.

"What a job," says the Magistrate. "I feel sorry for him."

"Are they any good?"

"The best of the best. An elite force. Incorruptible."

"And asleep on the job."

"Don't be deceived. Look . . . " The Magistrate picks up a pebble and flicks it in the direction of the guard. At the slight impact of the pebble hitting the ground, seemingly in one fluid motion, the carabiniere is up, crouched on the balls of his feet, his machine gun cocked, his eyes scanning the empty landscape.

"Scusi," the Magistrate calls.

"It is no problem, Signor Magistrato. I always sleep with one eye open for you. It is only right you should test me."

"Per favor, resume your rest." Then, to the old man, the Magistrate says, "You see, sempre fidelis."

"He is not from here?"

"No, from Rome. I am originally from Rome too, you know. I grew up there, went to school there, then university, and eventually to the Instituto Judicale. After getting my degree and passing a very difficult public examination to become a magistrate, I elected to come here."

"You must miss Rome, compared to this," the old man waves his hand at the barren countryside., empty as far as the distant silhouette of Mt. Etna, capped by an anvil-shaped cloud of volcanic dust.

"In a way, yes, but not for the obvious reasons. Rome is a great teacher. The city taught me the first essentials of life. Listen, I remember one summer my parents were away at the seaside and I was cooped up in our small house preparing for an exam. It was the evening and the doorbell rang while I was in the kitchen getting supper ready.. A fellow student of mine, a handsome chap from Milan, Francesco, who was cramming for the same exam and had come over to study with me, answered the door and presently came into the kitchen followed by a truly amazing woman and a taxi driver carrying her luggage.

'Pay the taxi,' she said.

'I beg your pardon?' I said.

'The taxi,' she said. 'Hmmm. What are you cooking? It smells delicious.'

'Who are you?' I said. 'Why are you in my house? I do not know you.'

'You must be Alessandro, yes? I saw you once, at your christening. Didn't your mother tell you I was coming? She invited me to stay for a few days. How very like her not to warn people. I am your notorious cousin Claudia, from Venice – ah, I see my name strikes a chord. Do not be alarmed. I promise I will not eat you . . . yet! I have an appointment in two days with Cardinal Fellini at the Vatican to annul one of my marriages.' So saying, she removed long black gloves and took off the very large black straw hat she was wearing. She had raven hair, a big hooked nose and the most wonderful dark eyes which seemed to laugh at you. She was covered in jewelry, gold bracelets, gold and ruby earrings, even a ruby stud in her left nostril. She was 35, maybe 37- years old, which from the perspective of my 24 years, made her almost a grandmother. I was very naïve then, but even I could tell that she had a sensational figure under the tight black watered-silk dress she was wearing. Francesco was not so naïve and the way he was staring at her made his interest more than clear, so, when she said, 'Aren't you going to offer me a glass of wine?' it was as if she'd jerked a puppet's strings and he was pouring her a glass before I could blink. Anyway, it ended up that we all sat down for supper, even the taxi driver, and this extraordinary woman held us spellbound with stories of the worldly life she led.

Eventually she said she was tired and ready for bed. 'Be a good boy, take my bags upstairs,' she said.

'You cannot sleep upstairs,' I said.

'It is where your mother told me to sleep, upstairs in her bedroom.'

'She did not know Francesco would be here. He's got my room and I'm using my parents"

'Indeed?' She eyed both of us. 'That leaves you with an interesting decision to make.' And off she goes upstairs.

Well, after a furious argument with Francesco, I lost my naiveté very quickly that night and learned I knew nothing about how to make love or the possibilities of certain orifices. In the morning, and all the following mornings until she left, I was tortured by one question: what to tell my parents?

'Tell them the truth,' my cousin Claudia said. 'Because if you don't, I will!'

I was horrified. 'What will you say?'

'That you show promise,' she said, laughing at me.

There is a long comfortable silence. Then the old man says: "Who paid the taxi?"

"Francesco. He kept asking me what it was like with my cousin until she slept with him to shut him up."

There is another long silence before the old man says: "So what did you say to them?"

"Nothing. By the time my parents returned, Francesco had left and I was back in my room. They never mentioned Claudia, so I didn't. In an odd way their silence made me feel guilty and, even more odd, it deprived me of the chance to tell the truth. I had always been a little secretive about women and sex and deflected any questions they had on the subject. In a perverse way this adventure made me bold, and if they had asked I would have told them, but I didn't feel I could just blurt it out. Maybe ten days after their return my mother got a 'thank you' card from Claudia, which she showed me, because of the postscript: 'Please tell my cousin Alessandro how much I enjoyed his company!'

'Funny you didn't mention her visit,' my mother said.

'Didn't I?' I said. 'Probably I was too busy studying.'

'Of course,' said my mother. 'Which explains why she put this exclamation mark at the end of her postscript.'"

Here the Magistrate stops. When he speaks again it is to suggest that perhaps it was time they return to the village. Nothing is said on the way back and it is only as they go into the schoolhouse that the old man says, "So you didn't take the chance?"

"No," says the Magistrate, "but I learned the lesson."

CHAPTER FOURTEEN

Signora Bombelli prayed for the safety of her husband. She had gone to Catania to have her hair done and to do some shopping and, being the frugal woman she was, she had taken the bus. Having finished her business in town, but being obliged to wait the greater part of an hour for the bus home, she took the opportunity, when finding herself walking in the heat of the day around the ruins of the Roman amphitheatre, to slip into the vast cool, interior of Sant'Agata alla Fornace , dip her fingers in the sacred water of the font, cross herself, buy a candle, light it in the nearly vacant Chapel of the Blessed Sacrament, look up at the painting of the martyred Agatha, cross herself again and kneel in a pew on the hard wooden shelf put there to accommodate the knees of the pious. Her faith was one of custom, an ingrained habit of prayer under stress, rallying the Almighty to her side to ward off an evil world intent on directly affecting the well-being of her family. She knew her husband regarded this as superstitious rot, so she prayed for forgiveness for him. It was a little bit like car insurance, you were safe if you had it but you could be sure some drunken fool would run into you the second it lapsed. She felt momentarily absolved, in the stillness of that large, quiet space, vaguely scented with incense and dust, and as her thoughts drifted off she paid no attention to two men standing discreetly to one side of the chapel, nor did she notice another kneeling woman, whose pale, veiled face could scarcely be made out in the shadow of her clasped hands.

+

"It's his wife!"

"You're sure?"

"Positive."

"Who else?"

"She's alone. Praying in the same chapel your wife uses."

"Who's on watch?"

"Vito. I'm using the telephone in the café across the street."

"You know what you have to do?"

"Si, Zu Angelo."

"Bene. Not in the church, you understand. Wait till she's in the street. Don't screw it up."

+

Signora Bombelli was still praying when he rejoined Vito. The two men whispered together, then settled down to wait. After what seemed an interminable time, they saw the woman cross herself, and, not without difficulty, get off her knees to sit back in the pew, where she paused long enough to gather up her purse and her shopping bags before edging her way to the aisle. In so doing she tripped on something in her way, stumbled and fell. From where they were, across the gloomy chapel, the men could not see what had impeded the Magistrate's wife, but now they clearly saw Don Angelo's wife suddenly stand up and help the other woman.

"Shit!" said Vito, under his breath.

+

"I am so sorry," said Don Angelo's wife. "Please, excuse me. I was not thinking when I put it down."

"It is nothing," said Signora Bombelli. "I am always clumsy. I hope I have not broken anything?"

"There's nothing to break. It's only my bag. Are you sure you are not hurt?"

"Grazie tante, I am fine."

"Let me help you with that."

"No, really, it's alright. I can manage."

"You look pale. Maybe you should sit down for a moment?"

"Yes, I think, perhaps, I should."

"I am truly sorry. It is my fault."

In the most natural way, Don Angelo's wife sat down with Signora Bombelli, took her hand in her own, to gently massage the back of it, and the two women shared a moment of calm.

"You are most kind," said Signora Bombelli eventually.

"Prego. Are you feeling better?"

"Much better, thank you." Signora Bombelli retrieved her hand. Then, as if an explanation were necessary, she said, "I was saying a prayer for my husband."

"So was I!"

"Do you suppose it helps?"

"Us or them?"

"That is the question." Signora Bombelli smiled. "If my husband knew he would say I had nothing better to do."

"Mine would immediately list all the things I should have done instead of wasting my time in here."

"They don't understand."

"No, how could they? Sometimes I wonder if they believe."

"That is true, more's the pity. Mine goes to Mass, but only to be seen talking afterwards with our priest."

"Mine sits in confession so the priest can tell him in confidence the secrets of his parish."

"Who are they kidding?"

"Because we're women they think we're dumb."

"But we can't do without them."

The comforting platitudes drifted off and the two women sat, shoulder-to-shoulder, each lost in her own thoughts. Finally Signora Bombelli sighed.

"I must go or I shall miss my bus," she said.

"Do you have far to go?"

"Not really. We live near Acireale."

"But that is on my way! I have a car. You must come with me."

"Oh, I couldn't do that. I'll be fine."

"Please, I insist."

"It is very kind of you, but please do not bother."

"Don't be silly. It is no trouble at all. Look, my driver is over there. We can sit in the back and continue our little chat."

"Are you sure this is not putting you out?"

"Not at all. I rarely get to meet interesting people. Well, what I mean, is somebody new. You make me feel I can tell you anything, as if I have always known you. It is strange, because we don't even know each other's name. I am Serafina Lividiani." Don Angelo's wife extended her hand to Signora Bombelli. After a fractional hesitation, the Magistrate's wife took the offered hand in hers.

"And I am Marina Bombelli," she said.

CHAPTER FIFTEEN

When she walked through her front door she found her husband on the telephone finishing a conversation with the coroner. She waited, not even putting down her shopping, until he hung up. Bombelli sensed her impatience, and though what he had just heard was of the first importance to his case, he paused, said 'Scuzi' into the mouthpiece before putting his hand over it, looked her over carefully, smiled and said: "Yes?"

"You will never guess who just drove me home? Serafina Lividiani!" she said.

"Good God! How on earth did you meet?"

"In church. I said a prayer for you and there she was sitting next to me . . . "

"And?"

"She looked so sad."

+

"You will never guess whom I just drove home?"

From his wheelchair behind his desk in his office, Don Angelo Lividiani looked across at his wife as she came through the door after knocking.

"Bombelli's wife," he said.

"Oh, . . . you know?"

"Of course," he said. "A man should always know what his wife is doing. It was kind of you."

"She had just done her shopping."

"So you gave her a lift."

"She was going to wait for the bus."

"You are a beautiful woman. I am glad I married you. We will discuss it later after my guest has left."

It was only then that Serafina saw a man sitting in a high-backed armchair to the left of her husband's desk. As he rose to acknowledge her, Don Angelo said, "I don't think you have met before. This is Signor Mazzini, our esteemed coroner."

"Signora." The man bowed, vaguely kissed the air over her proffered hand, and remained standing looking awkwardly from husband to wife.

"Signor Mazzini will be staying for lunch," Don Angelo finally said, dismissing his wife without a further glance. "Until then, please make sure we are not disturbed."

+

"As I was saying, it is a puzzle," the coroner said. "The two bodies are so badly burned, that if it were not for their dentures, it would not be possible to identify them. You have seen the pictures of the car? A complete wreck, upside down, inside and outside scorched. The police showed it to me. Normally it would not be my province, but I was trying to make sense of the only discrepancy in the autopsy - both had broken necks . . ."

"So?"

"In itself a broken neck in a violent car accident is not unusual. Even two broken necks. But the police are adamant the car did not crash . . . "

"I see." Don Angelo looked at the closed door for several minutes. "He has your report?"

"Bombelli? Of course. He called me on this very point. It was as bizarre to him as it is to me. He wants to see me."

"Who else knows of this?"

"The police, yourself and the magistrate. I've no way of knowing whom he would tell."

"Bene. After lunch it would be best if you were not seen leaving here."

"Capito," with the index and middle finger of his right hand the coroner tapped the side of his nose. "As you know, I am always careful. But I hear things. In Palermo there is talk of this old man who may be a witness for Bombelli. We have known each other a long time, Don Angelo, long enough for me to feel you will not be upset if I say to you in confidence that you too must be careful."

"Careful?"

"This business with the Batistero . . . "

"That was ten years ago?"

"Not the parents, the girl."

"What about her?"

"I'm sure you know."

"What the fuck are you talking about?"

The coroner frowned. "May I remind you I did the autopsy on her and left certain details out of my report? Your two fried clowns in my refrigerator couldn't help talking about what you did when you went out there. Men are worse gossips than women when it comes to it." The coroner paused. "I am merely the messenger here and I quote: 'La prego, gli dica di stare attento.' "

"Che cazzata! Telling me to watch out? Fuck them, fuck their message and fuck you!" His face suddenly white, shaking with rage, Angelo Lividiani, points at the door. "Get the fuck out of my house. You think I need lessons from rats who don't have the balls to say what they mean to my face? Si fottano tutti!"

+

The meeting takes place at night in the basement of an abandoned house in the eastern suburbs of Palermo, the doors and windows facing the street bricked up to prevent squatters.

"He actually said that - 'fottano tutti'?"

The speaker is a small grey man, with grey hair, in a grey suit and a grey shirt open at the neck. He has large ears and tiny black eyes buried under thick grey eyebrows. He has not shaved for several days. He is preparing the evening meal. He looks around the room at three men sitting

89

in a semicircle of chairs facing him where he stands peeling garlic at a wooden kitchen table. From a cracked ceiling dangles a lamp, laying down a slab of light on the table top. With the knife in his hand he points at the coroner who is standing by the sink. "He has balls, I'll give him that, more than brains."

"He was angry," the coroner said.

"He was stupid."

"Fucking stupid."

"Dangerously stupid, to do that. Che stronzo!"

The comments are volleyed in. The small grey man taps the knife blade against his teeth. "Remember he's a cripple. They always have something to prove, so, let's say he's stupidly proud. And for someone who has been so careful for so long . . . Does he really think this will just go away? That he can whack someone for that?"

"Il suo rispetto . . . " the coroner said.

"Fuck his respect. Think man. If he feels he can knock off every witness you're in danger and if Bombelli finds out what really happened how long d'you think it will take him to put the arsehole in chains?"

"He can't know now, can he? He's just sniffing around. The real question is who did knock over Lividiani's muscle, because we know we didn't and neither did the cops?"

"The old man?"

"Impossible."

"Are you sure? I remember this man from the war, after Luciano made his deal with the Americans and we collaborated with them, storing their ordinance and supplying them with intelligence. He led a group of saboteurs who came ashore from a submarine at Licata well ahead of the allied landing. Very secret, very professional. They drove the Nazis crazy demolishing their infrastructure, blowing up the airfields, their munitions dumps, seizing key bridges in support of the British Eighth Army. Cleverly done, as if they were partisans."

"That was then. The guy's in his eighties now."

"And he's rebuilt a Roman watch-tower by himself according to Paoli. More than any of us could do."

"So you think it's him?"

"Not necessarily. Best to keep an open mind," the small grey man waves the knife at the room, "and get me out of this rathole."

The irony of his comment is not lost on his audience, for this man whom the media call 'the capo di tutti capi', living in hidden squalor, is the richest, most powerful man in the city, as a matter of fact in all of Sicily, and, as they are well aware, the true target of the Magistrate's investigation.

CHAPTER SIXTEEN

INVESTIGATING MAGISTRATE: Someone will talk.

WITNESS: How can you be sure?

I.M: History. It's feudal. Contrary to popular belief omerta typically concerns outsiders; between themselves they talk. Inevitably one of the foot-soldiers will feel cheated or have his nose put out of joint. A capo will be slighted because another got promoted. And if the boss is in hiding it will be seen as both a weakness and an opportunity. Time is on our side.

W: How do you know he's hiding?

I.M: Simple really. He hasn't been seen. Normally from our snitches we get reports of sightings here and there; the odd funeral or marriage where he should show up but doesn't; safe houses hastily abandoned when we raid them.

W: You do?

I.M: You don't think I sit on my ass all day asking you questions? You've got to make it uncomfortable for them. Particularly the young ones, strutting about as if they own the place in their tight pants and fancy shirts. Make them doubt each other. They think they know everything because we have leaks in all our institutions, 'ears' in every room. I feed the rumours.

W: Like now?

I.M: Maybe . . .

W: You're on a mission, Bombelli, to bring down the mafia. Although I will help you as much as I can, objectively you must appreciate your war is not my war. I am not your recruit. I am a bystander caught in a web . . .

I.M.: Stronzata! Off the record. This is bullshit. Stop feeling sorry for yourself. Whether you like it or not you are a participant ever since that little girl saved your life, okay? Now let's go back. On the record. Lividiani gets the farm in '63; you start travelling around Europe with the girl in '65 after her adoption; she has various tutors when abroad, thrives on your cosmopolitan lifestyle, yet you kept returning here to finish your tower. Why?"

W: You forget, Bombelli, she is the native, Sicily is her home, I am the outsider. Even you are an outsider. Italians think Sicily is part of Italy - Sicilians do not. But when I ask myself your question, I have no sensible answer.

+

Like a drumbeat: why? why? why? Before going to sleep, on waking up, out for a walk, from nowhere between footsteps, the same question: why? Just to finish what I'd started? Ego? Ambition? Selfishness? Or because it was home, our home? You could see her excitement whenever we came back, it was that contagious. The taxi from the airport would stop 5 kilometres short of the tower as if by doing so nobody would know where we lived and we would walk in. 'Do you think everything will be the same?' she would say again and again, skipping ahead to be the first to confirm that nothing had changed, the unfinished tower still there guarded by the two old olive trees with the hammock waiting to be occupied, the sheep and goats nibbling whatever they could find on the distant hill, the odd seagull looking down on us seemingly motionless riding the thermals off the cliff. And always the smile of wondrous satisfaction on her face as she would gleefully turn and say 'We're home!' She was so proud of Sicily, proud that scarcely any major city in the world had remotely the ancestry or cultural history of her island and she would rattle off the names and intimate details of famous Sicilians, everyone from Archimedes, to the four Popes, Agatho, Leo II, Sergius I, all of them Saints, and Stephen III, who dealt with his rivals by blinding them and tearing out their tongues, to Luigi Pirandello and Salvatore Quasimodo, both Nobel Laureates, the poet, Maria Messina, Giuseppi Tomasi di Lampedusa, across whose land we used to walk, Dion, the tyrant of Syracuse and friend of Plato, in whose ruined palace she would play, Michelangelo's assistant, Jacobo Siciliano, in whose Chapel of the

Sacrament in Messina she would kneel to the memory of her parents, the painter whose name made her laugh, Antonio Barbalonga, pupil of Domenichino, Jawhar Al-Saqli, who conquered North Africa and founded the city of Cairo, the composers, Scarlatti and Bellini, whose overture to Norma she belted out whenever she was in a room with an echo, on and on, including in her list scabrous individuals like Giovanna Bonanno, a witch, who sold poison to women who wanted to murder their husbands. But she was most proud of the fact that our tower, our home, had been lived in hundreds of years before anyone ever lived in a place called London, Paris, Berlin, Geneva or even Rome, leave alone pretentious newcomers like New York and Los Angeles. She was convinced Caesar must have stood on our roof to survey the distant prospect of the coastline and the sea and I could hear her up there in conversation with him asking questions about what it was like to be Consul. In her imagination nothing was dead, just waiting to be resurrected by the infinite curiosity of a small girl.

Paradoxically, once home, her confident behaviour on the continent became the timidity of someone who knew her place and she reverted to being the farmer's daughter. Not for her the palaces of Palermo but the comfort of Paoli's sheep and goats and the ritual grind bringing up stones from the seabed for our tower.

I kept a diary, and in the daily recollection of unimportant things, facts, doings, thoughts, accidents, schedules, what was said and not said, the accumulation of the threads that made up our life, you could read how close we grew. So close together we knew each other's thoughts, dreamt dreams sharing the same pillow, shared every waking moment, every meal, washed each other's clothes and dishes, even washed each other's hair. Years of days. Of stretched out hours and minutes and seconds lived together as if they would go on forever as my life slowly evolved to accommodate the advent of this girl into it.

Each evening Sofia would watch me writing.

"What are you writing?" she said.

"Everything," I said. "What we do, what we say, the weather, memos to remind myself what we must buy, my thoughts and . . . "

"But you can't write what I think," she interrupted.

"No, I can't. But you can. Here." I gave her an empty journal. She looked at it for a long moment, as if weighing an important decision.

"What should I write?" she said.

"I don't know, whatever comes into your head that you think is important and that you would like to remember."

"Will you read what I write?"

"No. It's private for you. You're not writing to anybody, you're writing to yourself."

Apart from her name on the inside front cover, the journal stayed empty for two years.

Then one morning, she had just turned eleven, washing up after breakfast she announced, "I've started my journal."

"Good."

"You know the first thing I wrote?" she said.

"No. What?"

"Your smell when I hid behind your legs that day."

+

Sofia's memory of her life before that day was distilled by the five senses, sight, touch, sound, taste, smell. Each one, however haphazard or illusory, would trigger a response. Over time the responses began to fade as the chemical and physical stimuli of both her short-term and long-term memory overwrote what had gone before with ever renewed information and it was this that finally determined her to write down what she could remember before it vanished completely. The specific trigger was the smell of the essential oil the old man used after taking his daily shower, a mixture of jojoba and patchouli to repair the damage the sun and the sea-salt made to his skin, which smell permeated his clothes.

"You can only read one word and tell me if I have spelled it correctly," she said, pointing to the first word on the first page of her journal.

"P-a-t-c-h-o-u-l-i. Patchouli, yes. Correct."

"Thank you." She snapped the book shut. "When I was little and saw you walking through our farm I thought you were an old man and that you would smell like an old man, sweaty and dusty, not clean, like you'd peed in your pants . . . " she wrinkled her nose.

"Chi è quello?" she said to her father. She remembered standing on tiptoe just able to look out of the window in the kitchen overlooking the vegetable plot where her mother grew tomatoes and carrots and lettuce. "Who's that?"

'Il vecchio," her father said.

"He's very big," she said.

"He's a giant. Don't go near him, he might eat you up."

She giggled.

"Don't say that. You'll just frighten her," her Mama said.

"How can you be frightened of someone who brings us presents?" Her Papa laughed. It was true, every feast day, left anonymously on their doorstep, small packages, almond biscuits for Sant'Agata in February, fireworks for Martedi Grasso, chocolate Easter eggs for Pasqua, special wine for St. Rosalia in July, even more special fish in August to celebrate la Madonna della Luce, with tickets for the Passeggiata di Giganti in Messina, and in December presents for the Festa dell'Immacolata, for Santa Lucia, for Christmas and for the New Year.

"It's his way of saying thank you for the water," Papa said.

One day, it was her third birthday, there was a special package just for her. Inside, a raggedy doll with a mass of curly hair and pigtails, wearing a polka dot dress, white bloomers and red and white striped stockings. She called it Lorenzita.

Lorenzita was carried everywhere, by an arm or a leg, scrunched into a bag, sat on, walked on, tripped over, lost, found. Her hair came out, an eye went missing, the hem of her dress unravelled. Over the years, she slowly, slowly, disintegrated. No matter.

It was doubtful that Sofia even noticed. She and the doll were inseparable. Even in her sleep. However much she tossed and turned, whether the doll lay across her face or got pushed under the blanket to her feet, her first instinct on waking up, before she even opened her eyes, was to locate Lorenzita by touch, her fingertips running over the long, thin arms and legs, taking inventory of the yarn her mother used to darn holes and repair seams. Satisfied, she would say to the doll 'Indovina un po', - guess what? - and in whispered confidence relate what she could remember of a dream.

It was only after she started writing in her journal that Sofia realised that her memories before that day were mostly the snatched recall of such dreamlike fragments as told to the doll, as if the doll were the repository of a mythical landscape where fact and fiction cohabited in a non-linear realm.

'Guess what? I saw that giant again,' she said once. 'He was carrying a bag and talking to Papa and showing him what he had in the bag. Three black kittens! Their mother had died and he found the kittens under a rock and knew I always wanted one so he saved them for me.' Lorenzita said nothing. There was nothing to say. There were no kittens. It was a dream.

Another morning whispering in the semi-dark under her blanket she said to the doll, 'I saw Mama crying. She wouldn't tell me why. I think something's happened that has made her sad.' There was no way to tell a child of four that her mother had had a miscarriage, but she overheard a conversation between her parents which concluded with the words 'Thank God we have her' and then they hugged each other for the longest time just as she hugged Lorenzita.

Or the day she came back from her first communion. She was seven. 'You have to say your sins and stick your tongue out and eat a wafer which tastes like dust. You wouldn't like it,' Sofia told Lorenzita in confidence, who for once had been left at home despite all the fuss she made.

'What sin did you confess to?' her Papa said. As an unbeliever he had also stayed at home.

'It's a secret,' she said.

'Tell me in my ear,' he said. 'I won't tell anyone.'

'You promise?'

'I promise.'

She whispered in his ear, 'I said some bad things.'

'What did you say?'

'I asked the priest why the people in the windows in the church all had gold plates behind their heads and he said they're not plates they're haloes because they are holy saints and I said well they look like plates and if they're not careful they look like they may fall off and break and he made me say ten Hail Marys and ten Our Fathers as an act of contrition and repeat 'O my God, I am heartily sorry for having offended Thee, and I detest all my sins because of Thy just punishments' when I hadn't done anything and I told him so. Now he says he's coming to see you to complain about my attitude.'

Papa nearly fell off his chair laughing which made Mama say, 'Caro, it is not a laughing matter.'

When she was little the farm seemed enormous to her, the long rows of orange and lemon trees stretching away as far as she could see. Papa was very proud of his land, all 4 hectares, owned in fee, and thankful for the spring that allowed him to irrigate his crops. Most of his neighbours were sharecroppers who had small plots of poor land with little irrigation rented from the absentee-landlords who owned the latifundia, vast hereditary estates, some descended from Roman times. They grew wheat and most were desperately poor.

'Be thankful for Grandfather's wisdom in buying this place and leaving it to us,' Papa always said, even though it meant endless backbreaking work going up and down ladders 12 hours a day pruning the trees in the spring, eliminating sprouts and dead branches with sterilized shears, each stub cut down to the branch collar so smooth no pruning paint or sealant was needed for the tree to heal itself. She helped with weeding and laying on mulch and so did Mama and all three brought in the harvest with the help of migrants. Their fruit was sold in the open-air markets in Catania and Syracuse and sometimes Papa took her with him to stand behind his cart in the shade where the sun-tanned crowds came to finger the fruit and haggle over the price. Some of the wrinkled old ladies would pinch her cheek and say, 'Che bella!' or 'Ma come sei bella oggi' and with a smile say 'Complimenti, Signore' to Papa. It was a lot of work and not much money but the important thing was, as her Papa always said, 'We do not have to bow to anyone.'

There was one day, though, that she remembered vividly. It was the first time she saw her Papa angry, really angry. He was always such a quiet, gentle man that to see him get angry, really mad, made her frightened. She and Lorenzita had been playing in the dirt in the shade of an orange tree near the front door when a long black car drove up and the driver beeped his horn. She knew her Mama was at the back of the house doing the laundry and her Papa somewhere in the orchard and probably neither heard the horn beeping so she stood up to say something when the passenger door opened and a man dressed for the city with shiny black hair got out. He looked annoyed.

'Suonare di nuovo il clacson,' he told the driver. This time the horn blared out. Silence.

'Ancora!'

Silence.

She went to step out of the shade when a window in the rear of the car was wound down and a voice inside said, 'Try the front door.'

The city man went up the two steps to the door and, without knocking, opened it and shouted inside, 'Hallo! Pronto!'

Silence . . . which is when she found her voice, stepped forward and said, 'They're not here.'

'Who are you?' the city man said, walking towards her.

'Sofia,' she said.

He grabbed her arm. 'Where are they?'

'You're hurting me,' she said.

'I will if you don't tell me where they are,' he said - when a hurricane hit him. It was her father. He had heard the noise, came out of the orchard, saw a man molesting his child and in three furious strides was on the man. He picked him up and threw him violently into the side of the car with such great force the car rocked on its suspension. The man fell to the ground where her father kicked him in the face with his heavy work boots. 'Don't ever - EVER - touch my daughter!' Each word punctuated by the thud of his boot into the man's head.

'Enough!' The voice from inside the car stopped her father. '`We have not come for a fight. We have come for your answer.' It was said quietly.

It took all of Papa's self-control to contain his anger and reply, 'I do not like repeating myself. I have told you once and I will tell you again - my spring is not for sale. Neither is my land, or my farm. You are not welcome here, Lividiani, and I will kill any of this vermin who work for you if they so much as look at my daughter leave alone dare to touch her.'

'I apologise for that. He should not have touched her,' the quiet voice said. 'But I urge you. Reconsider. Think of your family.'

'Is that a threat? You think I'm afraid of you, Lividiani? Fuck you! Get off my property and take that sack of crap with you.' Then, turning to her, he said, 'Veni, Sofia. I am so sorry you had to see and hear that.'

This. This she remembered. She was scarcely six years old. Old enough to know she must never tell Lorenzita who, forgotten, lay in the dirt under the orange tree while Sofia and her Papa went to comfort Mama who had witnessed the whole scene from the pantry window.

+

INVESTIGATING MAGISTRATE: We're off the record. Go on.

WITNESS: "What can I say? She loved my stories of growing up in faraway places. I think they helped her escape the present." the old man said. "She would pile up our cushions, sit cross-legged on top, blue eyes wide open shining in anticipation, her long sun-bleached hair a veil hiding her skinny body, her chin in her cupped hands, a tiny golden gap-toothed Bhudda. "Poi?.." her inevitable curiosity eager for whatever came next. Nowadays nobody can remotely believe the lives we once led, but to those living them it was a commonplace in Shanghai or Singapore to meet a ruined Russian princess running a restaurant or an Archduke serving behind a bar or baccarat table. Life unplanned you could say, while in the background, unappreciated, the circus went by. Today the names are gone, sometimes even the places. Only remembered. Sofia said an interesting thing - why do we remember?"

"Why?"

"I don't know. My memory is like a sponge with holes in it. Sometimes I can't remember what I did yesterday and then for no reason in my mind I'm in 1903, when I was about 7 or 8, after we'd been backwards and forwards between Japan and China. How far back can you remember?"

"Last night. My wife's arancini al ragù."

"Stuffed rice balls?"

The Magistrate nodded, stretched, stood up, looked at his notes. "We can't have you saying there are holes in your memory; it's as well we're off the record. Let's take a break."

What a life, he thought, looking at his witness. So he said it. "What a life you've had. I could listen to your stories all day." And thought of the child who loved the same stories. "On your travels, who did they think she was?"

"Sofia? You mean in hotels? God knows, probably my granddaughter. When she was little we always had a suite with two bedrooms, a waste of money according to her since she never slept in her own bed. The nightmares were less frequent but no less devastating when they came. She could not go to sleep on her own as I told you and since there was no rational way to discuss, leave alone explain, the murder of her mother and father, I was at a loss how to help her overcome her grief and hoped time would heal what I could not. I failed her, Bombelli. She gave me her love and trust and look what happened."

Silence. The old man observed Bombelli watching him. After a moment it made him uncomfortable.

"What?" he said.

"What 'happened'? Nothing just 'happens'," Bombelli said.

"Maybe not for you acting like a forensic scientist. Reconstructing the crime scene. You see life as a series of facts, of serial events neatly knotted along a timeline. One following the other. Undo a knot and you think you can follow up and down the line until all the knots are undone and you understand what happened. It's more ambiguous than that."

The old man was dissatisfied with himself.

"When I recall anything it is images. And with them sometimes an atmosphere, even a smell. Things come in and out of focus . . . if it is more accurate than what you do, I don't know?"

Well maybe that was not quite accurate. Now he felt Bombelli was dissatisfied with his answers.

"Does any of this help you?" he said. "I'm never sure that you're satisfied with the answers I give to your questions."

Bombelli looked at him sharply. "What other answers would you give me?"

"None. Unless you would have me lie."

"Why would you lie?"

"Sometimes people don't want to hear the truth. I came up out of the sea one time with a hundred and fifty-kilo granite block roped in the sling, took off my face mask and mouthpiece, and looked up to see her on the rocks, a shrimp of a girl looking anxiously down at me and then between her legs where a dark thread of blood ran between her thighs.

'I'm not hurt, but I'm bleeding,' she said.

'Your period – it's finally started'. We had often discussed in detail what was happening to her body as it changed through puberty, explaining growing pains, the odd aches and the first signs of budding breasts. It simply never occurred to me to get in a supply of sanitary pads. Paoli solved the problem when I met him on my way into town to buy some. His daughter, Giulia, had gone through the same experience as Sofia and, upon learning what happened, he raced away to get her. She had what was needed and the two girls went off to confer in private.

That evening, just before going to bed, Sofia said, 'This is what Mama told me would happen.' A pause, then, 'One day I will be a woman, get married and have children.'

'Yes. Imagine that.'

'What will you do?'

'Do?'

'When I'm gone you'll be alone again. What will you do? Won't you be sad?'"

+

"Just thirteen, Bombelli, think on it."

But Bombelli was thinking what the schoolteacher said - you come around a corner, see what you should not have seen, your whole life changes.

CHAPTER SEVENTEEN

The police recording shows a time of 2.42am when the telephone rings in the Magistrate's house. It rings for nearly 3 minutes before Signora Bombelli's voice finally answers - Yes?

A male voice, heavily disguised, whispers - Bombelli?

Signora Bombelli - He's sleeping.

Male voice - Wake him up . . . now . . . quickly.

Signora Bombelli - Do you know what time it is? He's exhausted. Call back in the morning.

Male voice - No; don't argue. I must speak with him . . .

Bombelli (off) - Mio caro, who is it?

Signora Bombelli - Oh, I'm sorry . . . you're awake . . . it's a man who insists he must talk to you . . . you can hardly hear him . . .

A PAUSE.

Bombelli - Okay, give me the phone - Yes? Who is this?

Male voice - Just listen . . .

Bombelli - Try again . . .

Male voice - Shut up and listen, Bombelli. It's not what you think. But I will want something in exchange - shit, wait - (SILENCE 38 SECONDS) - ok, you still there?

Bombelli - Yes. Just so you know we have a trace on this call.

LAUGHTER.

Male voice - Una stronzata! Before you're out of bed I'm gone. PAUSE. The two pistolas cremated in the Alfa? . . . it's not whom you suspect. Ask yourself, who profits from this? . . .

PAUSE.

Bombelli - Well?

Male voice - Also ask yourself what did they do and what did they witness? . . . got it? . . . I'll call you.

Bombelli - Wait . . .

Male voice - Can't . . . remember, you'll owe me.".

CALL ENDS.

+

Weary, in rumpled pyjamas, his face a mask, the Magistrate takes off the headphones and hands them to the police technician at the switchboard. The listening post is in a dilapidated van parked in shadow on the lane behind the Magistrate's house.. At a bench along one wall of the van, two carabinieri still wearing headphones are making notes, their machine-pistols lying on the floor.

"I could do with another coffee."

"Pronto, Magistrato." The technician reaches for a thermos, pours steaming coffee into a paper cup and hands it over. "Prego."

"Grazie. Anybody have a clue or can I go back to bed now?"

"Maybe?" one of the officers drapes his headphones around his neck. "We've established the call came from a payphone in the lot behind the Marconi, the cinema in Palermo. Not that it helps much. But - and this is just a guess, because it doesn't matter how many times you listen to it, the voice is bloody well disguised - maybe he made a mistake. Here."

On a tape recorder he presses the rewind button, carefully watching a readout until it hits the desired location, where he again presses a button, this one marked 'Play', and through the speakers:

LAUGHTER.

He does it again. Press. Rewind. Press. Play.

LAUGHTER.

"He's laughing. So?" said the Magistrate.

"He can disguise his voice. Laughing's different. Much harder to disguise, more like a fingerprint. It's a long shot. Give me some time with the computers, and maybe . . . maybe we have a break."

CHAPTER EIGHTEEN

On a day of low pressure, which brought a welcome storm to Sicily, with heavy wind and rain, it was a surprise to see the old man walk past Rizzo's wearing one of his silk shirts plastered to his skin, a World War 2 desert-army forage cap pulled down on his head, the back flap dripping water, his trousers and boots sopping wet and covered in mud. He didn't come in for his usual coffee and Lividiani's children, there that day with their mother and two more of Lividiani's men, burst into a gaggle of comments. They were disappointed as they had been waiting for the storyteller to show up and carry on the fairytale. Frankly, so were we.

I was behind the bar, where Rizzo had a stove on which the communal soup was cooked in a large blackened pot, my role being to cut up, put in and endlessly stir an assortment of ingredients grudgingly contributed by whoever could spare the odd leek, potato, carrot or onion. To this ever-simmering concoction was added sprigs of thyme or rosemary, garlic, salt and pepper, vermicelli, rice, whatever, topped up occasionally with bits of what Rizzo said were the remains of old Charlotta's lost cat or a stray dog found run-over. It was Rizzo who judged if more water should go in and, if he was feeling generous, a hefty glass of house red - 'to give it body', as he liked to say. 'Un uomo di panza', as we liked to say.

Whenever you walked into the bar the smell of the soup was the first thing you noticed. For the hardcore of some thirty single men in our village, widowers or lifelong bachelors, down on their luck, more than likely broke, or, like me, existing on what the State was pleased to call a living pension, a contradiction if there ever was one, this broth was our daily lifeline, eaten quickly, out of thick, cracked, porcelain bowls. You could not help but feel guilty at accepting such endless charity and whatever task you were assigned by Rizzo to keep the place clean, tables cleared, dishes washed, dried and properly stacked, was undertaken quickly and gratefully because the man could not stand being thanked for feeding us. All he wanted was, 'Ciao, Rizzo.' as you left.

What a difference a few lira can make. My neighbour, an old hag whose unwashed body odour forced you to cross the street if you saw her approaching, had a daughter married off after the Armistice to an American G.I., which union produced a new child on average every two years, the result being an ever-increasing avalanche of gum-chewing spoiled brats, who came on regular holidays to the old country to visit la Nonna. This production line started in Chicago, and stopped years later, when the couple moved to San Diego, at child number nine, aged now two to nearly twenty. Obviously they could not all be accommodated in the ruin the hag called home, and, since I was a bachelor living in what she grandly called my palazzo, she assumed - rightly, I'm sorry to say - that I would gladly rent out some of my empty rooms to earn a few dollars. Since one American dollar was trading on the black-market for nearly 700 Lira, and my pension was 30,000 Lira a month, you did not have to be a mathematician to do the arithmetic. My parents, long dead, from whom I inherited the house, would have been appalled that their dear son had fallen so low.

For a few Lira more, three days a week whenever they were on the island, I rode my bicycle out to the old man's tower. He had heard, probably from Rizzo, that I was out of work and hired me as a private tutor for his daughter since there was no school nearby that she could attend. Our classroom was the stone patio in front of the tower where two rough chairs faced each other across a homemade table. She took her lessons seriously and expected me to do the same. She was eleven when we started and I came with the expectation I would have to teach her the rudiments of reading, writing and arithmetic only to find myself confronted with an intellectual demon who confounded me that first day by opening a battered copy of Archimedes 'On the Measurement of a Circle' and demanding an explanation on how he calculated the value of pi. Or the time she announced that if you spent 5 minutes a day brushing your teeth and lived to be 80 you used up 101 days cleaning them and her calculation that if I came three times a week to teach her that was a 30 kilometer round-trip times 3 which was 90 kilometres a week and if I cycled to see her on average 30 weeks a year over 5 years until she matriculated that would be the same as cycling from Messina to Rome 19 times or 6 times from Messina to London.

"I never said teaching her would be easy," the old man said.

For homework one day I set her the task of writing an essay using as a matrix Milne's poem that begins 'When I was One, I had just begun.' As a preamble she wrote:

'When I was Eight, I saw my parents murdered.

My then life ended, a new life began.

How many children can say the same?

I cowered in the dark afraid of the light

With days that grew longer, nightmares in the night.

I was found by a friend, a young man grown old,

And sheltered by his love lived mute in his home

A tower by the sea just for him and for me.

Then the day dawned when the warm sun shone in

And I was his daughter allowed to begin.

I am sixteen now in love with my life

Of sheep and a shepherd who wants me for wife.'

In all my years I never had a pupil like her and found myself excited whenever I pedalled over there rehearsing what I would say to her. I learned as much from her as she ever did from me.

Stirring soup your thoughts wander and it took me a minute to realise Lividiani's wife had given one of the new bodyguards an instruction. The man looked perplexed, sharing an anxious glance with his associate.

"A shirt, Senora?"

†

INVESTIGATING MAGISTRATE: "Off the record. She gave you a shirt?"

"Yes," the old man said. "Blue denim. I shouldn't have accepted it. It was so unexpected I didn't know what to do. The bodyguard came into Guglielmo's and just handed it to me. 'Dalla Senora,' he said."

There is a pause while the Magistrate digests this as he studies his witness. What had a sociopath like Lividiani thought when he learned what his wife had done? Talk about un affronto al suo rispetto. What got into her to do such a thing?

"Was it the right size?"

"Yes."

"What did you do with the silk one?"

"Guglielmo dried it for me."

"This is in '70."

"Yes. That autumn."

"Bizarre. Okay. Back on record . . . when you arrived in '43 did you make any local contacts?

W: I am not sure I understand your question. We were part of the army, obviously we came in contact with the local population.

I.M.: Can you be more specific? You have testified you were part of a specialised unit sent in ahead of the allied invasion -

W: I never said that.

I.M.: No. But this American you mentioned, Wilberforce, has been contacted through their Embassy and in an affidavit he has sworn you were part of a secret commando landed ahead of the invasion. Did you liaise with any group or individual after you landed?

W: Off the record?

I.M.: Very well. (To the Stenographer) Please give us a moment.

+

After the door closed behind the stenographer Bombelli got up to stretch, walk around his desk to come and sit on the bench next to the old man, the informality further enhanced by him pulling out a packet of cigarettes, lighting up, taking a hit of nicotine, before offering one to the old man who shook his head, no. Bombelli took his time, blew smoke through his nostrils, and eventually said, "So?"

"So where did you find Wilberforce?"

"In Washington. He works for something called the CIA."

"Water finds its own level."

"Whatever. He gave away very little."

"Because he couldn't. He really didn't know anything . . . wasn't in the loop back then as far as our operations went. Nobody was outside a very tight circle. Without going into details, in broad outline I can tell you this, we had a hard-nosed, cynical instructor, a Havildar Major seconded from one of the Gurkha regiments, about my age, who looked on us as a bunch of pampered sissies. 'War is not cricket, gentlemen, there are no boundaries, no MCC to interpret the rules,' he said. 'You don't want to hear me say this but each one of you is expendable. If you weren't here in front of me today and I had never met you I would still have a commando out in the field harassing the enemy. But I have you for better or worse. You are not natural born fighters, neither are the French - forget the Italians. To put one American soldier in the field costs a hundred thousand dollars per year, more than an entire Gurkha battalion. They have a preoccupation with getting three square meals a day, proper medical attention and preserving the lives of their soldiers. We Gurkhas, with the Pathans and the Sikhs, go into battle on rice and lentils and regard it a disgrace to be taken to hospital for anything short of a mortal wound. Our General Sam Bahadur said if a man says he is not afraid of dying, he is either lying or he is a Gurkha. Your Napoleon said an army marches on its stomach but if it has no fuel and no ammunition it doesn't matter what it has in its stomach, it can't fight. That is your goal, gentlemen, your singular objective. You are being trained to infiltrate and destroy the enemy's infrastructure. And you will take no prisoners."

For a moment the old man stopped, his eyes no longer focused on Bombelli, his thoughts far away. Then he said, "He meant it literally."

Bombelli said nothing and waited for the old man to go on.

"The problem with fuel and ammunition is that it has to be stored and it has to be stored in sufficient quantity and at such convenient locations as to be able to efficiently supply the troops that depend on it. In a war of attrition and constant movement it is nearly impossible for an ammo dump or fuel depot to be both accessible and perfectly protected. They are a locus for activity and cannot be completely hidden, particularly from the local population.

'From the native population your best recruit, gentlemen, is an orphan child,' the Havildar Major said. 'They sit on the edge of all games forever outsiders, but they see everything and their loyalty is easily won: recognition, food and somebody to pat them on the back of the head and say well done. Just remember if they tell you what they see, they also see what should not be told - who *you* are, *your* whereabouts, how *you* operate. As much as you would like them to be a friend, they are not. They are a tool - an expendable tool to be used and discarded when no longer needed. You are being inserted as partisans, soldiers of a Mafia that has been nearly wiped out by Mussolini and his facists. At heart the Sicilians will approve and support you but there will be reprisals that the Germans exact on the local population for giving such aid. It is not of your concern. We will only be on this island for a few weeks; the locals live here and they will have to live with what they do and what is done to them. Remember that. As Patton has said, our enemy is tenacious, his heart is in the Motherland, Germany. Our aim is to kill him from here all the way to our objective, Berlin."

Again the old man stopped.

"So who did you recruit?" Bombelli said.

"No names," the old man said. "You know I can't give you names. Anyway most of them are dead."

"How were you chosen?"

"To pass as a local you obviously had to speak Sicilian or at the very least have fluent Italian. You also had to look the part since we wore no uniform, but dressed as civilians with appropriate clothes and shoes bought in the flea market. Even our haircuts had to match. You know how easy it is to recognise a group of foreigners on holiday? We all do it almost subconsciously - look at those Yanks, look at those Frogs, look at those Krauts - leave alone the Brits who seem almost to go out of their way not to be mistaken for anybody else." The old man sniffed. "It's not just the clothes, it's the posture, the gestures, even the way you hold a cigarette.

Most of us had an Italian background of some sort and by sleeping in our clothes and acquiring three days of stubble we thought we would fit in. Wrong. Literally the first person we met when we came ashore at dawn, was a fisherman mending his nets, who said, "Americani? Inglesi?"

Bombelli laughed.

"You think it's funny, Bombelli," the old man said. "We were shitting bricks. In hindsight it's obvious. It was known the Allies were coming, just not where or when. A fisherman mending his nets looks up from his work to see four badly shaved strangers walking along the quay carrying backpacks immediately knows they are foreigners. He has never seen them before. He knows everybody who works on the waterfront. There are no tourists. And what are the odds on four men dressed as tramps all carrying backpacks? We were blown before we'd started.

Then the fisherman said, 'Sei fortunato. The German patrol only comes at 8 o'clock. Veni.' That was the start of our collaboration. Brave, unknown people who went out of their way to help us with little thought of the risks they ran. Perhaps a few survived and maybe one or two are still alive today, I don't know. But, if I did, you don't seriously imagine I would tell you who they are?"

Silence.

He knows, Bombelli thought, then said, "What was in the backpacks?"

"Our gear. Explosives, some Nobel 808, some Comp C and C2, pencil detonators, time lapse fuses, wire, pliers, couple of small voltage generators, the usual. We could do a lot of damage, with a shaped charge even cut through solid steel."

"You make it sound simple."

"It is if you're properly trained. The Havildar made sure of that. The bastard put us through the hoops. His mantra was Be Calm, Practise, Coordinate, Execute. Calm focused on breathing, controlling your heart-rate, which demanded fitness in body, mind and spirit. Practice was endless, repetitive replication of every gesture needed in handling the green plastique with the funny almond smell, moulding it, inserting the detonator, timing the explosion. Coordination determined the sequence of a small package of highly sensitive explosive, the detonator, that in turn set off the more stable, but more massive primary explosives, leading to Execution where, through the use of sympathetic explosions, a small bomb exploding in a munitions dump could lead to bigger explosions triggering the conflagration of a stockpile of fuel. 'Learn this properly, like riding a bicycle, let it be as natural as breathing, and you will be safe," the Havildar said. 'Be afraid, hasty, or impatient and you will be dead." To me he said, 'You have done this before, I think.' Years ago, I said, Loos, Ypres, Verdun. 'I was in Loos and Ypres,' he said, shaking my hand. 'Here's to survival.' He made me the leader of a platoon of four men and we set sail in a submarine from the North African coast bound for Sicily."

Nothing the old man said seemed to surprise the Magistrate, but before calling the stenographer back to work, he surprised him by saying: "Oh yes, my wife told me to ask you how you got into films?"

"The concierge, Madame Lucette. She knew Alice Guy, a pioneer in the industry at Gaumont in La Villette who was making movies before I was born and she got me jobs as an extra. One thing led to another and I started writing screenplays. Times were tough back then and America was overtaking Europe, so when I got the chance I went there."

"The way you tell it, it sounds like it happened yesterday."

The old man laughed. "In a sense it did. Alice only died a couple of years ago. Time telescopes everything, you know. But we're talking about 40 years ago! That's like looking through the wrong end of a kaleidoscope at specks that won't come into focus. Think, when I was born, Victoria was on the throne in England, the Tzar ruled Russia, and McKinley was the American President. Even as I say it I have to adjust a scale in my head. Since then we've had, what, three Kings and a Queen, thirteen Presidents, a Revolution, a bloody Dictatorship, countless Prime Ministers here, two World Wars and the world population going from 1.5 billion to 4 billion people. If I picture myself as a boy, the 3-year old boy I picture is unfamiliar, right down to the clothes I wore, pantaloons, with the top half of a sailor suit and my hair blond and curly. Don't laugh. It's what a sepia photograph shows, but do I - me, I - remember, or is it my memory of that old snap? A snap that is itself a refugee from a fire that burnt down our house and all the family heirlooms in it. But I don't recall a fire, or which house - we lived in so many - or even when or where my family lost all their estates."

"What estates?"

"Despoiled family estates amassed during the 50-year rule of Franz Joseph's Austro-Hungarian Empire. My mother's people owned a lot of stuff, trashed by the Communists after the revolution in '17, stolen by the Nazis, ruined by neglect, but still a pretty astonishing haul. Dozens of castles, palaces, chateau forts, entire hamlets, three or four villages, farms, houses and apartments too numerous to count, thousands of hectares of land in what was Hungary, Poland, Austria,Czechoslovakia, Bulgaria, Armenia, Azerbaijan, Latvia and even Africa to which we had title . . . all gone."

"Gone? My God! That's astonishing! Nothing's left?"

"Couple of things, mainly an old mansion in Genoa."

"So what do you live on?"

"This and that. We still have a few good pictures. I sell one occasionally."

On the pad in front of him Bombelli made a note. "I thought you said all the family heirlooms got burnt?"

"No, I said I don't recall a fire. However in my memory I carry a clear image of the fire, down to my playroom burning and melting my toy soldiers having listened to countless retellings of this tale across three continents by relatives from all over Mittel Europa who swore to me it was true. So it must have happened just as my memory thinks it remembers happening. Which I - ego - doubt."

"If the stenographer was in here I'd have her strike that paragraph."

"Why? It's true."

"Try and imagine what their attorneys would do to your testimony if you admit to doubting your own memory. Like I've said, we can't have that. Anyway, my wife wants you to come to dinner to tell her about Hollywood and then she wants you to finish the story of Fifine and the concierge."

+

"I love the cinema," Senora Bombelli said.

"She believes it's all true even if it's giant squid fighting spaceships," her husband said.

114

"Shut up, Bombelli, what do you know? Our guest is going to starve while you babble on. Sit," she said to the old man. "This will be ready in a minute."

'This' was pasta alla Norma, made with macaroni, tomatoes, sautéed aubergines and basil, topped with grated ricotta salata. "Sicilian diesel fuel," Senora Bombelli said, putting a huge bowl in front of the old man. "Eat."

Which is when the telephone rang. She swore, and she swore again at her husband when he went to answer it. "Pronto?" said the Magistrate.

"You worked it out yet?" A male voice, heavily disguised.

"Yes, it can only be Lividiani. Thank you for the clues. And I also know who you are."

"Il mio culo lo fai."

"A moment, please. Caro, I'm sorry, I have to take this call . . . thank you." As his grumpy wife put his plate back in the oven to keep it warm, Bombelli said into the phone, "We're watching home movies; all about a mafia chief hiding in a rathole."

The man laughed. "That I'd pay to see."

"Laugh some more and I'm sure you will. I have a screenwriter sitting two metres away - you can tell your story to him."

"If that poor bastard finds out the truth of what Lividiani did to her he'll never pick up a pen again." A long silence. "What? A cat's got your tongue?"

Without another word the Magistrate hung up. A minute later, when the phone rang he just looked at it until it stopped. Both his wife and their guest were watching him closely and he knew he had to say something. "Sorry to spoil dinner, but there are some things I must do.."

"That bad?" said the old man.

"You heard what he said?"

"Not clearly; but your face tells the story."

"I'm sorry."

"No problem. I'll be off."

"Not before you finish your plate," said Senora Bombelli. "Life has priorities and at my table no one walks away from a meal I have cooked for them!" She glared at her husband. "No one!"

"Caro . . ."

"Don't caro me, Bombelli. That rat is not going to destroy the few moments when I have you to myself. Now eat! And pour your guest some wine."

A long hour later they were tucking into homemade roasted almond and espresso cannoli with an aged amaretto to wash it down. "Bene," said Senora Bombelli, "now tell me how you conquered Hollywood."

The old man chuckled, caught a look from her husband, said, "It's late. With your permission, we'll save that for another time. Thank you both for dinner."

"Please, do me a favour," Bombelli said, "let my men escort you back."

The old man chuckled again. "You'll get an ulcer worrying about me."

CHAPTER NINETEEN

High on the path over the ridge from where the distant pyramid of Etna could be seen etched against the night sky , the old man paused, listened for a moment, his eyes scanning the way he had come by the light of a pale moon. Silence slowly filled in, nothing moved. It was from this very spot the other night that he had heard a distant explosion and looked down at something burning on the road a half mile away. It had been none of his business then. Now it paid to be cautious so he waited a few minutes longer. Nothing. Then, almost from out of his shadow, a fox silently crossed the path without looking at him.

The Magistrate's face fills his mind. As silent as the fox he continues walking while trying to make sense of what he half-heard. That it had to do with him and Sofia was certain, but the expression on Bombelli - no, not expression, revulsion - begged an explanation. He'd ask him. Walking on, unbidden, unsought, unwanted, he remembers what he was trying to bury and forget. His past. His guilt for the life he took more than 50 years ago. As the details unspool, unedited, a long forgotten tune . . . he shakes his head. The tune plays on, cannot be switched off, matching his footsteps. As he walks the memories flood in.

✝

Of hours spent with the women cutters editing on the Moviola and the new-fangled flatbed Steenbeck machines, running the film forwards and backwards, using the splicer, matching key numbers from the print to those on the negative, cutting in the war footage. He remembers repeated screenings of the workprint in the projection room, remembers the miles of outtakes on the cutting room floor. Sometimes holding strips up to the light to focus on individual frames - the machine-guns - the defrocked priest with the stolen golden crucifix - the tooth-marks in the Professor's Meerschaum pipe - the marquetry in the Train Bleu - the tell-tale crotch in the killer's borrowed trousers - the dribble of sand on the girl's back - the rows of empty shoes at the foot of the gangplank - and Louella, Louella Parsons, who in her gossip column titled "Script boy's Double-Header", told the story of his 'seducing, after lunch in El Jardin, Barbara Burns (née Blossom Ella Armstrong Schultz), who played the coloured girl, Pru, in 'Alias', and that evening, after dinner in the Brown Derby, his seduction by Goldie Grayford (originally Lilli-Ann Korlinski of Podunk, Iowa) who plays the lead Kate Sanbourne, in the same movie; the boy has stamina' - which memory of another lifetime as far removed from Sicily as possible is now a blur since he was drunk that day but remembers how a scene could have been rewritten, how Lartigue wanted it framed. Walking, he remembers how much of the story is, was, or might have been real. And remembers the young Jasper Johns' take - 'Interesting, if true.' - truth a troubling concept in the movies. Worse in real life.

Walks on. And out of nowhere his memory skips. To the campfire.

One evening Sofia said, "Did you know my name means wisdom in Greek? From the word 'sophos'? My lucky number is 5. And that I'm adventurous, adaptable, easy going, progressive, sensual and intellectual."

"Who told you that?"

"It says it here. Look."

She was reading her horoscope in a woman's magazine. "February 17, see, so I'm Aquarius. And if you are Aquarius with my name then this is what you're like. So am I?"

"What?"

"Adventurous?"

"Yes."

"Adaptable?"

"Yes."

"Easy going?"

"Hmmm, tricky. Have to think about that."

Sofia stuck out her tongue. "Progressive?"

"So-so."

"Sensual?"

"Very."

"Intellectual?"

"Not if you believe that stuff."

Sofia threw the magazine in the fire. "I know it's rubbish. But what do you think I'm like?"

"Honestly?"

"Yes."

"I think for a wise fifteen- year old you are intellectually progressive, sensually easy going, adventurously adaptable, and . . . " and in the ensuing wrestling match he allowed her to pin him to the floor.

She was laughing when the old man found himself looking up at her and realized that never in all his life had he seen eyes that were so intelligent, so human, so full of kindness and love. Vasily's epigram arrived unbidden: 'Everything passes, time alone remains; everything remains, time alone passes.'

He remained but there was nothing left of him and she had gone. What happened to our time together, he thought, the time that was just for us? Where had that time gone?

"Give up?" she said.

Everything. He would give up everything to have her back. On the empty path he now walks alone. The word screams in his head. Alone! No hand in his. No voice to hear. No laugh to share. A girl gone. Eternally lost. How was it possible? Above him the silent sky filled with indifferent stars uncaring of his loss. Below his feet the fallen leaves of countless autumns past. Without her nothing mattered. He felt his grief would last forever with her in the cemetery of his thoughts. And . . . and what he thought safely suppressed, buried in his mind, bursts, overwhelms him, and once again he is holding the bruised and bloody lifeless body of his daughter with its shattered limbs and torn fingernails. He could not count the number of empty days that followed her death and feels a force crushing his heart.

He only stops when he realises that, untold, his feet have brought him back to his empty tower, to a vacant life, where no light burns, and he hears her voice.

"I'm sorry," she said. "I'm sorry."

Tears pouring down his face he howls into the blank space of night, howls as he did at the bottom of the cliff two years before, howls until he feels his vocal cords about to rupture, and for the thousandth time feels the pain of utter loneliness wash over him; an immense sadness; an acute awareness of time passing, things left unsaid, that he is no longer a player in Hollywood or anywhere else, no longer 30 years old looking forward to turning the page to see what the next adventure would bring, but a washed-up old man looking back, who after such a long, adventurous life, finds his refuge, his unsought safe-harbour, the miracle of Sofia, forever gone. His throat hurts him. His head aches.

He sits in the dark with his thoughts. Hours pass. Then abruptly he switches on the lights, goes to the bookshelf and takes down, one after the other, nine books, daily diaries, in the pages of which she still lives. He reads through the night . . .

+

December 24, 1962 - Woke up to our first Christmas together. It is early, the sun not up but S is already awake, her nose six inches from mine on our pillow, her eyes wide open, her first words 'É venuto?' Did Father Christmas come? Non lo so, I say. Go and look. Under one of the olive trees the toys I made for her are wrapped in aluminium cooking foil tied with string. She is ecstatic, particularly with the wooden pig who is introduced to Lorenzita.

July 1, 1963 - Rizzo with the news: a car bomb planted in Ciaculli intended for Angelo Lividiani's capo, Salvatore Greco, has instead killed several carabinieri and two soldiers. The Mafia boss of Acquasanta, Michele Cavataio, is supposedly the perp having lost out to Greco's Sicilian Mafia Commission's control of wholesale heroin traffic in Palermo. The cognoscenti in the bar opine 'They'll get him however long it takes'. The schoolteacher's opinion is that Cavataio, whatever his murderous reputation and penchant for bombs, would not have the authority for such a hit and the man who would must be Pietro Torretta, the purported capo of Palermo Centro.

October 10, 1963 - On our way out to visit Peggy G to see her collection in Palazzo Leoni when the concierge here in the Danieli informs us of the disaster at Langarone yesterday where a landslide has caused a wave 250-metres high to sweep over the top of the new Vajont Dam and drown the villages downstream and the thousands living in them. Out in Piazza San Marco S points at the campanile. 'Was it that high?' No, I told her, the wave was two and a half times higher. It is beyond her comprehension and she is silent all day - I don't think she looked at the pictures; in the evening she says a prayer for the children that died and cries herself to sleep.

__February 17, 1964__ - For her 10th b'day I have made S a chess set out of black and white pebbles scoured smooth by the sea. The pawns are small, circular, with bevelled edges, slightly domed, a lowercase 'p' painted in the middle. So that they are identical I have made a stencil of the letter and painted it white on the black stones and black on the white. The pieces are bigger, with the knights, bishops and rooks two pebbles high, with a hole bored in the middle bolted together with countersunk screws and nuts, and 'k', 'b' and 'r' painted in the appropriate colours. The Queens and the Kings are respectively three and four pebbles tall, also bolted together, with a painted coronet surrounding the capital 'Q' on the Queen and a painted Maltese cross to designate the King. The board is a thing of beauty, a thick piece of bleached driftwood sanded down, the 64 squares for the pieces stained into it using two different coloured varnishes, a pale ivory and a dark honey. Making the set took a couple of months, diving for the right pebbles the hardest part. S kept saying 'what are you making?' and I said 'you'll see. Don't peek.' 'Is it for me?' 'Wait and see.' Question and answer like a ping-pong match and it was a job hiding what I was doing. When it was finished and wrapped and ready to be opened she circled the package pretending to know what was inside but in fact really curious. I'll have to teach her how to play. Particularly the Sicilian.

Later - she's lying in bed trying to play both sides, talking to the pieces, aiming them at their targets. She thinks the King is stupid because it cannot move more than one square at a time and is always hiding.

__September 20, 1964__ - In Milan for the last days of the Triennial, staying with W in his mini palace on Via Fatebenefratelli, who tells us a horror story of how his brother has ruined the family. S, fascinated, wants all the details. Exactly how did he commit suicide? Why did he shoot his dog? How could he leave an ex-wife with whom he had two kids? And the current wife pregnant? How do you gamble on the Borsa? What are stocks and shares? Why do they go up and down to make you lose all your money? Wide-eyed in bed S says 'if they have none left how will they buy food to eat tomorrow? Why do so many bad *things happen?' Across the street is the monastery of Santa Maria delle Grazie and by bribing the guard we get in to see Leonardo's fresco 'The Last Supper' which is in terrible condition. S wants to know why there are no women in the picture. She loved the Italian Pavilion and meeting Gae Aulenti. Now she wants to be an architect. Then, after we see Clint Eastwood in Serge Leone's spaghetti western 'Per un pugno di dollari' she wants to be a villain like Gian Maria Volonté and she walks around with a black eye-patch I have to make.*

January 3, 1965 - *Sofia woke up shivering, pale, with a fever. Put her to bed on a diet of soup.*

Two sentences - the start of a panicked nightmare. Sofia, her face grey, trying to twist around in the sweat-stained sheets to look at the lump on the back of her thigh, said, "It looks like a bite." She ran her fingers over the lump. "It feels hot. Feel?"

It felt hot and swollen. Much more than an ordinary insect bite. For two days I had been taking her temperature which was all over the place, with a high of 104°, and I was giving her aspirin ground up in water to no avail. "I feel so shivery. And tired," she said. She fell back on her pillow, her eyes huge, looking up at me. I felt useless and tried not to show how worried I was. From under the tented groundsheet I could see to the top of our hill and kept hoping for a sight of Paoli to send for help. No such luck. It got cooler that evening so I put another blanket on Sofia. She slept fitfully holding my hand.

At dawn one of Paoli's dogs was sitting by Sofia when I woke up. It ran off when it saw I was awake. Sofia was soaked in sweat, with a nasty yellow cast to her eyes and face, almost looks like she had malaria. Bite mark now horribly swollen, feels hot as if about to burst. 'It hurts,' she said without opening her eyes. Can't be mosquitos, no stagnant water. Spider? Feel bloody useless. Can't leave her to go for help. She is in no shape to be carried. Think. Think, man think. No bloody telephone. Signal?

Of course, cretino. How dumb. This is a watchtower, make a fire, send up smoke you fucking idiot. Easier said than done, but finally I got a damp fire going on the roof when I heard Sofia calling for me. Go down. The dog was back, staring at Sofia, whose eyes were open and who said in the faintest voice, "Maybe I am going to meet Mama and Papa." Her eyes close. Weeping, I hold her hand. What to do? Water. She must drink water. I help her sit up and force her to drink a little. We are exhausted. I lie down next to her and when I next wake up, hours later, Paoli has arrived with his son, Matteo, and the dogs. "I saw the smoke," he says.

"The child needs help," I say. "A doctor."

"I know, the dog told me," he says. "Help is coming. Andare." This to Matteo. "Go!"

Late that evening it is not a doctor but Paoli's wife who the boy brings back, carrying a basket of assorted herbs and poultices, even leeches in a jar (I flinch on seeing them), and she applies them to the now purple-black puss-filled swollen bite mark on the back of Sofia's left thigh. Every half hour, as they become satiated with Sofia's blood Paoli's wife detaches them with her fingernail and applies more. Meanwhile a herbal broth she has made puts Sofia to sleep. "Take some. You need it too," she says to me.

When I retell this nobody believes it. It takes three days but the fever has finally broken and the obscene bite on her leg is little more than a memory. Sofia is thin as a nail file, just skin and bones, but her eyes are clear and the yellow gunk has gone, a tired smile written across her face. A talking dog, herbs and leeches in the middle of the 20th century, a health prescription from the Middle Ages? Paoli's wife, in her shapeless black dress and black headscarf, who has kept a vigil over us for the past forty-eight hours, says, ' Leeches reduce swelling in tissue and promote healing, you know. Their secretions contain an analgesic that's anti-inflammatory and antimicrobial. It is not their fault that we think they are ugly. The girl is young. Given rest and time she will be fine.' She packs up her basket and refuses my offer of compensation, my thanks shrugged off - what are neighbours for? And the doctor? 'He's a quack. All he does is prescribe drugs to earn a commission from the pharmacy.'

May 31, 1965 - S going around trying out her new name. 'Now you're my daughter, you'll have to sleep in your own bed,' I tell her. She grins. 'Now I'm your daughter you can't kick me out,' she says. In Catania see Fellini's 8 ½. Cashier not sure S old enough but let's us in anyway.

July 23, 1965 - They've finally got the tunnel under Mont Blanc open. We drove through from Courmayeur to Chamonix, had lunch, and drove back. 11 kilometres each way. Didn't even show my passport. S gets car sick.

August 1, 1965 - *First day of school for S with the teacher from Rizzo's. Arrives on a bicycle. Mondays, Wednesdays and Fridays. Out on the patio 9 - 12, lunch, 2 - 4.*

August 15, 1965 - *Somehow S has heard there will be a Formula 1 race in Pergusa and badgers me to take her to see it. Not my thing. Pain in the arse getting to the track stuck in the middle of the island. Pretty lake. She couldn't believe the howl of the engines as the cars went past us on the first lap, Jim Clark leading in a Lotus. By 60 laps she was stoned on the noise. Siffert won. We both fell asleep on the bus back to Catania and the taxi home. It was dark walking in, no moon but an amazing sky filled with stars which we tried to identify. Everytime we saw a shooting star S yelled 'There's one!' And when I told her they were just bits of rock, meteors, burning up in the earth's atmosphere she said 'How do you know? Maybe they're aliens coming to see us. Paoli told me he's met one.'*

Feb. 23, 1966 - *Moro voted back in to form an organic centre-left government, whatever that is. It's his third go-round; Italy's 21st cabinet since the war! Of all the ministries, the Ministry for Extraordinary Acts in the South takes the cake, a re-branded version of the Cassa del Mezzogiorno, a third of whose funds have been nicked by the Mafia dixit the schoolteacher.*

April 10, 1966 - *Take Hovercraft from Calais to Ramsgate. Hard to believe we are on an air cushion sailing just above the water. S excited (so am I). She's reading Evelyn Waugh, 'Black Mischief', and loves the bit where Basil Seal eats the remains of his girlfriend, Prudence, in a stew. When we get up to London it was a sad coincidence to learn Waugh died today! Remember: buy tickets for Wimbledon.*

July 2, 1966 - *Who would have backed Santana to win? But then who would have imagined him playing Ralston in the Final. S thinks the Ladies champion, Billie Jean King, could have beaten both of them in the same afternoon.*

August 1, 1966 - *Progress report from the tutor after 1 year: 'She learns faster than I can teach.'*

September 29, 1966 - *Go to Palermo to see Blow-up by Antonioni - in English! Following which I have to buy S a camera so she can snoop around taking pictures à la Hemmings. With nowhere to get stuff developed and printed at home she has to wait till we go to town to see what she has photographed. She has some good pictures of goats finding shelter from the sun in the shade of a stone wall.*

__November 6, 1966__ - We are up to our knees in water, well I am, S is up to her waist. The water is filthy, contaminated by busted oil and sewage pipelines. It's been pissing down for days. Luckily it's stopped for now. They say it was 20 metres high in the Piazza del Duomo. Poor Florence. Everyone and his aunt who knows anything about restoration is on their way here to help. We are called the angeli del fango - the mud angels. We are assigned to salvage what we can in the Biblioteca Vieusseux where tens of thousands of priceless antique books and manuscripts are submerged, sodden, plastered together on walls and ceilings. Mould is the greatest fear and to stop it spreading between the pages of the books we use everything from blotting paper to hair dryers. S insisted on coming and worked with grim determination. We are camped out in the San Michele along with Richard Burton who is making a documentary with Franco Zeffirelli about the aftermath of this flood. What a disaster! In the Biblioteca Nazionale they say 1,500,000 items are destroyed. God knows how many years it will take to get back to normal.

__May 18, 1967__ - Longchamp for the races. Pouring down, regular bloody monsoon. Everywhere we go it's the same. Last meeting of the year, invited by Suzy Volterra who has one of the favourites entered. She was there with Maurice Chevalier. In the paddock S fancied the look of a 3-year old grey, Little Caesar, mainly because the racing silk the jockey wore was an eye-stabbing pink slashed across the chest with a broad orangey-gold stripe. I gave her some francs to bet with one of the bookmakers. Huge crowds swanning about oblivious of the weather, including the Aga Khan + entourage, the men resplendent in tophats and tails, the women in dresses of every colour of the rainbow from all the grand couturiers. Umbrellas up everywhere. Track soaked, v. soft going. At the start S couldn't see over the people jammed in the box in front of us and I had to lift her up onto my shoulders from where she called the race like a pro, my binoculars glued to her eyes - 'And they're off, Mon Coeur leading from Dynamite, trailed by Pretty Boy and Jojo Joie . . . at the first furlong it's Dynamite, Dynamite leading Pretty Boy and Jojo, Mon Coeur already fading . . . Little Caesar is last . . . at the halfway mark Avenger is making a move on the outside, it's Pretty Boy from Avenger with Dynamite third and Tantôt in fourth a length behind. At the tail Little

Caesar is going wide, Little Caesar is making a move going into the back-straight . . . the field is tightly bunched around the bend, its anybody's race with Avenger now ahead, Avenger from Jojo, Avenger showing daylight . . . oh! . . . and HERE COMES LITTLE CAESAR . . . on the outside, LITTLE CAESAR, now fifth, now fourth, LITTLE CAESAR, past Tantôt, past Pretty Boy, catching Jojo . . . two furlongs to go, Avenger and Little Caesar are neck and neck, neck and neck, one furlong, COME ON LITTLE CAESAR . . . COME ON!!!' The horse wins of course. The crowd goes crazy, whether for the horse or the small girl screaming out her lungs nobody knows. When she goes to collect her winnings the bookie proudly gives her a lollipop and gives me a substantial pile of loot and a wink. 'Against government regulations for a child to be betting, Monsieur,' the bookie says.

May 31, 1967 - Meeting chez UBS, Geneva. M.Huber absent, assistant manager, M.Bachmann goes over accounts. 1.3M SwsFr net after sale of the Dürer. Give S rare gold Maria Theresa thaler from stash in deposit box - she's impressed by the buxom portrait of the empress on the obverse with the initials underneath D.G.R.IMP.HU.BO.REG and the Habsburg Double Eagle on the reverse with ARCHID.AVST.DUX BURG.CO.TYR and the date, 1780. Weighs it in her hand. 'Wow. What do all these letters mean?' Dei Gratia Romanorum Imperatrix, Hungariae Bohemiaeque Regina, Archidux Austriae, Dux Burgundiae, Comes Tyrolis. It's Latin, I say. Can you work it out? With a bit of help from her friend she says 'By the Grace of God, Empress of the Romans, Queen of Hungary and Bohemia, Archduchess of Austria, Duchess of Burgundy, Countess of Tyrol. Now she is really impressed. And when I tell her Maria Theresa was the only female to rule the Habsburg Empire and that my ancestor, Pyotr Alexis Bélanopeç, was the interpreter to her grandfather, Leopold 1, the Holy Roman Emperor, S stares at the coin for a long time then gives it to M. Bachmann. 'I think you should put it back in the box because I am sure to lose it.' Bachmann does a little ceremony, has her sign the registration book for the deposit boxes, puts the coin back where it came from, shakes her hand and with the kind of avuncular kindness bred into generations of Swiss bankers tells his new client she can come and visit her coin whenever she's in town. When we leave the bank, on the way up the Rue du Rhone, she says 'Am I rich now?' Very, I say, and to celebrate we go ice skating at the Patinoire des Vernets, a first for her. Hilarious. Falls over a hundred times, gets up laughing another hundred.

Stay on to watch a men's hockey match, Geneve-Servette vs Davos, to show her how it's really done.

__July 27, 1967__ - 5th anniversary of the murders. S shows no sign she remembers that day so I keep quiet. Don't know what I would say anyway. She's reading Don Quixote which she tells me is the best book ever written and that I am uniquely suited to be Sancho Panza (obviously with her as the Don mooning about daydreaming) She has the nutty lingo down pat: 'As a Hidalgo of the First Order, you Panza will obey me by performing your duties in a humble manner, never turning your back on me, speaking with a low courteous voice only telling me those things I want to hear since my brain is dry . . . 'etc. Keeps me in stitches.

__September 8, 1967__ - 'Belle de Jour' gets the Lion d'Or in Venice. Bunuel didn't look all that happy. S wants to know: 'What does a prostitute do in the day that she can't do at night?' Standing at the rail holding hands on the vaporetto back to Mestre to catch our train, out of the blue, she says 'I'm not a little girl anymore, you know. I think we should stop holding hands.' Makes me feel incredibly old and sad. But she's right.

He stops reading for a moment, looks at his hands, remembers what followed:

"Ok. But since you're not a little girl anymore, you're old enough to sleep in your own bed."

It made her think.

"No."

"Not no, yes. If you can walk by yourself, you can sleep by yourself."

"I can't."

"Why?"

"You know why." Pause. "I get scared in the night."

There it was. An opening to what could not be discussed - her fears - which was put on hold because they had to disembark and then postponed when she said, "But I'll try."

Then she added, "We'll still be friends, won't we?"

"Certo."

"Friends can hold hands," she said, taking his hand. "And if I'm frightened in the dark can I still come to you?"

"Always. You're my daughter."

November 10, 1967 *- Nasty dream reliving S sick like she was two years ago, growing smaller and thinner until she became a tiny transparent 'thing' about to disappear when I sit up to find her holding my hands, comforting me, saying, 'it's alright, it's only a dream, I'm here.' I was so frightened I had lost her.*

January 14, 1968 *- Woken just after midnight by a strong earthquake. Luckily we are outside under the groundsheet. Succession of aftershocks . . . daylight shows we only lost a broken glass. S slept through it all.*

January 15, 1968 *- Centre of quake is at the other end of the island around Belice. 5.5 on the Richter, aftershocks continuing all 5. + Check tower. A few cracks but nothing worse. Paoli over to see we are OK. Tells us of several hundred dead, many injured and thousands homeless. His family live in the west, in Poggioreale which has been destroyed, their home collapsed, but, praise God, none of his people so much as scratched. He and his boy must go to their help and ask if he can leave his flock with us in the care of the dogs and S. 'Con il tuo permesso?' he says. The protegé shepherdess leaps to her feet. 'Say yes!' she yells and rushes off to find her stick.*

January 16, 1968 *- To the manner born, S takes her duties very seriously. Up at the crack of dawn to whistle and chivvy the herd helped by the dogs, she's gone most of the day foraging for fresh patches of grass along the ridge line of hills. I worry needlessly about my responsibility in letting her do this and am cheered when I see my little ragamuffin return at dusk covered in dust with the news 'we saw a black snake but the dogs chased it away!'*

January 23, 1968 *- Paoli is back to reclaim his animals. Matteo and S go off for him to hear her account of her adventures with the flock. Privately Paoli says to me, 'They get on well, I think. If there is a prettier, more intelligent child than Sofia, I never heard of her. She is a miracle. God's gift to you, Signore.' S asks if Matteo can join her private tutoring. Why not? The Professore advises against it. 'He's a nice boy, but intellectually nowhere near her.' And adds an interesting comment: 'It will simply hold her back and undermine his confidence.'*

April 5, 1968 *- A preliminary report in the aftermath of January's quake blames 'ill preparedness at local and provincial levels in planning for disasters, exacerbated by excessive bureaucracy, lack of supplies and suspicion of outsiders* *who volunteer their help.' Also, 'non delivery of prefabricated housing units, despite their having been paid for' and 'no government reconstruction grants although the funds have been approved and disbursed.' Really? They never hear of the Mafia in Rome?*

July 14, 1968 *- Back from France, interesting to hear the denizen's debate in Rizzo's denouncing the students, the general strike and what they're calling 'imitazioni', the Italian students copycatting the French calls for less work, more pay - as if anyone in Rizzo's (except the man himself) did any work. Rizzo is predicting a hot Autumn with no reference to the weather. I have a gut feeling this Sessantotto movement or moment has legs and the conflict it will inevitably bring might breathe fresh air into the bogged down political scene here.*

October 4, 1968 *- Shopping in Syracuse for clothes for S who grows out of stuff seemingly before we leave the store. She refuses to wear a bra and only consents to dresses if they are wildly colourful, starting with turquoise, fuchsia, lemon yellow, pink, cyan, and acid green, and the hems as short as legally possible. At least shoes aren't a problem since she goes around barefoot all the time.*

February 20, 1969 *- S quotes from an article she's been reading about the age of consent in Europe, currently 14 in Italy. 'So, now I am old enough we can do it without you committing a crime,' she said. 'Nonsense. Show me that.' But it's there, in black-and-white . . . where's this going? 'Anyway, forget it, you're my daughter now.' She laughs. 'Keep reading. You'll get to the bit where I have to wait till I'm 16 if I'm under the influence of an adoptive parent. What will you do then?' Good question. And I realise how blind I have been - she is no longer a child. At least she sleeps in her own bed even if it's only on the pallet on the floor next to mine.*

June 13, 1969 *- As a treat for us, get seats in the old Greek theatre in Taormina where they are re-running Le Petit Monde de Don Camillo during the outdoor film festival. Can Matteo come with us? S asks. Yes. Tell the youngsters they are sitting on a seat first occupied 2000 years ago and S immediately stands up to touch the stone under her bottom. She loves Fernandel. When we leave we can see against the night sky the red glow from lava flowing down Etna. Soon it will be the anniversary of the murders. Not sure how carefully S is tracking time. Should I tell her? Matteo sleeps over.*

July 22, 1969 - *S First trip outside Europe. We arrive in New York the day after Americans walk on the moon. NYC is the moon for S, who cannot get over how tall the skyscrapers are and how short the skirts on the girls in the Village. We've rented a flat for a month on Beekman Place facing the East river, with a deli a block away on the corner of 1st where we have breakfast every morning, surrounded by the Hari Krishna people in their orange robes getting fueled on coffee before they go off chanting and ringing bells and gongs. In the Voice S reads about a concert to be held somewhere called Woodstock on a farm in upstate NY. All her favourites are scheduled to play. Never heard of some of them. Buy tickets. Vendor warns ' get there early or not at all' What's that supposed to mean?*

July 29, 1969 - *So far we've done the Met, the Whitney, the Frick, MOMA, and the Natural History Museum - in a week! S likes the Frick best and imagines living like that. Says maybe we should move to the City. The countermen at Pete's, our deli, have adopted her and compete to bring her treats when the boss is not watching.*

July 30, 1969 - *Our flat boasts a huge window from where we watch the tug-boats and barges going about their business on the river, and looking to the right, the United Nations building with endless fleets of long black limos ferrying diplomats. Everyday we walk miles up and down the island. S loves Grand Central Station looking down from the Main Concourse at the swarms of people scurrying for trains or bolting down food in the Dining Concourse, and up at the celestial mural painted with constellations, some of which she recognises and can name. It's a short walk from there to the Waldorf.*

October 2, 1969 - *S driving me nuts practising on a flute Matteo gave her. He made it out of a piece of bamboo. Even the dogs cringe.*

November 17, 1969 - *Finally finished decorating our bedroom with the bamboo poles on which to hang S's dresses. Very colourful. We no longer sleep outside. Took a while for us to get used to it. We've made real beds out of cedar which stand side-by-side in the middle of the room. With a couple of windows open the draft makes the dresses undulate which for some reason is v. satisfying. S now an authentic died-in-the-wool hippie Woodstock-veteran, is into her Janis Joplin act singing (make that screaming) 'You don't know what it's like, you don't know what it's like, to love somebody, to love somebody, the way I love you!'*

Again he stops reading. Love.

Love.

The word rebounds.

Echos in the hollow chamber of his heart.

He closes his eyes and sees her.

Opens them and she is gone.

He reads on.

December 12, 1969 - *Overhear gossip in Rizzo's relayed with relish by the schoolteacher: as he predicted, in Palermo a combined Mafia hit squad including the Bagarellas, Gaetano Grado, one of the Provenzanos etc have knocked off Michele Cavataio in Viale Lazio, the bomber fingered for the massacre in Ciaculli back in '63 which kick-started the Mafia war. Too bad it's not Lividiani.*

February 22, 1970 - *We're invited over for dinner by Paoli. This is a first. We only see him in his role as a shepherd, never really imagine him with a family home. He and his wife and two children live in an isolated stone crofter's cottage in the hills 7 kilometres from us and he is at pains apologising for the modesty of their abode and the meal we are to share. It's true, the place is tiny, basically two rooms, an all-purpose living-dining-kitchen area and a bedroom for the parents, the daughter sleeping on a pullout couch and their son on the floor. The boy's incredibly shy, like a shadow watching his sister and S huddle in a corner, whispering (why do girls do this?) We are served a ragout of lamb which is delicious, as is the wine that accompanies it. In no time at all we feel at home and on our walk back that evening, with a cold wind coming in from the east, S says 'Next time let's ask them to come to us. I'll cook. You can do the washing up.' Quite the grownup.*

May 5, 1970 - *Christ it's hot. Summer already and no breeze. Six months to go with the sun clamped down on us, S practically living in the water, even swims with the jellyfish. She's been stung so often to all intents she's immune, like me. From the rocks catch some sea bass on a handline. Grilled, with just olive oil and lemon. Make plans to go to the Alps, get us out of the heat.*

June 2, 1970 - *Rent small flat in the ramparts of Briançon, an ancient fortified town 1800m up in the French Alps on the border with Italy. Caesar, on his way to conquer Gaul, camped here. Magic panorama of mountains,* *amazingly some still with snow on top. We come and go by the Grand Rue, a v.steep, narrow road running between the houses up the town centre, in the middle of which is a so-called gargouille, le grand Béal, which the inhabitants use as a drain. Watched an ancient crone all in black, hoist up her skirts to straddle this ditch and have a pee. S, of course, has to imitate her. Quel scandale!*

June 5 - 8, 1970 *- 3-day hike through the Vallée de Névache to Mont Thabor, rock-hopping along the ridgeline looking down into Italy. S plays her flute as we walk, a haunting melody that flows across the hills. We are so used to sleeping out under the stars it has become second nature to us. Walking 10-12 hours per day, I am a bit footsore despite bathing in the freezing waters of La Clarée and when we get back. S, fresh as the proverbial daisy, says 'I thought you were tough. Don't tell me you're getting old?' No. I won't.*

August 2, 1970 *- The schoolteacher advises enrolling S in university. 'In all honesty there is nothing more I can teach her. She is a prodigy. Whatever excites her interest is devoured. I have spoken about her to my alma mater in Catania. Despite her youth they would gladly welcome her.' Food for thought.*

October 1, 1970 *- In Milan for the Rolling Stones gig at the Palazzo Dello Sport. Getting in was a riot with cops using tear gas battling fans without tickets trying to gatecrash. S, una bomba, in a mini skirt, chatted up by the crew. 'They want me to go backstage after the show, Dad.' Dad? She loves Jumpin' Jack Flash, Brown Sugar, Honky Tonk Women and Charlie Watts on the drums. If getting in was difficult, getting out was worse, the audience going crazy applauding loud and long enough to attempt to keep the Stones on stage. S is a bit shaken by the noise and a spooky undercurrent in the crowd. We left as soon as we could.*

New Year's Day, 1971 *- Slept in. Rare for us. Maybe because we had a row - no, not a row, a heated misunderstanding perhaps, my fault, which ended with each of us going on seperate walkabouts far into the night, missing midnight, the champagne we bought for the occasion and seeing in the New Year together. Never happened before. It all started innocently. We had made supper, laid the table with the tablecloth she embroidered and she lit the candles, but before sitting down to eat she said 'Excuse me. I have a surprise for you,' and went upstairs to change out of shorts and a T-shirt to come back down wearing a skin-tight full-length white silk dress I had never seen on her before. She was breathtaking, full of a loveliness far beyond beauty. She smiled at the* *effect she was having and I was speechless and could only stare at her as she held out her arms to be taken and I am the idiot who whistled and said, 'Wow!' A pause. 'Sweet sixteen!' (Even writing this I am embarrassed). As soon as the words left my mouth I knew it was an idiotic thing to say. For a moment she still held out her arms, then let them fall to her side, and with a sadness mixed with contempt, finished the quote ' . . . and never been kissed!' adding 'What a fool!' - referring to herself or to me I don't know - turned on her heel and walked out of the tower leaving our tasty meal to get cold on the table. I went after her but in the night I did not see her and when I got back home after hours searching there she was asleep in her own bed. This morning she came down after me wearing her shorts and T-shirt again.*

__January 3, 1971__ - It's been difficult. We try to behave normally but when I catch her looking at me her smile is tinged with melancholy, her eyes sad. As much as possible she keeps to herself. She won't go near the sea with me and boycotts our nightly campfire. Meals are a sad, silent affair with all manner of stuff unsaid, but like the cold food left on the table, our thoughts are scrapped. Time and again I say I'm sorry and feel like an idiot saying it. What's going on? How can this happen? In a month she will be seventeen. Is this a teenage thing? How could she think I would accept her offer? If that's what it was. Try a feeble reference to Jung: 'The transference of affection to the father-figure.' I feel my head bursting. Need to talk to someone. Paoli says, 'Talk to my wife. She understands these things.' Instead I send S over there. She spends the night.

__Jan 4, 1971__ - S back. Says 'Is it because there's someone else?'

Someone else? Which may be the explanation to why he finally gave way one morning and took her with him to Rizzo's. No hint of danger, leave alone tragedy. Nine books, one for each year of their life together. Three thousand two hundred and eight-five pages. He has re-read excerpts from the diaries many times and every time is different - but the guilt is the same, why, why did he take her? It would never have happened if he hadn't given way. The heartache is also the same for what was and is now not, the chronicle written with no sense of closure, no hint of mortality to interrupt their plans. It is dawn when the old man closes the last one and gets up to make coffee. Drinking it out on the terrace, he is blind to the long vista of the sea stretching away at his feet where they once worked and played, and he remembers what a yogi had told him - life is not measured by what you get but by what you give, just as it is not about how long you live, it is about how much you live - and he has the distinct feeling Sofia is standing next to him holding his hand to ease the anguish he feels. Thinking to erase the pain, he makes an abrupt decision he will regret for the rest of his life. He takes the diaries to the roof of the tower, pours oil on them and sets them on fire.

CHAPTER TWENTY

Closing the door to the schoolroom and returning to his desk, the Investigating Magistrate said, "I've asked the stenographer to wait outside. I have an odd question for you - could you kill someone?"

"What do you think we did during the war?" the old man said.

"I don't mean in a war. In cold blood."

"What a question. Depending on the circumstance anybody could."

"For instance?"

"To save your skin."

"Yes. That's the crux of it. Lividiani killed his own men - well, had them killed, we're not yet sure who had the contract"

"Why? It doesn't make sense."

"In their world it does. They witnessed something he did and they ended up talking about it."

"Just as you predicted. Does that mean I'm no longer your chief suspect?"

Bombelli shook his head. "Per favore. Do not treat this lightly. You seem to assume that by being nonchalant it gives you some sort of advantage. Think. These two men were family to him. He knew them intimately. Despite all the years they worked for him, and all they saw him do, even trusted by him with guarding his wife and his children, he now has them executed. What triggers such a decision? And why now?"

"You said he did something? What could he do that could not have been talked about? Over the years they must have seen and talked in-house about every imaginable crime."

"And if the crime is unimaginable?"

"What are you on about?"

"This country. These people. What you can and cannot do. A code of conduct that still forbids certain things. 'Non toccare ma figlia.' You know this expression? Don't touch my daughter. They say this is where the Mafia gets its name. Lividiani betrayed his own oath."

The Magistrate put his elbows on his desk and, over steepled fingers, looked at the old man for a long, silent moment.

"You are in grave danger, my friend." Bombelli said. "Lividiani is ruthless and will do anything to protect himself. He may have laughed at you before but he knows you are here being questioned. In his mind you will inevitably be a witness in court against him for the murder of Batistero and his wife - don't shrug - what I am trying to impress on you is that with all the other participants dead it is your word against his. There is no one else who can place him at the scene of the parents' assassination and testify he gave the order to kill them. To be clear, if he can eliminate you there is no case against him."

The old man smiled but there was no smile in his eyes when he said, "To do that he would have to catch me."

"Don't smile," Bombelli said. "I am serious."

"Tell you what, Bombelli. Let's play a game. You say your men are the best. Yes?" From his pocket the old man pulled out four small polished pebbles, two white and two black, the letter P painted in the middle of each one. "These are pawns, part of a chess set I made for Sofia. When I leave here you will instruct your men to try and trail me on my way home. They can work singly or they can work as a team. They win if any one of them can touch me on the shoulder. This evening call them together. See what they have to say. Let's see how good they really are."

"A game? This is not a game. There is more to this than a game." the Magistrate said.

✝

I was sitting on the narrow bench outside the door of Rizzo's enjoying the sun-warmed wall at my back when the old man walked past carrying

136

some groceries and supplies, said 'Ciao, Professore', and carried on out of town as was his custom. He was followed by the Magistrate's escort, four armed men, the carabinieri, who conversed briefly then split up to go in different directions. I thought nothing of it until the Magistrate came from the schoolhouse to sit on the bench next to me, lit up a cigarette, inhaled slowly, stretched out his legs and also said 'Ciao'. Curious. I had never seen him go about unprotected but he seemed to enjoy the warm wall as much as I did. Before I could ask the obvious question he supplied the answer. "We're playing a game," he said.

Which is when Rizzo came out of his bar unasked, carrying a tray and two glasses of red wine which he placed on a small rusting cast-iron table between us. "Alla salute!" he said.

Sometimes it is best not to be curious but accept a free drink when it is offered to you. "Grazie, Rizzo," I said. The Magistrate nodded. "Salute," he said.

✝

When next they met the Magistrate gave the four polished pebbles back to the old man. "How did you do it? Is it a trick?" he said.

"Simplicity itself," the old man said. "I let them walk past me and then followed each one. You seem to forget, Bombelli, I have been walking these hills for the past 20 years and know every shrub, rock, dip and dale. Your men are from Rome, what can they know of the country?"

"You embarrassed them. They could not understand how you got close enough to give each of them a stone?"

"Training. Seven years in the army. Didn't I tell you I had certain talents? You have to get up close to slit someone's throat. Don't worry about me, okay. You said there was more?"

"There *is* more." Bombelli paused. "I am reluctant to discuss what I must do now, as I fear your reaction. It concerns Sofia."

His voice froze the old man. He stared at Bombelli. Moments later, he managed to say, "She is dead. I buried her two years ago. Apart from the shepherd and his family, the priest, the schoolteacher and Rizzo hardly anyone came to her funeral. You know this. What can 'concern' her in the grave?"

"Her death was recorded as a suicide."

"Bullshit. She would never kill herself."

"You do not know that. There were no witnesses. But she either fell or jumped off your parapet wall fifty metres to that ledge halfway down the cliff where she was found. The impact killed her. The coroner's report is clear. What I am attempting to do is ascertain her state of mind."

"Bollocks. There is no way she fell and she certainly did not jump. You never met Sofia, you don't know what she was like. She loved life. She . . . " his voice choked. Tears swelled in the old man's eyes. "Why are you telling me this now?"

"I need to know where you were when she died?" Bombelli said.

+

In Rizzo's, the moment before Paoli burst in. The usual tableau: half a dozen balding heads bent over the morning paper, the old man at the bar with his ristretto, me stirring the soup, dust being moved around by Rizzo's woman with a mop; a quiet morning, no mafioso's wife and children We all looked at the distraught face of the shepherd as he rushed up to the old man. It was obvious his news was dramatic since he could barely speak having run nearly 15 kilometres. Finally he got it out.

He had been grazing his flock on the old man's land in the dell on the small hill behind the tower when he distinctly heard a scream cut short. From where he was he could see nothing, but alert to his pledge to look out for Sofia, he left his dogs to herd the sheep and ran as fast as he could up out of the dell, over the top of the hill, down the path to the tower. There was nothing to be seen but a spiral of leaves twisting slowly in the wind. He called out for Sofia. Stopped running to listen. Nothing. "Sofia!" he was now shouting. Again nothing but a couple of seagulls cawing and a distant car changing gear. The front door of the tower was open which meant she could not be far off, but the fact that she was not in the doorway - it frightened him and he screamed her name - SOFIA! And immediately thought of the work she did bringing rocks up from the seabed and ran to the edge of the terrace to look down the face of the cliff, and - his voice shook - he saw Sofia lying sprawled out unnaturally on the ledge half way down in a pool of blood. There was no way for him to climb down to her. He called her name again and again but she did not move. He was reluctant to leave her but he had no one he could ask for help so, in a panic, he began to run to Rizzo's, and - Paoli staggered and the old man cut him off.

"Sit down, Paoli," he said, "or you will collapse." To Rizzo he said, "Your van's outside?" And to me he said, "Please call the doctor and an ambulance and the police." Then he left with Rizzo in the van with a couple of the men and I did as he asked. And remembered the first and only day she came to the bar - who could forget it? Or what happened?

As in the theatre all the supporting characters were again in place for Act 1, Rizzo doing an inventory of the bottles on a shelf, his woman cleaning the floor, two or three men at a table nursing hangovers, Signora Lividiani and her children at their table, their bodyguards smoking in a corner, and I, behind the bar, making soup, when, on cue, the old man came through the bead curtain. But, this time, not alone. An apparition walked in with him, my pupil, whom I hadn't seen for a couple of months since their return from the continent, transformed into una meravigliosa creatura, something you only saw in fashion magazines or on the TV, an impossible combination of long blonde hair, laughing blue eyes, tight jeans, an amply curved white T-shirt, thin, young, beautiful and perfect. Un sogno bagnato - a wet dream. It was so incongruous for a girl like this to come into a dump like Rizzo's that everybody stopped what they were doing as she slowly looked us over, pausing momentarily on the children and their mother, then followed the old man to the bar for his 'ristretto'. To me she said, "Ciao, Professore."

Act 2, was curious. It didn't take long. From where they stood, shoulder to shoulder, chatting quietly at the bar, their backs turned to everyone but me, I caught the old man glancing in the long speckled mirror on the wall behind me to catch the eye of Signora Lividiani, and I swear she shook her head, no. But here's what was odd, the girl caught the look too. Then the old man finished his coffee, turned to the children and said, "Cominciamo?"

'One day, Wonderful, her elbows on the window-ledge of her bedroom in the castle, chin cupped in her hands, her one blue eye gazing glumly through the leaded glass at dripping moss hanging from the eaves under endless ranks of drizzling clouds marching in unbroken order to a gloomy horizon, thought to herself, when will it ever stop? It won't, said a spider, twenty-five feet above her from the safety of its web in the rafters, unless you do something.

Yes, but what? thought Wonderful, which is when a butterfly flew past her nose and then came back to land on the tip of her little finger, where it slowly flexed its blue and yellow iridescent wings and looked her in the eye. Look at me, it seemed to say as it opened its wings wide and she saw that the wings were covered in hundreds of thousand of tiny scales and the wing veins were hollow. She stared as an idea grew in her mind. How do you keep dry when it's so wet outside? she said. My wings repel water, but as the water molecules roll off the surface they also clean my wings, said the butterfly.

"I know what she's thinking," the little boy said. "She's going to make a kite." The old man nodded. "A special kite."

It took Wonderful a long time and many experiments but she had learned to be patient and with the help of the insects and the animals she finally got it right and it flew up, up through the clouds. The kite was the colour of gold and on its upper surface she painted a smile to greet the Sun and underneath an arrow for him to see the miles of string hundreds of spiders had made out of spider silk with a tensile strength much greater than steel and weighing nothing in comparison and which the Sun had to follow down through the clouds to the ground. In the end the castle, its inhabitants and all the surrounding land was bathed in bright sunshine and they all lived happily ever after.'

"Is that the end?" said the little boy.

"For now," said the old man.

He and the girl turned to leave at the same moment that the Signora, her children and the bodyguards stood up to go. There was a jostle at the door over who should take precedence on the way out, and - *uno scherzo del destino* - a twist of fate, led to Act 3.

Lividiani's car pulled up just as the group came through the door. Nobody knew why he had come back after seeing his wife dropped off in her car that morning, but, destino, there he was, immaculate, groomed, waiting with the window down, watching as first, one of the bodyguards, then his children, then the girl, then his wife, then the old man and finally the second bodyguard filed out into the street. Being crippled he couldn't get out of his car without help, but he was polite. Leaning toward the window of his car he said to the old man, "Buongiorno, signore," and to the girl, "Signorina, buongiorno," in the same moderate tone he had used to say 'ucciderli' all those years ago.

Then it happened, after an atom of suspended time, a nanosecond of recollection, Sofia stepped past the old man and spat in the face of the gangster. "Assassino!" she said, sealing her fate. "Murderer!"

This outrageous affront, to a man of respect, before his wife, his children and his men . . .

✝

INVESTIGATING MAGISTRATE: Back on record. This is in '71?

WITNESS: Yes. You already knew all this, right?

I.M.: Yes. I interviewed the schoolteacher. He said - a moment please (To the Stenographer) the teacher's file? Thank you. Let me see . . . yes, here it is, he testified, I quote, 'Don Angelo took a handkerchief from his coat pocket to wipe his face, ignored the girl, looked at il vecchio for a moment before saying to him "You understand this is your responsibility?" He then ordered his wife and children to get into their car and the two cars drove away.' Is that how you remember it?

W: Yes.

I.M.: What did Lividiani mean by 'your responsibility'.

W: God knows.

I.M.: Was it a threat?

W: How can you ask me that? It would be pure speculation.

I.M.: Well what do you think he meant?

W: That I had failed to keep my part of the bargain he made when he spared our lives all those years ago.

I.M.: When he killed the parents?

W: Murdered. We've already been through this.

I.M.: What did you do?

W: Do?

I.M.: After Lividiani drove off?

W: What could we do? What was done was done. We walked home.

I.M.: Did you see them again?

W: In Rizzo's? No.

I.M.: What was Sofia's reaction?

W: She said 'I'm sorry.'

I.M.: Sorry?

W: Off the record?

The Magistrate made a note.

"Bene," he said, and added to the stenographer, "per favore, aspetta fuori."

+

Once the door was closed behind the departed stenographer the old man stood up and turned his back on the Magistrate and went to the only window in the room. There was nothing to see outside but the empty road and a row of shuttered buildings opposite the school. Bombelli's reflection behind him could just be made out in the windowpane. To the reflection the old man said, "There are some things I do not want written down. I tell them to you but they are not for repetition in a courthouse or for questioning." Pause. "I need your agreement."

After a long silence Bombelli said, "Agreed."

The old man turned to face him. "Try to fathom the quantum ethical distance, leave alone judicial distance, between the murder of two innocent people, spitting in the murderer's face and saying 'I'm sorry.'"

Pause.

"She's not sorry for spitting in that man's face. No. No. Not at all. Even as I said you have nothing to be sorry for, she said I have put you in danger. She's sorry for putting me in danger. *Me.* She was thinking of me, Bombelli. Can you imagine that?"

142

'What have I done?' she said. Her voice was trembling. "I couldn't stop myself. I hate him. What have I done?" she repeated.

"You have done what all of us in our hearts wished we could have done but did not have the courage to do," I said.

"No," she said, " now everything's changed. Everything." She shook her head. "What will he do?"

"Nothing," I said, "he's a coward." But even as I said it I knew it was not true and that she was right, everything had changed. The equation was out of whack. In the eyes of this madman two murders did not equate to getting spat on. The spit was a greater affront than killing two people. How does that work? Since our lives were now undoubtedly upended my instinct was to quit Sicily and on our long walk home we discussed this option.

Sofia shook her head. She said, "No. It would mean we could never come back because we were afraid of him."

Which was the truth. I was afraid. Not of anything he could do to me, but of what he might do to her. A die was cast. As we walked Sofia took my hand, no longer the confident teenager but a child once more. "I'm sorry," she said again.

+

"Where I failed her, Bombelli - this is hard to say - I failed because I was too proud of her courage and I did not have the guts to tell her that her bravado was misplaced and the wiser course was to leave and hope that by us not being there, over time, Lividiani would come to his senses or that he'd get himself killed. It was my fault. I should have been more forceful," the old man said, turning back to look out of the window again, "- there is no justification that words can bring. I am responsible. As I told you I failed to protect my daughter. I am guilty. Do you understand this, Magistrato?"

"Nonsense," Bombelli said. "Please spare me wringing your hands and wallowing in self-pity. We need to get on with my interrogation or we will never be done with this bloody business. Would you say your daughter was distraught at the thought that what she had done endangered you?"

143

"Distraught?"

"Unbalanced. Enough to harm herself?"

"Don't be ridiculous. I've told you, that's bullshit. She did not commit suicide. Get the notion out of your head. And she did not fall. She could climb the cliff in her sleep. Someone did this to her. So . . . "

+

I.M.: So. On record. You were in Rizzo's bar when the shepherd brought the news of discovering your adopted daughter's body on the rock shelf half way down the cliff below your tower and you went in Rizzo's van with him and a couple of men to the tower. Please answer Yes or no.

W: Yes.

I.M.: Upon arrival you immediately rappelled down the cliff face to the ledge and were joined there subsequently by Rizzo, two men from the ambulance brigade, both with medical training, and a policeman. Together you ascertained that your daughter was dead. Yes or no?

W: Yes.

I.M.: Did you move your daughter?

W: Of course. I tried to see if by some miracle she was alive.

I.M.: If you touched her body did you also adjust the position of her limbs?

W: I cradled her head . . . I was -

I.M.: What?

W: Howling.

PAUSE.

I.M.: Take your time.

W: Sorry. I was devastated. Screaming. I thought my lungs would burst . . .

The old man shuts his eyes as once again he relives the horror of holding the shattered body of his daughter in his arms, looking up the cliff-face and realising what he had to do. Rizzo had a builder's ladder on the roof-rack of his van and this was improvised as a stretcher that was lowered down the cliff-face onto which Sofia's body was laid out and winched back up. A sheet taken from the tower was laid over the body and he found himself riding in the back of the van completely crushed, hollowed out, unable to grasp her non-existence, his hand clamped on the foot of the ladder to stop the jostling in the van from hurting her, not hearing the policeman saying 'please, Signore, let go' when they reached the morgue . . . it takes him a moment to hear the Magistrate.

I.M.: Shall we continue?

W: Yes. Sorry. Carry on.

I.M.: Did you photograph her body the way you found it before cradling her head? Yes or No.

W: Are you crazy?

I.M.: Please answer Yes or No.

W: No!

I.M.: Did the policeman or either of the ambulance men photograph the body before it was disturbed, touched, moved or 'cradled'?

W: No!

I.M.: Did anyone make a diagram of the position in which the body was found?

W: No!

I.M.: Was there anything to suggest how she got there?

W: No!

I.M.: Were you given a copy of the autopsy with the photgraphs?

W: Yes. I still have it.

I.M.: You read it?

W: Of course.

I.M.: Just yes or no will do. Now please think carefully. Was there something, anything, in the copy of the autopsy you were given that struck you as significant or unusual?

W: Yes. It says she committed suicide but if nobody saw her how do they know? Also, I meant to tell you this - bearing in mind I am not a medical man and I can't say I understood much of the medical jargon - it was not what was *in* the autopsy that struck me, it was what was missing. Nowhere does it mention the bruises on her arms or her torn fingernails.

The Magistrate makes a note.

I.M.: The body was then placed on a stretcher, strapped in, and winched up approximately 50 metres to the platform forming the terrace that surrounds the tower.

W: Yes.

I.M.: Before the doctor arrived?

W: He never showed up.

I.M.: What do you mean, he never showed up?

W: He didn't. He called the ambulance guys to meet him at the hospital. Anyway, what could he have done? She was dead.

I.M.: None of you thought it important to establish the place and time of death

which the doctor could have estimated by an examination of the body in situ?

W: What the bloody hell are you trying to imply?

I.M.: Off the record. Look, please bear with me and please refrain from editorial comments and asking rhetorical questions. Okay? On the record. That day, when did you last see your daughter alive?

W: That morning before setting off to the village.

I.M.: Is there someone who saw you with her and saw you leave her there that morning.

W: You mean a witness? How could there be a witness in the tower with just the two of us living there? We had breakfast; I said goodbye and took off.

I.M.: So no one actually saw her alive before you left.

W: Except for Paoli, the shepherd.

I.M: I thought you said there were just the two of you there?

W: He was 150 metres up on the hill, sitting in the shade with his sheep and goats. He waved to me. I waved back, indicated the tower and pointed at him to keep a look-out. He laughed and made a wolf whistle and pointed at the tower himself . I turned to see what had attracted his attention. There, tiny in the distance, was Sofia ready for work, naked as the day she was born, getting the ropes and pulleys set up above the parapet wall.

I.M.: And that was the last time you saw her alive?

W: Yes.

I.M.: About Paoli - what in your opinion was his relationship to your daughter?

W: Paoli? You must be sick. He's a million years old. The man worshipped her. He'd known her since birth. She played with his lambs and goats. Called them by name. Even his dogs loved her, slobbering all over her face when she was little.

I.M.: We are not talking about her as a child but as a young woman who by your own description earned a 'wolf whistle' from Paoli.

W: What are you suggesting, she jumped off the terrace to escape him?

I.M.: It's possible.

W: Of course. And then he ran 15 kilometres to get help.

I.M.: To give himself an alibi.

W: You really are sick.

I.M.: No. I am impartial and look down every avenue of enquiry, even if they end in a cul de sac. What about his son?

W: His son? Matteo? He wasn't even there.

I.M.: Precisely. Where was he?

W: I have no idea.

I.M.: What was his relationship to her?

W: They were friends.

I.M.: Just friends?

W: They were nearly the same age. They knew each other since they were babies. He taught her to play the flute. I don't understand? What are you trying to get me to say?

I.M.: He was a year older. What did he do?

W: Do? You mean a job? He was studying to join the police force I think. Ask his father.

I.M.: Never mind.

The Magistrate makes a note.

I.M.: I see you don't wear a watch.

W: I don't have one, no.

I.M.: But could you say what time it was when you last saw your daughter?

W: Exactly, no. This all happened more than two years ago. Can you remember what you did at a specific time on a specific day two years ago?

I.M.: With respect, I will ask the questions. Be as accurate as you can.

W: We were always up early. By the time we'd had breakfast and cleaned up, I'd say 8.30.

I.M.: How long did it take you to walk to the village that morning?

W: Couple of hours or so, the usual.

I.M.: How long had you been in the bar before the shepherd ran in?

W: In the bar? Half an hour perhaps, after I'd picked up some supplies and ordered some stuff from Guglielmo's.

I.M.: Would you say you had been in the village for an hour then, before Paoli got there?

W: Roughly speaking, yes. More or less.

+

This is where my case is weak. Look at all these approximations. Every feeble qualifying word will be seized on by his lawyers. 'More or less'. 'Roughly'. 'Perhaps'. The Magistrate underlined the words on his copy of the transcription of the interrogation. Momentarily he looked out of the car, his eyes unseeing, then back down to the document on his lap. Had he overestimated his witness? And they'd have a field day with the way the body was moved. I wonder about that boy, Matteo.

"Scuzi, Magistrato," his driver interrupts.

"Si?" Their eyes lock in the rearview mirror.

"That Alfa is back on our tail."

"Chi cazzo! Don't they have anything better to do? Fuck 'em. Just carry on."

His pencil trailed the words he was reading. If the old man had been in the village an hour before the shepherd got there . . . and the shepherd ran the fifteen kilometres . . .

148

"How fast could you run fifteen kilometres?" he asks his driver.

"Me, Magistrato? On a good day six minutes per kilometre, say an hour and a half on a track."

"Not on a track, through these hills?"

"At least two hours."

"And you're fit."

But so was the shepherd. Call it two hours running, no way the old man could have walked it in the same time. He leaves at 8.30, gets to the village at best at 11, spends an hour, 12, when the shepherd gets there, which means that the shepherd left the tower at 10. So whatever happened to the girl happened between 8.30 and 10 o'clock that morning. One hour and thirty minutes. Time enough. Which poses the question: where was Lividiani that morning, specifically between 8.30 and 10, and how do I prove it if the only two witnesses are burned dead? Starting another if - if the rumours of what they said they did are true? Which begs the question, why would they lie?

+

As he walked the familiar trail home, the old man remembers Rizzo persuading him to get out of the van, Rizzo helping him with the papers he had to sign in the morgue identifying the body and Rizzo volunteering to drive him home and stay with him overnight and when in the morning Rizzo had to leave he remembers he never thanked Rizzo for his help and remembers how he found himself alone staring at her bed unable to understand how she could not be there, would never be there again, never hear her voice say 'Guess what?' as he relives their last morning together, the perfect whiteness of Sofia's teeth munching through toast and marmalade, her blue eyes quickened by knowledge.

"Guess what?" Sofia said. "As we sit here we are moving. Infinitely slowly, but moving. Did you know that? The teacher told me Sicily is part of the southern edge of the Eurasian plate, a tectonic plate pushing against the Arabian plate which is why we have Etna and Stormboli, part of the mantle that covers the Earth, pushed up by the convergence of the two plates. And did you know it is 6300 kilometres to the centre of the Earth where there is a solid inner core and a liquid outer core and it is incredibly hot? Nearly 5000 celsius! Just think the deepest mine we have dug only goes down 3 kilometres where the rock face temperature reaches 60° and has to be air conditioned so we can work down there. Isn't that amazing?"

And why had he ducked the questions about Matteo. Poor Matteo. Shattered by the death of Sofia. He remembers Paoli's words - 'They get on well, I think'. A father's comment. At the time he made nothing of it. Failed to note how much time they spent together. In the hills herding the goats and the sheep. But he remembers all too well the day father and son called on him, dressed as if for church on Sunday, to ask for Sofia's hand. It had startled him. She was still asleep and did not hear the early morning knock on the door. The sight of the two of them in their Sunday-best, standing awkwardly out on the patio, the son half-hidden by the father. No dogs. No sheep. No goats.

"Paoli!" he says.

"Ci scusi, signore." Paoli pulling off a filthy hat. "Excuse us for disturbing you. We have not made an appointment but it is something of importance we would discuss with you." He looks at his son. "Matteo?"

The boy is so frightened he can scarcely speak. He drops his head, looks at his shoes, the ground, twists his hands.

"I am your friend, Matteo," the old man says, guessing what was coming. "Speak freely. You have nothing to fear."

"I -" the boy starts. Blushes. Clears his throat.

"Coraggio, figlio," his father says.

"Please, signore. I have . . . I have come . . . to ask you for your daughter . . . "

His father nudges him.

"For your daughter's hand . . . "

His father nudges him again.

"In marriage!" Matteo can scarcely get the word out.

Playing for time the old man says to Paoli, "I thought the father traditionally asked the question."

"In the old days," Paoli says. "It is not the modern way."

"She's not yet sixteen, you know. Her birthday is tomorrow. How old is your son?

Paoli nudges his son.

"Seventeen," Matteo says.

"Have you spoken to her?"

Embarrassed, Matteo looks at the ground, shakes his head, no.

"Well, if you come back tomorrow we can celebrate her birthday and you can ask her yourself - the modern way."

And they did that, they came dressed in their Sunday-best as before. Matteo and Sofia went off to confer and when they came back she was smiling. "We have talked it over," she said. "We both agree we are too young to make such an important decision now. We will see how we feel in a year."

The modern way.

Paoli raised his eyes to the heavens, sighed, shrugged, and simply said to the old man, "Tra un anno allora." And to his son, "Veni."

When they had left, Sofia, still smiling, twisting the ring on her finger, looked at the old man. "In a year, what will you do if I say yes?" she said.

+

He didn't know what to say to that she later wrote in her journal and remembered the day they went to see Snow White who sings 'Someday my Prince will come' and how she squeezed the old man's arm there in the darkness of the movie theatre and whispered to him 'You are my Prince' leaving him at a loss for words. Write that down a voice in her head said. So she did. *I was twelve* she wrote *and he was my father but also my friend and my Prince and just as the seven dwarfs loved Snow White I loved him. I also love Matteo and maybe one day he will be my husband but my friend will always be my Prince.*

CHAPTER TWENTY-ONE

"Forgive me Father for I have sinned."

Head bowed, on her knees in the confessional of the great cathedral, the Duomo di Siracusa, the penitent, a middle-aged woman of character, dressed severely in black, wearing an ivory crucifix on a fine chain around her neck, looks up at the wooden screen behind which sits a young priest. She hesitates to go on.

"Allora?", said the priest, trying not to sound impatient. It had been a long day and he was sore from sitting for hours on a hard wooden bench listening to a list of petty woes, minor crimes and the paltry failings of his congregation. It crossed his mind that his impatience, given his calling, was itself a sin.

"I am guilty of the sin of omission," the woman said. "I carry the knowledge of great harm done to an innocent person, now dead, by another person who is now also dead. I have had this on my conscience for two years and have not told anyone when I should have done so long ago. It disturbs my day, my thoughts and my sleep and I seek absolution that I may once again be at peace."

It takes the young priest a moment to absorb this information and with it the realisation that he is out of his depth. He falls back on what he learned in seminar.

"My child," says the priest, "a person may be guilty of a sin of omission if they fail to do what they are able to do and ought to do because they are in, or have been put into, a state or situation where they are unable or unwilling to complete the action. Did not James, the brother of Jesus, say 'Whoever knows the right thing to do and fails to do it, for him it is sin?"

"Then I have sinned, even though he was my husband."

This complication rattles the young priest. "Who was?"

The woman is crying softly and it is hard to make out what she says: "He worked for Don Angelo, for years. For years doing whatever he was ordered to do. And when he came home that day with his face all scratched . . . you must know this. My husband may not have come to confession often but when he felt the need he came here. Now they've killed him."

Momentarily the priest is lost. Then he says, "Are you confessing to me what a penitent has already confessed to God? If it is so I cannot hear you, I cannot violate the seal of confession."

"I am his wife. He told me in the privacy of our home the abominable things Lividiani did that day and made him do that day! I must confess this." The woman's voice was louder.

"Please, Signora, respect where you are," the priest reprimanded her. "For a person to violate the secrecy of another person's confession is a mortal sin, wherever heard, even by chance, wife or not. You could be excommunicated. Just listening to you repeating what may have been in another penitent's confession would be a mortal sin for me. I am deeply troubled and ask your forgiveness because I cannot give you the absolution you seek." And he crossed himself.

+

"Forgive me Father for I have sinned."

The words repeat themselves endlessly in the mind of the young priest. It has taken him two weeks to get an appointment with his Bishop at the Jesuit Mother-house in Palermo. To get there he had to take the bus from Syracuse, through the barren hills, a long, hot journey during which he constantly reviewed what he felt he had to do and say. Arriving outside the massive walls of the monastery he had nearly turned back, such was the doubt and confusion in his mind. The Bishop's secretary, an austere deacon, with the beaked nose of a vulture, kept him waiting and when he was finally admitted to his Excellency's presence, the bare chapel he was shown into, striking in contrast to the Baroque splendour of the rest of Casa Professa, made him feel he was somehow intruding. His head bowed, eyes cast down, he remained silent and it was the deacon who said, "You have written to us asking for an audience with his Most Reverend Excellency. What do you have to say?"

The young priest makes the Sign of the Cross before looking up.

"I feel I have failed with respect to the obligations which you have presented to me, Your Excellency. I am confused and seek to confess myself."

"Being confused, in and of itself, is not a sin. We all have obligations in life and these can be confusing," said the Bishop, a moderate prelate with a certain style in dress and bearing, with a penchant for compromise. He also felt obscurely flattered by this appeal to his understanding.

"Explain yourself," he said.

"My confusion did not permit me to give absolution to a penitent seeking to confess herself of something she was told by her husband. Apparently the husband was a participant in a crime which led to the death of an innocent person."

"When did this happen?"

"Approximately two years ago."

"Two years! Why did she not go to the police at the time?"

"Because of the man her husband worked for."

"Who is this man?"

"I cannot say his name."

"That is not a response you can make to His Excellency," the deacon said.

"This is part of my confusion. The woman repeated what she said her husband told her he had confessed in the Duomo. I believe she has put herself in dire jeopardy of excommunication by repeating what she was told and that I in turn would be in jeopardy if I listened to her confession and would put you in jeopardy if I repeated to you what I heard from her. I believe the woman to be sincere. I am concerned that by acting the way I did I was only thinking of how to protect myself, and not of the woman's real torment, nor that by refusing her absolution, I betrayed my holy vow to serve The Church."

"As a practical matter," said the pragmatic Bishop, "this can be readily resolved. Have her husband confess and ask for forgiveness for putting his wife in the situation you describe."

"Unfortunately that is impossible."

"What impertinence! How dare you contradict His Excellency's suggestion!" said the deacon.

"It is impossible because the husband is dead."

"Dead?"

"Yes. Killed by the man he worked for - so she claims."

"And you know this man's name?" said the Bishop.

The young priest hesitates, drops his eyes to the floor, and unsure if he might be transgressing, finally says, "Yes, she blurted it out."

"But not in confession?"

"No."

The Bishop thought for a moment, looked at the deacon and with his eyes and a slight flick of his index finger, indicated the door. After the deacon's somewhat reluctant withdrawal, he studied the young priest.

"There is more?" the Bishop said, more as a statement than as a question. "Let me guess: I know this man?"

The young priest can only nod.

"I will hear your confession," said the Bishop.

CHAPTER TWENTY-TWO

It is early and Paoli has brought the smell of his sheep with him into the classroom, caught in the filthy grey duster he wears over ragged trousers and a washed-out sweater. His hair hangs like seaweed down to his shoulders, covered by a once-handsome, battered fedora stained by years of sweat. Through the grimy window he can see his flock filling the street, the odd stray being harried by his dogs, while the Magistrate's car sits trapped, with a couple of goats peering in at him through an open window much to his amusement and the annoyance of his escort.

Paoli opens the classroom door and whistles a high-pitched sound which stills the commotion. He walks through his herd to rescue the Magistrate, who says 'Tante grazie', and together they walk back into the schoolroom, where the Magistrate goes to his desk, picks up his notepad, runs his finger down a column, finds what he is looking for, seats himself and indicates where the shepherd should sit.

Paoli says, "I would rather stand."

"As you wish. This won't take long. In fact I should apologise for making you come all this way with your sheep for just one question. You said in your statement, that when you were running to where you thought you had heard the girl scream, and I quote, you 'heard a car changing gears in the distance.'

"Yes?"

"But there is no road out near that tower."

"No. Just the dirt track, the path to the tower, it's drivable."

"Then in your view this car must have been on that path?"

"Yes."

"Can you say how far away?"

"No. You can see for at least three or four hundred metres before the path curls around the hill, so it was beyond that or I would have seen it. Why is this important? I barely heard the car."

"In this enquiry everything is of importance. Who used that path or track? Does it go somewhere else?"

"No, nobody. The path stops at the tower."

"So if it could not have been somebody going somewhere else..?" Bombelli drums his fingers on his desktop, for a moment lost in thought. " . . . And if they weren't driving towards the tower then they must have been driving away from the tower. But for them to be driving away from the tower pre-supposes they had driven to it first . . . you only heard the car that one time, right?"

"Yes, faintly in the distance, changing gear."

"Yes, changing gear." Bombelli makes a note in his pad. "You were alone?"

"Alone?"

"Your son was not with you?"

"Matteo? No, he was at the police academy in Catania. Still is. He's a cadet."

"I thought he was apprenticed to you?"

"What for? You think there's money in this?" Paoli gestures at his flock.

"I see." The Magistrate studies the shepherd. "Please do not be offended if I ask you what was the relationship between your son and the old man's daughter?"

"Matteo and Sofia? They were friends."

"Good friends?"

"Close friends."

"Da uomo a uomo. How close?"

For a moment Paoli says nothing. Then, "Man to man, this is important?"

"Very important."

"They were like this -" Paoli holds up his right hand and crosses his middle finger over the index finger. "Made for each other."

"You think . . ?"

"Of course. They were like healthy animals, young and beautiful, couldn't keep their hands off each other. Seeing them together would've made a saint jealous."

"Did the old man know?"

"Maybe, maybe not."

"Perhaps he didn't want to know?"

"Perhaps." The shepherd shrugs. "Why speculate? It won't bring her back. My son is inconsolable, poor lad."

"I am deeply sorry," the Magistrate says. "Now, one last question and then you can go. Can you say at what time you heard the car that morning?"

"Exactly, no. But it was at least an hour after il vecchio had left for the village."

"Bene. Tell me, does he have a motor-car?"

"The old man?" Paoli laughs. "He walks everywhere. I don't think he knows how to drive."

+

When the stenographer came into the schoolroom she could not help herself sniffing at the foreign smell inside and it took a moment for her to remember where she had smelled it before.

"Good morning, Magistrato. The shepherd was here?" she said.

"Yes, good morning. He could only come early, and left soon after." Bombelli smiled. "Generously leaving us this stench."

"You should have told me. I would have . . . "

"Nessun problema. I needed to clear up a point from his testimony."

"Should it not go in the record?"

"Non c'è problema. I have to go out now and will be back after lunch." Bombelli stood, put his notepad in his pocket and called for his guards.

"I could type up your notes while you are out," the stenographer said.

"You are very kind, " said the Magistrate, "but that will not be necessary.

+

That afternoon, on the dirt track approaching the tower, Bombelli felt his pulse quicken and surprised himself, he who was usually so calm, by how excited he was in anticipation of his visit to - why did he hesitate? - 'the scene of the crime'. Even as the cliché ran through his mind, it was shadowed by the thought that the rumors were true, inexplicable, but true; not a suicide; here in this sunny place something terrible had happened. He shivered.

"Stop when you see the tower,' he said to his driver.

"Si, Magistrato."

The car, trailing dust, came around a bend and stopped. To the left was a barren stony hill with a stand of scraggly olive trees nearly at the summit. Away down the path was the tower and beyond that the Mediterranean Sea, glittering in the sun to a distant horizon. As the dust drifted over the now stationary car, the Magistrate said, "How far is that?"

"I would estimate less than four hundred meters," said his driver.

"Good." The Magistrate got out of the car, followed by the two carabinieri sitting in the back. "Mark this spot," he said to one, and to the other he said, "Walk, counting your steps, to the tower." Then he got back in the car. "Andiamo," he told the driver.

They reached the tower in silence and both got out. There was no one there, the front door was shut, the terrace empty but for a worn wooden workbench with an equally worn wooden chair behind it, on which was draped faded blue overalls, their owner, absent. Two antique olive trees, with a hammock slung between them, guarded entry to the terrace. In the stillness all that could be heard was the breath of a gentle breeze, the buzz of insects, the steady clomp of the approaching carabinieri's footsteps and the murmur of his voice as he counted.

"Three hundred and eighty-seven paces, Magistrato," he said, when finally he got there.

159

Bombelli nodded. "Grazie," he said, shading his eyes to make out the distant figure of the other carabinieri. Then, to his driver he said, "Go and pick him up and continue slowly round the bend and when you have to change gear, probably when you start climbing the slope of the hill, have him get out of the car and mark the spot. He is then to walk back to where you picked him up, carefully counting his footsteps. Got it?"

"Si, Magistrato."

"Also time how long it takes you. Then come back and drive the same distance quickly and time that as well."

"Pronto."

The driver got back in the car and drove away.

"Now we listen," said the Magistrate.

"For what, Magistrato?"

"I want to know the precise moment when you hear the car change gears, so listen carefully. It will be out of sight but when you hear the change say 'now!'

They both listened, leaning slightly forward as if that would help. They saw the car stop to pick up the carabinieri, then drive slowly away to disappear around the bend, and it was a long, tantalising minute before they both, almost simultaneously, said 'Now!'

Which is when a voice behind them said, "What on earth are you doing?"

Startled, they turned to find the old man, standing naked, dripping water onto his terrace, holding a stonemason's mace in one hand and a stone chisel in the other. A thought flashed into Bombelli's mind: this is exactly what an ageing Hercules would look like, right down to the mace.

CHAPTER TWENTY-THREE

"Please forgive the intrusion," Bombelli said. "I have a theory which requires me to prove an unknown event happened at a date and time certain to which there are no witnesses."

"But you know where it happened," said the old man.

"Yes. Here."

"So you concede she did not fall and she did not jump and that it was not an accident."

"Yes."

"It was deliberate then. Somebody did this to her and now you think you know who did?"

"This needs to be discussed in private. And before we go on, perhaps you should dry yourself and get dressed. I am not comfortable talking to a naked man in front of his house."

Without a word the old man, still wet, picked the overalls off the back of the wooden chair, put them on, went to the door into the tower, pushed it open, and said, "Come in. Perhaps you will be more comfortable with a glass in your hand."

"Don't you have a key?"

"What for? Nobody comes here. Anyway there's nothing to steal." The old man walked through the doorway leaving Bombelli to station his men in a defensive perimeter around the terrace. Then, curious to see for himself, the Magistrate went to the edge of the parapet to look down the cliff face at the ledge fifty metres below. The sight was so vertiginous he instinctively flinched away, but managed to force himself to look back down again to comprehend the impact of a body hitting granite from that height. To his surprise, carved into the ledge, he saw the outline of a torso. His face was pale when he entered the tower and found himself in a surprisingly cool circular chamber with whitewashed walls, a flagstone floor with a refectory table standing in the middle of it, benches on either side, a stone sink set under a window looking out to sea, an ancient wood-burning cast-iron oven to the left of it and to the right a draining board, cupboards above both, all of it cleverly cut into and made part of the impressively thick walls. The staircase to the first floor was not immediately obvious as it too was cut into the wall, the treads finished in polished olivewood, as were the shelves packed with books beneath it.

"You alright?" the old man said. 'You look like you've seen a ghost."

"I looked down your cliff. It scared me, I must admit."

On a curved ebony credenza to the left of the stairs was a sculpture in modelling clay of a young woman's sleeping torso, with long hair framing, yet hiding, her face.

"Is this..?" Bombelli said.

"A maquette of what I'm making down there? Yes."

"I hope you'll show me when it's done."

"If you're still here in a year. Chiselling granite takes time, you know."

Other than a kilim rug under the table and three seemingly identical framed photographs on the wall, there were no other decorations. Meticulously clean, it made Bombelli realise he had misjudged the old man.

"I am impressed," he said. "I had expected something much more rustic. This is almost modern. My wife would love to see what you've done."

"It's mostly Sofia. That tatty table and chair you saw outside did for me here before she came along and sorted me out." From a cupboard the old man produced a bottle of red wine and a couple of glasses, which he filled, handed one to the Magistrate, took the other for himself, said 'Cheers!', took a sip, said 'ça va', and, 'some cheese, I think', which he fished out of another cupboard, put on a wooden chopping block, cut a couple of thick slices, said, 'here you go', speared a slice and gave it to Bombelli and said, 'let's sit', and, suiting action to his words, pulled out a bench and sat down at the refectory table, all the while studying the Magistrate and wondering what was so important it had to be said in private.

For some reason nervous, Bombelli stayed standing. Sipping his wine, he glanced out of the window, then roamed around the room to where the three photographs hung on the wall. "May I?" he said.

"Go ahead," said the old man, "take a look."

The three pictures showed a girl sitting in, sitting on and standing next to an open two-seater sports-car. It was the same girl in each picture but differently dressed in each one, just as it was the same car in each picture but painted a different colour in each one. Only the background of each picture was different.

"Is this . . ?" said Bombelli.

"Yes, Sofia. That's her car. I taught her to drive in it."

"You know how to drive?"

"Of course I do, been doing it for fifty-odd years. What a funny thing to say?"

"Never mind, something somebody said. How old is she here?"

"They're taken a year apart. Fourteen in the one on the left, then fifteen, then sixteen when she got her licence."

"I thought you had to be eighteen?"

"Not in America."

"I am not very good on cars, but isn't this a Fer . . . ?

"Ferrari, yes. A 250 Spyder California."

"How could she afford a Ferrari?"

"I bought it for her. It was cheap, ten years old, but with under thirty thousand kilometres on the clock. Remember May '68, the general strike in France? Well the bloody garbage cleaners thought it their civic duty to empty a truck full of garbage into that car as their contribution to the redistribution of wealth and protest against capitalism."

+

Was it really five years ago? She loved the Hotel du Cap and she loved the owner, André Sella. When they first met they made an unlikely couple, the tall

163

hotelier with the big nose and straw hat, and the tiny girl. She had the run of the place and whenever she went missing you could be sure she would end up in his office, painting watercolours while he was working on his accounts. He was justifiably proud of his hotel and found the perfect audience in Sofia for the stories he had to tell about the fabled guests who had stayed there over the years. 'He told me how you met,' she said one day. 'That you were poor and came on a green bicycle all the way from Paris. Is that true?' It was. I rode a dark green bicycle with no gears when I first went there back in the day. I was a young bum after the war working for the summer holidays at a petrol station outside La Bocca on the coast road as you came into Cannes and in our downtime at lunch, cheese, a baguette, a bunch of grapes, un coup de rouge, reading gossip on the back pages of a paper lying around, there was always an article about the glamorous life of the rich and famous at Eden Roc. One Sunday, my day off, I decided to hop on my bike and peddle over to the Cap d'Antibes to see for myself not realising that there was nothing to see because the whole place was screened off from the road by thick shrubbery and an iron fence. Trying to find a spot where I could look in I heard a celestial voice on the road behind me saying, "De dehors on ne voit rien," and turned to find an exceptionally tall, elderly man, wearing an old-fashioned straw boater, looking down at me. "Donnez-moi votre véhicule," he said. "Venez." He took my bike by the handlebar and I followed him through wrought-iron gates down a gravel driveway into the forecourt of a large faded building, painted beige with pale grey shutters, well past its premiére jeunesse but still striking, a grande dame slowly coming to the end of her fortune.

The entrance was up a short narrow staircase and you came into a stone-flagged hallway around the open cage of a rather elegant lift serving the upper floors. My host turned out to be André Sella, the owner, as I was told by the concierge, a Monsieur Irondelle, who was directed to show me around. "Montrez Monsieur notre parc!" was the imperious instruction, to which Sella added, "Mais qu'il ne touche rien."

From his station at a wooden counter on the left, Irondelle walked me through the lobby to exit at the top of a wide flight of stairs overlooking a marvellous panorama of a long carpeted walkway down to a distant sea framed by lanky umbrella pines and palms and cypress trees. Taking a quick look over his shoulder, Irondelle said, "Right, you heard what he said, don't touch anything. Walk around. See me before you leave."

It was impressive, the park I mean, as I suppose it was meant to be, but curiously I immediately felt at home wandering around with my hands in my pockets past the clay tennis courts, the dog's cemetery, the rose garden, the cabanas and the pool cut into pink rocks jutting into the sea. When I got back up to the hotel an hour had gone by, Irondelle was not behind his desk and for a moment it seemed nobody was there. Then I saw long legs stuck out through the doorway of a tiny office to the right of the lift, Sella's. The man himself was head-down examining some papers, but looked up over the top of the spectacles on the tip of his nose. "Alors?" he said to me.

For a moment I did not know how to reply, then heard myself say with a nonchalance that came out of nowhere, "I feel at home. How much does it cost to stay here?"

Sella stopped what he was doing, took off his glasses the better to inspect me and having made an inventory of everything from my uncut hair to my dusty sandals, he said, "Vous avez combien en poche, jeune homme?"

I had been paid the previous day so I fished out the few francs I had earned for inspection just as Irondelle hove into view to count what was on my palm. The owner and his concierge exchanged a glance and Monsieur André Sella said, "Show him one of the maid's rooms over the garage." Funny to think we would shoot a movie there one day.

Now, with the Hotel du Cap closed because of the strike, we had rented a small house in Haut de Cagnes, which came with a maid, an eccentric Hungarian woman of a certain age, a former circus performer, bent as a pretzel, with an undeniable talent for mixing cocktails. She was also crazy about cars.

The town was made for exploring and I can still hear the tinkle of the bell above the door of an antique shop we entered on the ground floor of a handsome house facing the castle across the Place du Chateau. Age had not been kind to the woman who came to greet us from out of the gloomy interior. Her hair hidden by a curious pink and black silk turban tied in a fashion popular in the 1920s, wearing the tailored uniform of an Admiral of the Fleet, nothing could hide multiple chins, and no amount of makeup camouflage the mottled skin and basketweave of frowns and wrinkles etched into her face, in stark contrast to the scores of portraits of herself filling every inch of wall space from floor to ceiling, portraits of a striking beauty, of youth, of vitality, of the hauteur of a woman of pleasure and carnal knowledge, who gave and took as she pleased from women and men whatever gratification she desired, sure that she would never be denied.

"Ah, the old hippy returns," she said. "Still alive?" And it was only then that she saw Sofia, backlit by the sun, making a halo of the ringlets of her blonde hair crowned with a ribbon of flowers, wearing cut-off jeans, a ruffled white blouse, beads and her ban-the-bomb necklace, a fringed-leather chamois jacket and long, long suntanned legs down to bare feet. She gasped. She, Suzy Solidor, born in the opening year of the 20th century, now nearly 70 years old, who thought she had seen - and been - with every kind of beauty, she actually gaped.

"Good God," she said, "the original flower child."

"This is my daughter, Sofia."

"Don't tell me you fathered her! All of France shuts down and you walk in with God's greatest creation. What are you doing here? I heard you were rescuing a Mayan temple or something."

"A Roman watchtower."

"Whatever. Sofia, is it true? Is he your father?"

Sofia began to smile, then, a twinkle in her cornflower blue eyes, she said, "Yes. Sort of. I wish."

"Make up your mind. He's not your boyfriend I hope. How old are you?"

"Fourteen."

"Unreal." Suzy Solidor shook her head. "You are a miracle, Sofia. Let me look at you." At arm's length, holding Sofia with both hands at the waist, she minutely inspected Sofia front and back, like a connoisseur debating the value of a precious object. Between the sun and the salt in the sea Sofia's hair was bleached into a light, airy golden nimbus about her head with her skin tanned and taut and she would say to me sometimes I wish I were a boy; I don't like the way men look at me. Not so with Suzy. "Chérie, if I were younger I would never let you out of my sight. Never. And you, you old reprobate, get to live with this divine creature. Truly, there is no justice."

"Are you going to invite us in or blather on out here?" said the old man. "Or maybe you're on strike?"

"Of course, pardon, come in, come in." Taking Sofia by the hand, she lead them through an obstacle course of antique furniture, lamps, mirrors, bibelots, escritoires and what-nots of doubtful provenance, into another, more intimate,

room, done up in various tones of grey, the walls of which were covered in still more portraits, where an elegant art-deco bar had pride of place.

"Sit. Let's out the bubbly and begin the beguine as the English say."

"Cole Porter was hardly English."

"Fuss. Fuss. This man never stops, Sofia. He's not English at all and here he's giving lessons. Has he told you he changes his name like he changes his shirts?" From behind the bar she produced a suitably iced bottle, popped the cork with familiar expertise and poured out three crystal glasses of champagne. As each glass was taken up, she said: "A toast: to our horses, to our men and to those who mount them. Skol!"

It took Sofia a moment to work this out and when she did she blushed. She had never met a woman like Suzy, never thought that such a woman existed. She was curious and bursting with questions to ask her.

"May I ask you a question?" she said. In exchange she caught a quick glance pass between the old man and Suzy, who then nodded to her. "Why do you wear a man's Navy suit?", she said.

"Don't you like it?" said Suzy; "No? Well if you must know, I'm too fat now to wear a dress. Anyway, sometimes I like dressing up as a man." She waved her glass at all the portraits on the walls. "Look how long I was a woman. Come on, I'll introduce you. This is my Foujita, and this is my Van Dongen - he really loved me - this one is by Jean-Gabriel Domerque. Here is my Marie Laurencin, and this one is by Marcel Vértes - "

"Didn't Barbezat pay for that?" the old man said.

"Parce qu'il voulait me baiser, le pauvre Maurice. Sorry, Chérie, it's sad but true.

"I don't understand, "said Sofia.

"Ça fait rien. All history now. Never mind. Look. That one's by Francis Picabia"

"Why did so many men want to paint you?" Sofia said.

"Because that's what I wanted to collect, pictures of me. It was a privilege for some of them and a commission for others, in cash or kind."

Again Sofia was not sure what that meant but decided against asking. So many pictures were quite overwhelming and she felt a little the way she did when she ate too much. However, there was no stopping La Grande Dame.

"You like that one, it's by Kisling? And that's by that dirty Englishman, Bacon; not my favourite. Tchikosky did that one during the war. The photographs, which I love, are by Man Ray. And this is my masterpiece, by Tamara de Lempicka."

"It is beautiful," said Sofia, her voice barely a wistful sigh. Painted in a soft golden tone, the artist shows Suzy Solidor full face, her naked torso turned to the right with her right arm raised curled over her inclined head, the nipple of her bared right breast aimed straight at the viewer, while with her left hand she is either about to cover her breast with a green silk shawl or, more likely, has just dropped the shawl to show her breast. There is an enigmatic expression on her face, sleepy-eyed, pouting, fine red lips (the only bright colour in the picture), as if saying to the viewer 'Is this what you want?' Hypnotised, Sofia cannot stop staring at the picture.

"Alors? You begin to understand?" Suzy said.

"A little bit," said Sofia. "It's just - do you like being naked for everyone to see?"

"When you decide to go to bed with someone you take off your clothes. What does it matter what people see or think afterwards?" Suzy stopped to listen. "Can you hear a telephone? Oh dear, I hate answering the phone. Would you go and see who that is?"

"Me?", said Sofia.

"Yes. Be an angel. The phone's in the office back there. Ask who it is and what they want; merci, Chérie."

+

It was a Mrs. Dunn on the phone, a wealthy American friend and companion of Suzy's, who lived in St. Paul de Vence and needed help because the garbage collectors had vandalised her shopping car. She was nearly hysterical and it was only when the old man volunteered Sofia to drive Suzy up the hill to the Colombe d'Or to meet her that she finally calmed down. They took the old man's white Buick 226 Electra convertible which he kept year-round in the garage of the Hotel du Cap, and, in a leisurely manner with the top down and the radio on, drove along the deserted roads in lovely afternoon sunshine, going past a couple of barricaded petrol stations with striking garage attendants glaring at them and yelling insults when they saw a young girl driving.

"We'll be lucky not to get lynched," said Suzy. "Opps!", as Sofia straightened out a wiggle, "Well done, darling. How come you have petrol for this car?"

"M. Pavetto."

"Who is . . ?"

"A crook. The kind you need when there's a general strike and no petrol." The old man was sitting comfortably in the back stretched out across the rear seats. "The restaurant will be closed you know."

"To you, not to me. The Roux's live there; strike or no strike they'll be in the kitchen and we'll join them for lunch, you'll see. I bet Molly's there already ordering that wonderful Chateau Rayas she loves."

+

Molly Dunn was from San Antonio, Texas, and when she ordered wine she ordered magnums. It was said that her wine bill alone paid for the replacement of the provençal roof tiles on the hotel. Like everyone else it was love at first sight the second she saw Sofia and she refused to believe that soon we would go back to Sicily. "I was there once in my boat, never again. What a godforsaken bare-assed bone dry place that is. You have got to be crazy to go back. They're all thievin', lyin', murderin' sons-a-bitches, all of them, including the cops. I never saw so much dishonesty. In port in Messina they stole the outboard motors off the tender, in Catania they ripped us off for fuel, and in Syracuse, where we anchored to go off exploring inland, by the time we got back they'd looted so much of the rigging and stays that the masts nearly fell down. I guess they saw a rich bitch ripe for milking. It's hard to believe that it's out there in the Med instead of where it should be - stuck in the Middle Ages. God knows what you see in the place. May I make a suggestion, leave Sofia here with us". . . and on she went, listing all the advantages to be had for a young girl growing up in a loving lesbian household.

Lunch that day at the Colombe finished around 5 o'clock in the afternoon, and after the usual hearty round of goodbye kisses to Patron and staff, Molly was poured back into the Buick and we drove her the few hundred metres to her home and the vandalised shopping car parked in the driveway, difficult to recognize under a huge mound of rotting refuse.

"What is it?" the old man said. "I can't even see its colour."

169

+

"Long story, short," said the old man to Bombelli, " after we dug it out of all that rubbish, there it was, the Ferrari in those pictures. Sofia went nuts when she saw it, so I swapped it for my Buick which Mrs Dunn loved because it was a nearly new automatic with power steering, not 'a piece of Italian junk, with a shifter you'ld need to be a weightlifter to shove in the clutch, always fucking breaking down.' Ten years before she'd bought it new for $9000, so secondhand it was worth what the Buick cost me and we were both happy. Ilona, our eccentric Hungarian, stopped being a maid and became a mechanic, with Sofia as her assistant. They shovelled the rubbish out, hosed down the interior, stripped everything off, every nut and bolt, door panels, carpets, dash, the lot, down to bare metal, which is where we found spots of rust in the firewall and floor-plate. The leather interior was a complete write-off, but fortunately the engine was fine. The car had a weird aubergine colour which we didn't like, so we shipped the whole shebang off to the factory at Modena and had them re-build it and paint it her choice, which you see there in the first picture, Porsche Bahama Yellow."

"Well I'm glad that's the short version," the Magistrate said. "I won't ask why it's white in the next picture and red in the last. Where's the car now?"

"How could I enjoy riding in her car after what happened? I sold it."

+

It wasn't true, I still had the car, hidden away in Monaco, locked in an underground garage full of rare cars, each shrouded in mystery under anonymous dust covers. I don't know why I lied about it to Bombelli, who was probably shrewd enough to guess I did not want to share every memory I had of Sofia. I was reading in bed that night when she came out of the shower, having spent half an hour scrubbing off the dirt and smell of rotting garbage after digging out the Ferrari. She wore a towel around her waist and had her hair wrapped in another and sat on the end of the bed and said, "What a strange day. In the shower I was thinking that that was the first time in my life that someone has spoken to me as an equal."

I looked at her over my book. "Really?"

"Not you, silly. Suzy spoke to me as if there was no age difference between us. And she didn't bat an eye when you told her I was going to drive. What did she mean about you having as many names as shirts?"

"She remembers when I was a spy."

"A spy? How exciting. Could I be one?"

"No. For a start you would have to grow a moustache."

"But . . . oh, you're teasing me again. I know you were once a soldier, Major Hart, right? - but a spy? How come you've never told me that?"

"I haven't known you long enough."

"Don't tease. You've known me for nearly half my life."

"And Suzy's known me for more than half of mine."

That made her think. I could see her mentally calculating back.

"Then you knew her when she looked like she did in those pictures?" she said.

"Even before that. She wasn't much older than you are, 17 or 18, driving an ambulance that picked me up at the triage centre after I got wounded outside Ornes, near Verdun, during the Great War."

"So she's also brave. You would never think it to look at her. Why does she prefer women to men?"

"You'll have to ask her."

"Are you sorry you gave that American lady your motorcar?"

Keeping up with the way Sofia's mind worked needed the skill of a slalom racer linked to all the knowledge in an encyclopaedia. I put the book down: "No. I think we got a bargain."

"She said some bad things about Sicily, it's not like that. If she saw the castles and palaces in Palermo or even how we live do you think she'd change her mind?"

"No, probably not. Castles and palaces aren't real; nobody lives like that today. Her reality is the life she leads, like most people's. If you fly around in a private aeroplane you don't think about the lives of the people on the ground below you and they don't think about yours up in the sky. We all live in one world at the same time, however different each world is. It might be night there and day here. All our different lives are lived singularly and simultaneously,

each moment important to each individual, but unknowable, because you can't be them or they you. C'è solo ora - there is only now . . . something like that."

Taking off the towel she started drying her hair. "If I let you, how would you paint me? Like this?" Smiling, she tried a pose. "Or like this?" and tried to imitate the Lempicka. And then threw a bomb. "Do you think about those three men still alive?"

I was speechless.

"In my nightmares I don't dream about what happened; I dream about revenge; about what I will do to them," she said, and began to cry. "It's horrible and each night I want to make it worse for them."

+

"Just fourteen, Bombelli. Her parents are murdered in front of her, she ends up living with an old man through no fault of hers, and dreams of revenge . . . " the old man broke off as he saw Bombelli eyeing the staircase. "You want to see upstairs? Go ahead," he said and while Bombelli went up he started to clear away the wine glasses and the remainder of the cheese. It was a moment before he distinctly heard Bombelli gasp.

+

I, Bombelli, gasped in awe. A masterpiece. I had no idea what I expected to see climbing the staircase to the bedroom but I did not expect to see the full length portrait of a girl looking at me as I came into the room. She was life-size, wearing a faded blue kaftan with a turquoise-green and coral necklace, a long stick held in her right hand. She was standing on a rock in a field on the ridge of a hill surrounded by a herd of goats and sheep, in the far distance the sea, the sea a teal-blue and this same colour extended into the rock, the whole dividing the picture, making a horizon with a sky painted a uniform turquoise-blue. The figure was strangely backlit as if the sun was setting behind her but no shadow was cast in front of her. Her abundant golden hair, blown by the wind, with a nod in the direction of Botticelli's 'Venus', outlined her torso, with her left hand pushing back strands from her forehead. The head, on the strong pillar of her neck, was turned a few degrees away but the eyes of a startling cornflower blue looked back with a distinct sense of humour. I sat down on the foot of one of the twin beds facing the painting and did not hear the old man come up the stairs into the room behind me.

"She would never let me paint her while she was alive," he said. "But I had all those sketches and with their help I did it from memory."

A pause.

I was at a loss of what to say and went to get up.

"No. No. It's alright, sit," the old man said.

"Sorry. I am overwhelmed. It's a wonderful painting. She seems to be in the room with us," I finally said.

"What makes you think she isn't?"

"Pardon? . . . "

"As long as I am alive and remember her, she lives, Bombelli."

Another, longer, pause.

"When I'm dead and forgotten my memory of her will still be there living in that picture." The old man nodded, then made a curious gesture pressing his palms together in front of his lips and bowing his head to the painting.

"It's why I made it," he said.

I looked about the room which had a most curious arrangement. Large windows faced the four cardinal points of the compass, with the two beds in the middle. Suspended from the ceiling of what was a circular chamber, squaring the compass in fact, were thick poles of golden bamboo that at a distance framed the beds and accentuated the direction in which they were oriented. An astonishing array of dozens of colourful dresses on hangers hung down from the bamboo such that they both curtained the beds and channelled the view towards the windows and the painting. There was a faint, ambiguous odour I could not quite identify. The smell of the sea and something . . .

"The scent?"

"Mine; patchouli. It lingers on stuff."

I again gazed at the painting, drinking it in through my eyes, trying to understand.

"She appears to be enjoying herself," I said.

"Oh, she is. She's laughing at us. Take a good look, Bombelli. How could you possibly believe she would kill herself?" he said. "Anyway, what was so important you had to tell me in private?"

"Our snitches tell us there is rumour of a coup. Something will be done to stop my investigation."

"By the mob or the politicians?"

"I don't know. Maybe both. I didn't want to say it outside in front of my men, you understand. They work under enough strain as it is."

"What will you do?"

"Carry on. With the focus on the parents. Circumstantial evidence being what it is, since there are no witnesses to whatever happened to Sofia, in practical terms there is little the law can do. I am sorry to tell you this, Signore, but it is best to be truthful. A terrible crime was committed here; what we think we know points at the only possible culprit whom I promise to pursue. But to nail the bastard I need you. Alive, if possible. And, as long as it takes, I need you to be patient. What was done was terrible. I cannot imagine your pain."

"No, you can't. There is not a day that passes that I think of all the things I should have done, could have done, to make a difference. She filled this place with life, with joy and laughter. I had no idea what a bleak miserable existence I was living until she came along. She changed my life. From being a miserable old sod bent on redemption for what I perceived were my sins, she showed me how to face tragedy by living life at what she called full tilt boogie. It's ironic, isn't it, even if it is self-evident, that you miss someone the most when they are no longer there. You walk off one morning to do the shopping and when you come home they're gone. Your whole world has collapsed. They say time heals but that's wrong. If anything it is the opposite. You have no idea how much I miss her." He turned away. "Now please forgive me, I am tired and it is time for my siesta. I know who did it and so do you. But if there were no witnesses and the law cannot take its course, what justice can there be?" Here he paused, then added, "The one thing you haven't asked yourself is this - if I had never met you, if you were not here investigating this case, do you really think that I would stand by and do nothing?"

On this note the Magistrate left, carrying with him not just the questions but also an image of the painting and of the tears he saw welling up in the old man's eyes as he turned away . . . and . . . And . . . dreams of revenge.' Like the scent, an echo.

The echo of what the old man said lingers on long after he has made his siesta-time an excuse to break off their talk. There is an intangible something nagging at the Magistrate - Sofia's words - and it is only after he has gathered up his driver and guards and they have started on the drive back and he has made the driver stop on the slope behind the hill at the first gear change, gotten out of the car to look back down the slope, made the driver turn around, switch the engine off, put the car in neutral and coast silently back down the slope to within 50 metres of the tower, waited to see if the sound of their return brought the old man out of his bed, and when it didn't, turned the car and was halfway to his home that a synapse closed, the thought stuck: two witnesses!

Of course! There had always been two, the old man and the child. You forget the child, until the child grows up. And remembers. No, forget remembers - never forgets. Has thoughts of revenge. And is killed.

Murdered!

One witness. Left.

The old man.

Which is when his mind makes an extraordinary leap. What was it his wife had said? 'She looked so sad.' Lividiani's wife. In the church...

She knew what happened to Sofia!

CHAPTER TWENTY-FOUR

The famed domed ceiling of the Archbishop's dining room was so high above the black-and-white chequered marble floor that it was doubtful anybody had been up there to clean it since the scaffolding, erected two hundred years previously, was removed upon completion of the frescoes. Smoke, rising from thousands of candles and countless wood fires which had illuminated and warmed this huge space over the centuries, had left a dark patina of neglect, hiding the nymphs and cherubs camboling in a cerulean blue sky from the four diners seated below at a long rectangular marble table. The young priest was not sure why his Bishop had insisted he come to sit silently through an elaborate meal orchestrated and commentated by their host, the Archbishop of Palermo, for the benefit of his principal guest, a visiting Cardinal from Rome, handsome in his red cassock.

"If it pleases Your Eminence, this fagioli all'uccelletto follows a family recipe from my home in Umbria."

"Ah, the farm where you were brought up?"

"Born and brought up, Sua Eminenza, and proud of the fact if I may be permitted?"

"Surely not in a manger?" The Cardinal's Italian was perfect even though he hailed from Toronto.

"Signor Cardinale, I would never be so presumptuous to suggest . . . "

"Eccellenza, a small joke, se sono permesso - if I am permitted?"

"Scuzi, Most Reverend Eminence, a joke, of course." The Archbishop's bleak smile hardly hid the thought: fucking foreigner. "So, to prepare the cannellini and beans, they must be soaked in cold water overnight."

"Really?"

"In the morning they must be drained, then combined with olive oil and fresh sage leaves, put in a pan and covered in cold water by five centimetres at least."

"Exactly five?"

"No salt."

"No salt?"

"No, none. It would toughen the beans. The pan must be covered and goes in the oven at a moderate temperature until most of the liquid is absorbed, say one and a half hours."

"So long?"

"During this time you prepare and peel garlic and two large ripe tomatoes, seeded and chopped - they come from our garden here in the town."

"Molto alla moda."

"Take a few more fresh sage leaves and gently sauté them with the garlic in olive oil for two minutes . . . "

"Two minutes."

". . . add them to the beans; then add the tomatoes, some salt to taste and cook for ten minutes, being careful not to brown them. Ecco!" With a good natured flourish, the Archbishop waved an episcopal hand at this modest dish. "Buon appetito!"

Thus encouraged they tucked in and it was indeed excellent fare, as were all the subsequent courses, each accompanied by a gustatory explanation washed down fortuitously by appropriate wines from the cellars beneath the Archbishop's Palace, served by novices overseen by a stern major d'uomo. Satisfied, with dusk darkening the little light coming through the tall curtained windows which gave onto the Cathedral, the Cardinal pushed back his chair, stood up, stretched his back, and, making the sign of the Cross, said, "Blessed be The Lord for his bounty to us his humble servants. Amen."

"Amen," the three prelates echoed in unison.

"Now, to business. Father," the Cardinal said to the young priest, "be so kind as to usher them out -" a glance indicated the novices and their master clearing up the last plates - "close the door and station yourself outside that none may hear what we have to discuss."

This done, he resumed his seat at the head of the table and, all joviality set aside, said to the Archbishop, "I have read your letter. It is most disquieting. You allude to an overheard conversation of someone's confession to a beastly crime implicating a major contributor to the finances of our Holy Catholic Church, this man, Lividiani, the cripple."

"Yes."

"You are sure of your facts? This is a heinous charge if true and for the Church to be impugned, even by innocent association, will give our enemies the ammunition they seek to condemn us."

"If I may?" said the Bishop to the Archbishop, who nodded. "As we know them, the facts are these: The woman, whose husband worked for Lividiani as his bodyguard, sought absolution from our brother outside that door for not informing the authorities two years ago of a crime he told her he confessed to in the Duomo in Syracuse."

"What are the details of this so-called crime?"

"We do not know exactly as there are no living witnesses, and short of questioning Lividiani and of him confessing to what he did -"

"Which is not going to happen."

"—which is not going to happen, other than her word, we only have the following circumstantial evidence: one, a report from our informant inside the Camorra in Naples of the safe return of a hit squad contracted he believes by Lividiani to eliminate two of his own men, one of them the husband of this woman; two, a copy from our agent in the telephone exchange of a recording of what is believed to be the voice of the capofamiglia, the Godfather himself, giving information to the Investigating Magistrate Bombelli, condemning Lividiani for what he did as unacceptable to their codice di condotta professionale, he actually used that term 'code of professional conduct' -"

"Unbelievable."

"—yes, unbelievable. Three, and I must qualify this as a deduction we have made to what they regard as unacceptable in their so-called code, according to this capo di tutti capi twelve years ago Lividiani murdered a couple. Their daughter, their only child, who witnessed the crime, was spared by Lividiani, who allowed an old man, a neighbour of the murdered couple, to care for and adopt the child. By doing so, according to their code, Lividiani implicitly protected her and him from all harm exactly as if they were members of his own family. The child grows, becomes a young woman, a beautiful young woman we are told, and, supposedly still a virgin, just shy of her eighteenth birthday, for reasons we do not know, Lividiani orders his two bodyguards to hunt her down and help him violate her. In the ensuing struggle she supposedly got away from them and jumped to her death when they tried to prevent her escape. The coroner has reported her death as a suicide. Afterwards, inevitably, the two bodyguards could not resist discussing this at home. Rumours regarding them began circulating. This is what the husband told his wife he confessed in church."

"May God have mercy on the soul of that innocent girl!" The Cardinal's face was taut white in anger. "And God damn this mafia to hell! How can we accept money, MONEY!, from such vermin?"

The Bishop and Archbishop sit silent; they know and they know the Cardinal knows of the Church's desperate need for funds. The three men confront la vita e destino, life and fate, impenetrable, implacable, inequitable. The silence that followed was long, then, finally, the Cardinal said, "What of this old man? Where was he?"

CHAPTER TWENTY-FIVE

The old man walked up the street towards the Magistrate's driver and guards who stood quietly talking and smoking in a group outside the schoolhouse. Theirs was the usual talk of men of a breed, lean men, over-familiar with one another; talk of the peccadillos of family life, being away from home, the outlook for favourite soccer clubs, the aspirations of men whose duty required them to accept long hours, poor pay and the stressful obligation, like animals in the wild, to always be alert. In chorus they greeted the old man, "Buon giorno", and each man shook his hand and watched him go inside.

"Povero stronzo," Gianni, the driver, said. "Talk about a walking target. Fuck if I'd hang about." Gianni was forty-seven and longed for the day he could retire to Ostia where his family had an ice cream concession on the beach, the kids could play and he could watch the girls in bikinis.

"He doesn't act scared, I'll give him that," said Luca, recently married, one child already and another on the way.

"Why should he be," said Luigi, putting down his machine-gun to light another cigarette. "He was a front-line soldier."

"So?"

"You ever ask yourself the essential quality of a front-line soldier? What they are all taught and trained to do? I'll tell you - to kill. They're all killers."

"So what. The guy must be nearly eighty."

"Yeah? You know many eighty year-olds still walk like that? Have you noticed, not a sound, like he's gliding, doing thirty kilos a day the way you and I would go down the street to buy a sigaretta. I think he's more fit than any of us."

"Won't stop a bullet."

"C'mon, knock it off. It's all speculative bullshit," said Giorgio, who had just received a letter from his bank that morning, refusing to extend his mortgage, included in another from his wife complaining about it.

"What's got into you?" said Gianni. "You're pissed because none of us caught him playing the Magistrate's game?"

"Fuck you."

Little did they realise this was the first sign of their undermining, that from that moment, invisibly, began the decline of their own vigilance.

†

INVESTIGATING MAGISTRATE: Off the record. I am sorry to inform you that I am called away to a meeting in Palermo and we must postpone our audition.

WITNESS: There is a problem? Is this part of the coup?

I.M.: No. I don't think so. Just some busybodies from the Consiglio Superiore della Magistratura, the CSM; in theory they are supposed to protect our independence, but they usually only show up if someone complains.

W: And somebody has?

I.M.: Yes. A Cardinal from Rome. The Church trumps the State; I am sorry but I must go. Before I do, my wife is wondering if you care to dine with us

again so you can finish telling her who killed Mlle. Fifine?

†

The conference in Palermo with the CSM was held in the Fountain Room of the Castello della Zisa, a 12th-century palace on the Via Guglielmo il Buono. Despite renovation work going on to restore the northern wall of the castle, this location was chosen as being smaller and more discreet than the Norman Palace where the Sicilian Regional

Assembly met and where crowds of tourists gathered daily to view the Palatine Chapel. However modest in scale, the Fountain Room, 700-years old, two stories high, elaborately embellished by Arabian craftsmen, was a perfect foil for the Cardinal, dressed in a cassock, black with scarlet piping, silk stitching and scarlet buttons defining the robe, a black, scarlet-lined cape on his shoulders and a broad silk scarlet sash about his waist, a gold pectoral cross on a gold chain, with a scarlet zucchetto on the back of his head. He chaired the meeting and, after perfunctory prayers, stated its purpose: "We are gathered here in confidence, a small committee, to ascertain such facts as we can in the matter and manner of the death of a young girl. You, Signor Presidente della Corte," and here he addressed the Magistrate formally, "you, I believe, have been conducting an investigation that could perhaps shed light on this for us?"

The Cardinal was fully aware of the imposition he was placing on the Magistrate and had deliberately kept his audience reduced to its smallest practical number to restrict the possibility of the slightest information of what was being discussed seeping out to the general public. Only the key prelates of the diocese and the CSM were present, just 9 in number, including himself, the Metropolitan Archbishop, the diocesan Bishop and his Vicar General, his Judicial Vicar, his Chancellor, the Prosecutor General of the CSM and a togate Judge from the same body, and, causa est omnium - the cause of it all - the young priest.

They all perfectly understood the meaning of the words 'in confidence', thought the Magistrate. He, the Cardinal, had come with a full team to cover every base, legal, liturgical, financial, ecclesiastical, and God forbid any of them should speak out of turn. They were there to observe, not to comment. And I am here alone.

"Your Eminence, it is true that I am conducting an enquiry," the Magistrate said, "and her death is part of my investigation, which is ongoing, that I can tell you. Unfortunately, by law, I cannot share any details with Your Eminence of where I am, where I am going, who does or does not interest me or the conclusions I have reached, if any."

"Your position does not help us," said the Cardinal.

"Yes, Your Eminence. It is regrettable." And thought to himself, your move.

Unfazed, the Cardinal turned to the togate Judge of the CSM, "Excellence, may we have your view?"

The Judge had not climbed to the rank he held by being naive, or by an inability to adapt. He was a veteran of many campaigns designed to finesse the powers constitutionally given to his organisation and had refined a manner of calm placidity designed to avoid confrontation or threats. He admired the subtlety of the Cardinal's mind, knowing, before he asked, that the Magistrate would refuse his request, would be obliged to refuse his request, and with a polite pirouette, put the onus on the CSM to enforce obedience. Start slowly with a bit of history, he thought.

"Your Eminence is aware that Sicily is considered to be a disadvantaged location by the Judicial Office. Fully 50% of staff positions here are unfilled, due in no small part to the activities of organised crime. Courageously, the Judge Magistrate has volunteered to this post. He has our confidence and support. He has full autonomy to conduct his enquiry as he sees fit, guaranteed to him by Article 101.2 of the Constitution."

Here we go, thought the Cardinal.

"But surely, as I understand the reading of it, according to Article 134 of the Constitution, you have the power to adjudicate a conflict of interests?" he said.

"134, and I quote," said the togate Judge, adjusting his soutane as if it was a real toga and he in the Roman Senate defending a client before Caesar, 'relates to controversies on the constitutional legitimacy of laws issued by the State'. Surely Your Eminence is not suggesting that by adhering to the law the Magistrate is conducting an illegitimate enquiry?"

Check, thought Bombelli, somewhat surprised that the Judge was going in to bat for him.

"Of course not," said the Cardinal, "but 101 allows you to make requests. I am suggesting that as an adjudicator it would be uncontroversial and perfectly legitimate for you to request your Judge Magistrate to share the information he has with us today in the confines of this closed forum."

Nice move, thought Bombelli.

"Notwithstanding the powers and functions we have," said the Judge, "there is a constitutional boundary that limits our competence to 'request'.

It is enshrined in the phrase that guarantees the independence of judges from all other powers saying they 'are subject *only* to the law.'

Mate, thought Bombelli.

At which point the Cardinal changed the game. "If he cannot share with us, we can share with him. This is what we know . . . "

+

In his car that evening, being driven home, the Magistrate was lost in thought. Little had been gained by the meeting, though it was useful to confirm the rumour about the hit squad from Naples; worrisome, but not surprising, the Church had infiltrated the telephone company; surprising, but not of his concern, that they anguished over the role of the young priest in re-telling what the woman had told him her husband supposedly confessed in church and . . . when the machine-gun bullets ripped into the car he felt momentarily distracted before diving to the floor.

+

Arriving promptly for his dinner invitation, the old man paused outside the front door of the Magistrate's house to take in the cops, the shot-up car and a mechanic examining the damage. Then he knocked. Senora Bombelli answered the door wearing a flour-stained apron and a strained smile.

"Welcome," she said. "I am so glad you could come. He'll be down in a minute. Come, sit, have a drink. I need one even if you don't."

They went into the kitchen and the evocative smell of spezzatino di vitello, which was nearly ready having already cooked for hours on a low fire.

"Let me guess," said the old man by way of diversion, lifting the lid of the large pot bubbling gently on the stove and sniffing an uprise of scented vapour while peering in at the contents. "I see diced carrots and celery and tomatoes, chopped shallots, a couple of bay leaves, what looks like lemon peel..?" Senora Bombelli nodded, more than willing to play along " . . . and fresh rosemary..? Another nod as she sipped her wine. " . . . and, veal cubes in a broth of chicken with a little flour? Olive oil. White wine?"

"Dry white wine; some salt and pepper. Bravo. Fifteen minutes more and it should be done. Now, while we wait, tell me about Madame Lucette, the concierge, and Mlle. Fifine. How does it end?"

"Ah, yes," said the old man, " where were we?"

"The tea cup and M. le Comte."

+

'Through the little window in my door,' said Madame Lucette, 'I saw his butler, always stinking up the place with his fags, sneak out to bury something in the flooded garden, glass by the sound of it. But the man is careless. While others speculate, I know his prints are on the cup - doesn't mean he killed her of course, but still. Next morning, the clouds roll away, the sun comes out and Paris is itself again. The papers now report the cops are looking for the driver of an abandoned Fiat found in the Bois. An elderly couple out for a stroll after lunch saw a cat locked inside. Connecting the dotted lines, the cops make enquiries which seem to be innocent but lead to a large office owned by an eccentric woman in the 16th, a curious combination art gallery-cum-fashion-house-cum-property company. Very odd. She owns the freehold on these buildings. "What do you want?" she says to the cops.*

"We are the police, Madame. It is about a murder in a property you own."

"You think I kill my tenants? I need them to pay rent, not get killed."

"Do you own a Fiat?"

"Yes. It's missing. Have you found it?"

"When did you last see the car?"

"I lent it to a friend. He said it had been stolen."

"Did you report the theft?"

"No. I assumed he did."

"And who is 'he'?"

"That chess player - the Grandmaster. You know?"

"No."

"Damn. His name is on the tip of my tongue. Chantal?"

Chantal is her personal assistant. She says, "Oui, Madame?"

"Tell the Inspector who that man is."*

185

"I'm sorry, Madame, which man?"

"You know, the one who plays chess."

"Do you mean . . ?"

"Of course. Excuse me, Inspector. I am very busy. Chantal will help you. Au revoir."

"How may I help you, Inspector?" Chantal says.

"You are . . ?"

"Madame's personal assistant."

"So, do you have the name?"

"I think she means Ivanov."

"The Ivanov?"

"Yes. Grandmaster Ivanov."

"But surely he's dead?"

"That I don't know."

"How could she lend a car to a dead man?"

"You don't know Madame."

Which is when Bombelli comes into the kitchen his hair still wet from the shower. "I could hear you laughing upstairs," he says to his wife.

"Better than getting shot at," she says. "Don't interrupt. It's about Fifine. We have a suspect, Grandmaster Ivanov, but he may be dead. Go on," she says to the old man.

'Ivanov has invited himself to a country house in Provence,' said Madame Lucette, 'hidden in a forest of umbrella pines a hundred meters from a sandy beach. He gets a joyous welcome from his friends and can't help noticing the two or three pretty houseguests giving him the eye. Lovely country walks keep him busy between flirting with the ladies and dallying over long, lazy afternoons full of good food and better wine, while the splendid skies of the Midi inspire his painterly instincts to the point he forgets what he has done in Paris while lounging on a yacht of classical proportions and immaculate trim. But suddenly, inexplicably, he feels homesick and decides to send a postcard. To me. Listen. Chère Madame Lucette, juste un petit mot pour dire bonjour. I know you hate your job. Hand in your notice and join me here. Signed, Ton Ami. It's tempting of course, a life by the sea, with a friendly sun to warm my bones instead of sitting in the pissing rain. But how could he be so stupid? If the world thinks

you are dead you do not send postcards from the grave. Stupid. Does he really think his dreamy life on the Côte d'Azur is going to stop me going to the cops. Besides I liked Mlle. Fifine. So I'm sending this answer - Sadly, M. Ivanov, thank you for the offer, but I must say . . . NO!'

+

Pause.

"And then . . . ?" said Senora Bombelli.

"That's it," the old man said.

"That's it?" said Bombelli.

"I love Madame Lucette," said Senora Bombelli.

"She got me a job as Father Christmas one year in the Galeries Lafayette. Good money until some kid sitting on my knee said the Father Christmas at Printemps was better and spat in my face. I clouted him over the ear and got fired."

For a long moment the Bombellis just stared at him. Then the Magistrate clapped the old man on the back. "Let's eat," he said.

Garnished with grated lemon zest and chopped parsley, the stew was eaten slowly with orzo al dente and the wine drunk with respect. As the meal progressed a sombre mood settled on the diners. Nobody mentioned the attempted hit, as if to acknowledge the danger and escape would somehow pollute the evening. But there were no more stories, their conversation was brittle, eyes sliding away from the unsaid, the unsayable, and it was with mutual relief that they agreed it was getting late and the old man stood to say goodnight.

"Before you go," said Bombelli, "I have a request. I need you to show me where you buried the Batisteros."

"I told you, it's near the spring on their farm which now belongs to Lividiani. How will you get in? He's closed the right of way, fenced off the whole area with barbed wire."

"Not to worry. I have a court order to exhume the bodies. There's nothing he can do."

+

Late in a sleepless night, Bombelli sat up and switched on the lamp on his side of the bed.

"Cara," he said, "if we can't sleep and just toss and turn, let's talk this out."

"What's there to talk about? You said it, you were lucky." His wife lay facing away from him."

"I was." Then he thought of his men. "Well, we were. Lucky. They fired over fifty rounds and hit nobody."

"Are you boasting?" His wife turned to look at him.

"They're idiots firing a machine-pistol from a motorbike. I'm amazed they even hit the car, leave alone making a hole in it."

"Ci fai o ci sei - are you out of your mind, Bombelli!" His wife sat up. "How many times do I have to go through this? Your car's a wreck, the windshield is blown out, the tires are shredded, and it's a miracle the petrol tank didn't blow up. What's the matter with you? Just because it's armour-plated? I'm terrified and you come home talking about luck. Don't you get it? When will you listen? How often do you have to hear it: you have to be lucky all the time, they only have to be lucky once! I'm frightened! Scared! I jump at every sound. I can hardly breathe thinking about it. I don't want you to die!" She had no idea her voice had ridden up into a shriek and then she was shaking, sobbing, falling back into the pillows with her husband staring down at her helplessly.

+

The Cardinal took the phone call; it was the Archbishop telling him the Magistrate had requested a transfer back to Rome. His reason? His wife had collapsed in fear. Of what? That he would be killed by the Mafia.

"What would he do in Rome? If they wanted to, they'd kill him there. No, no, we need him where he is," said the Cardinal. "We are sure your Excellence shares our genuine admiration for a most rare, brave, intelligent, incorruptible man. He volunteered to come here; it is his duty to stay. Please convey to him the honour it has been to meet such a devoted public servant and that until his investigation is complete we have to regretfully ask him to delay his return to Rome." Then, after a pause, reverting to the first person singular, and a broad Canadian accent, he said, "I am right in assuming you have only called me after canvassing your brothers and there is no article lurking in the Constitution to allow this man to go home?"

CHAPTER TWENTY-SIX

We knew something was amiss when we saw the Magistrate's new car and the morning paper carried the details of the attack and his fortuitous escape in the kind of exultant prose journalists use to sell bad news. As expected a follow-up story recounted the death of one of the would-be motorcycle assassins and the hunt in the mountains for the other. What was unexpected was the Magistrate coming into Rizzo's to join the old man for coffee one day as if that was his habit. We tried to be quiet to overhear what they were saying but other than a reference to some old film we could not decipher a word. When they left, Rizzo came to me behind the bar, whispered "é cattivo - it's bad" in the conspiratorial tone of an insider with special knowledge.

"Stai attento."

What did he mean, watch yourself? What did he know that we couldn't guess? The opaque, asymmetric war between different factions of the Mafia? Exacerbated by the Magistrate's enquiry? Like a virus in a once healthy body, growing hotter every day, the ever increasing heat inevitably erupts in pustules of angry retaliatory action. For the most part unsanctioned by any of the Families?

I like to think of myself as something of a connoisseur in the matter, an interested bystander to gratuitous violence committed by the unspeakable on the ungodly and good riddance to the lot. The anomaly was Don Angelo Lividiani, he of the cool detachment of a practised undertaker, the careful appraiser of risk, the unpanicked quiet voice of command, the iron fist in the velvet glove ruling over us; what had so unhinged him? But I kept my curiosity to myself, so 'stai attento' to what?

Restless, unable to sleep, Serafina Lividiani was at a window of her apartment on the first floor of the vast mansion her husband called home. Looking down into a shadowed courtyard she acknowledged that despite all the outward appearance of a genteel lifestyle of considerable wealth and comfort to all intents she was a prisoner at the beck and call of a psychopath with no other solution than to accept her fate. She feared for her children, for the day that inevitably would come when they were old enough to understand who their father was and grasp what he did. A profound sense of sadness overwhelmed her. She saw herself when she was 14, with her world about to change though there was no way she could have known it. In bare feet on the cool tiled floor she stands paralysed by her thoughts . . . on a Saturday afternoon she had come home with her mother from a morning spent shopping in Palermo to have lunch with an aging aunt . . . her mind shudders at what lies buried . . . and was surprised to see her father there with a man in a wheelchair. This is Don Angelo, her father said. Don Angelo, this is my daughter, Serafina. I was examined. He nodded. Apparently his wife had recently died. He needed someone to replace her and my father needed money to buy more land. A bargain had been made. Three years later I was just 17 when my parents married me off to him. 17, an innocent raised in a tradition of strict obedience, barely conscious of the ways of the world. He was 30 years older than me and if I'm honest my parents had traded me to a cripple about whose private life they knew nothing. There were certain things he could not do or could only do with help and on our wedding night he said to me come here I have to show you what you must do. He had the softest voice and a lovely smile when he was gentle. He never raised his voice but it was clear that I had to do whatever he told me . . . ho un dolce suggerimento per te, per favore, togliti i vestiti . . . please take off your clothes . . . her mind rocked . . . now, he said, turn around . . . slowly, turn around . . . watching me while he unbuttoned his trousers and took it out and started masturbating with his right hand and said, come, stand here and slid his left hand up between my legs and put his fingers inside . . . 'Vuoi che sia il tuo migliore amico e che ti scopi, che ti tratti bene, te lecchi la fica?' . . . the remembered words hissed through her mind . . . then he said, 'Vieni qui' - come here - 'ora leccalo' - now lick it. 'Leccare mio cazzo . . . lentamente, lentamente . . . slowly, slowly . . . molto lentamente' . . . holding me down by the back of my neck while I knelt in front of him licking . . . and when it had swollen to its full height 'adesso, voglio che tu mi succhi il cazzo'. And . . . I did . . . suck. And when he came he said, 'Ingoialo' - swallow it - and I did.

I hid - I hide - what he made me do in a compartment of my mind locked away. Now yawning open. In the bed, contorted in front of the wheelchair while he made it go backwards and forwards. She desperately tries to shut out the images. Nobody in the outside world can remotely imagine what she has to do while those black impenetrable eyes of his watch, unblinking. No emotion, leave alone words of encouragement or love - or even thanks.

Thank God our bedrooms are separate at each end of this very large house and I am only to go to his room if summoned by him, less since the birth of the children. Sometimes at night looking out of my window I see strange women leaving the house escorted by one of the bodyguards. At breakfast he tells me what he does to them. 'You are my wife. I want there to be no secrets between us. I sometimes feel you do not satisfy me and so I resort to these women. It is of no importance.' Although in my heart I know what he does and what is going on there's no escape so I feign ignorance, particularly at meal times when he says to me, 'What is this? I do not like your melancholic look. You will smile when you greet me and in all ways behave as the mother of my children should be seen to behave, particularly in public.' Said softly. Always this soft voice of his saying the most abominable things and making me obey. Her mind rockets back to the most foul day of her life.

Two years ago. Already two years . . .

She was in the music room watching her children taking their piano lesson when one of the bodyguards came in. He wants you, he said and it was the way he said it, not looking me in the eye, his eyes afraid, looking down, but it was a summons that had to be obeyed and when I turned to leave my daughter, Allegra, said Mammina I want you to listen to me and I said I'll be back in a moment my child, then, walking across the house to his study the bodyguard said, No, Signora, Don Angelo is in his bedroom, and for some reason I thought he must be sick but when I opened the door he was in his wheelchair facing me, masturbating.

Vieni qui, he said. Lick it.

He knew I hated it and to make matters worse he now said, Slowly, lick it slowly and then, just as I did on my wedding night, on my knees, I had to take his swollen member into my mouth and lick and suck it slowly while he caressed my hair and told me a horror story while he pushed my head up-and-down on his hard bloated member.

'I want you to know this my darling, because I want there to be no secrets between us. This morning we caught that bitch as she came out of the water and though she fought like a maniac my men held her and I fucked her with what you now have in your mouth and fucked her and fucked her, and do you know - don't stop, suck - and do you know, she was a virgin and with blood coming out of her cunt, I sodomised her as well and then the men took turns and when we were finished we threw her over the wall down the cliff - no, keep sucking. You will suck until I come and if you repeat any part of this story of what happened to that girl the same will happen to you' Then he came in an endless gushing stream into my mouth and forced me to swallow. She is back in the living hell of that moment, forever defiled.

'And you know,' Lividiani said in his soft voice, 'when I had her, as I fucked her, I knew I was getting what was promised to that old man, your phantom hero wearing your blue shirt - you think for one moment I don't know what's going on in that brainless head of yours? We'll do him when I'm ready.'

Her life eaten with self-loathing, if it wasn't for the children who knows what she might do, and for a second she relived the instant she first saw the old man as he came into the café, stopped sucking to look up, saw Lividiani's face harden and never saw the slap that knocked her off her knees to the floor.

Now, in the turmoil of her thoughts, in front of her window, she raises her hand to her cheek where the memory of that blow is imprinted, to wipe the tears running down her face, not sure if she is crying for Sofia or for herself as a door opens behind her and, unasked, her crippled husband wheels into the room.

"Cosa c'é, mio amore?" says Angelo Lividiani. "Vieni qui. I want you to read this. Bombelli's stenographer brought it to me."

++++

"Ah, Dottore Mazzini, we meet again. Thank you for finding time in your busy schedule to visit me here."

The Magistrate stood up to shake hands with the coroner. "I apologise for our rather unconventional surroundings," he waved a hand at the old schoolroom, "but we must make do with what we have. Please be seated."

Mazzini looked at the school bench to which the Magistrate pointed.

"On that?" he said.

"Yes," Magistrato Bombelli smiled. "It will remind you of when you were a boy. Anyway this won't take long."

The fastidious coroner took a handkerchief from the breast pocket of his immaculate suit and dusted the bench, then sat on it as if unsure it would support his weight.

"Good," Bombelli said. "Let us begin." He nodded, then tapped some files on the desk in front of him. "These are the unredacted original coroner's reports you have sent me relating to a car accident on June 16 of this year. Do you identify them as such?" With his fingertips Bombelli pushed the files a centimetre across his desk in the direction of the coroner. The coroner raised himself a fraction on the school bench, looked down on the files with hooded eyes, shrugged his shoulders, and settled back with a nod.

"Yes," he said.

"You identified the deceased, the date and place of death and the causes and circumstances of death. Yes or no?"

"Yes."

"Thank you. Your report is based on certain appended documents, am I correct?"

"Yes."

"A toxicology report, a medical record and an autopsy report, correct?

"Yes."

"Who conducted the autopsy?"

194

"I did."

"Were you assisted?"

"Of course."

The Magistrate made a note, picked up the report, turned a page and said, "In your report you state, and I quote, a 43-year-old Caucasian, white, male was in a car accident on the road to Catania. He was pronounced dead at the scene of the accident. Were you at the scene?"

"No."

"I see. Who made the report?"

"The police and the firemen called to the scene."

"Thank you. When and where did you see the cadaver?"

"In the morgue."

"How soon after the accident?"

"Three days."

"So this is post rigour?"

"Yes the body had been refrigerated."

"You report heavily charred remains, particularly over the head, moderately over the neck and left side of the body, the left extremities, with postmortem thermal fracturing of the left forearm and left lower leg and foot, and traumatic antemortem fractures of the skull, three vertebrae in the neck, the right arm, right forearm and right femur, hemorrhagic displaced fractures of the right greater horn of the hyoid bone, hemorrhagic fractures of the left and interior third through eighth ribs, anterior lung contusions, no signs of smoke inhalation, massive bilateral bright red traumatic hemothorax, 450cc left 400 cc right, extensive laceration of the parietal pericardium and mediastinal pleura. Avulsion of the base of the heart with complete transverse avulsion of the atria and superior and inferior vena cava. The cadaver is so badly burned it had to be identified by its teeth. Correct?"

"Yes."

"And from these findings you ascribe the death to traumatic injuries, correct?"

"Yes."

"In a like manner and in the same burned-out car a second male Caucasian, aged 48, is pronounced dead with very similar traumatic injuries, correct?"

"Yes."

"You also prepared the autopsy report on this cadaver, correct?"

"Yes."

"In your professional opinion were the postmortem and antemortem fractures consistent with the theory of a car accident?"

"Yes. The car overturns causing the antemortem fractures and when the car burns the heat causes the postmortem fractures."

"The two men are dead prior to the postmortem fractures?"

"Probably given their injuries. It is impossible to say definitively."

"Well let us hope so. In your professional opinion, was there any evidence to suggest foul play?"

"None."

"Even though the police in their report state the car was not in an accident?"

"The cops are not always right. The car did not turn itself over."

"Precisely. As a matter of procedure, if you were not at the morgue when the deceased were brought in, who received them?"

"My assistant."

"Who does what exactly?"

"He labels the bodies if the identity is known, photographs them front and back, undresses them, takes more pictures of the naked corpses and any apparent injuries, washes them and puts them in the freezer -"

"Even if they're charred beyond recognition?"

"Charred meat keeps just as well as fresh."

"I see. You are a man of considerable experience. As an expert traumatologist I imagine you have seen just about every kind of injury. Now, I have here another unredacted original copy of another autopsy you made two years ago in 1971 on the death of a young female, Sofia Belanopek, née Batistero. It was found fortuitously in the files of your assistant. It is signed and

dated by you." The Magistrate, face blank, voice neutral, looked at the coroner. "Please confirm your signature and that this is your report."

For a moment the coroner hesitated.

"Yes or no?"

Reluctantly the coroner said, "Yes." Then added, "We've been over this before."

"And we will go over it again. Please speak up. The stenographer needs to hear you. Thank you" The Magistrate opened the report. "You identified the deceased, I quote, as a 'white, Caucasian female, 17 years old, a virgin, weight 54 Kgs, height 1m75cms.' Correct?"

"Yes."

"You performed an autopsy on the deceased. Correct?"

"Yes."

"You have calculated that the velocity on impact of a body falling unimpeded onto a granite ledge from 50 metres would be circa 112 kilometres per hour and that death would be instantaneous. Correct?"

"Yes."

"You are sure?"

"Yes. A falling body accelerates constantly at 32 ft./s per second. It is 50 metres down to that granite ledge. After one second it is travelling at 19 km an hour. After two seconds it is travelling at nearly 70 km an hour. After 3.19 seconds, travelling now at 112.70 km an hour, it hits the granite ledge. The energy at impact: 26,460 joules."

"Remarkable. I am impressed by the professionalism of your report."

The coroner shrugged aside the compliment. "It is what we do," he said, then added, "I've already told you the terminal velocity on impact ruptured all the internal organs. It would be worse than getting hit by a car going that fast."

"Yes, I see. You state that the ilium, ischium and pubis of the acetabulum on the left outer surface of the hip bone was shattered by the impact, with multiple complex fractures. Correct?"

"Yes."

"You detail concomitant spinal injuries, significant thoracolumbar fractures, disc herniation, compressed and bursting vertebrae, injury to the

osseous pelvic ring and the thorax and chain fractures of the left leg, ankle and foot consistent with a high velocity fall. Correct?"

"Yes."

"Further, you detail multiple open fractures in the left forearm, distal radius and ulna and severe compound fractures of the skull with lacerations tearing the epidermis and the meninges and depressed bone fragments in the brain. You write that the body position at impact is crucial and posit that in this case the victim landed at an oblique angle on her left side. Correct?"

"Yes."

"A blood sample was taken for toxicological examination for drugs or alcohol concentrations. None was found. And there was no sign of menstruation. Correct?

"Yes."

"In your professional opinion was there any evidence to suggest foul play?"

The coroner hesitated again, then said, "None."

"None? I see. You would not like to reconsider your opinion?"

Silence.

"No?" The Magistrate makes a note. "Now, under Cause of Death you have written 'Suicide'. Correct?"

"Yes."

"How did you ascertain that she committed suicide?"

"Her body was found on that ledge half way down the cliff."

"Found by whom? By you?"

"No."

"Did you see the body on the ledge?"

"No."

"Did you see a photograph of the body on the ledge?"

"No."

"A drawing, a sketch, a diagram?"

"No."

"And yet you concluded she committed suicide? Why?"

"How else to explain how she got there?"

"She could have fallen?"

"It is possible. Unlikely but possible. Apparently she habitually climbed up and down that cliff face for years."

"Where did you first see the body?"

"In the morgue."

"Did you receive the body in the morgue?"

"No."

"Who did?"

"My assistant."

"Is this your modus operandi? Your assistant always receives the cadavers brought in?"

"If I am not available, yes."

"And I suppose this assistant then performed the same duties as you have already described for the cadavers in the car crash?"

"Yes."

"He took these photographs?" The Magistrate extracted a sheaf of photographs from the report he held in his hand and spread them across the desk. In stark anatomical detail they showed the severely mutilated body of a naked young female.

The coroner barely glanced at the pictures, shrugged and said, "Yes."

"Following his usual routine?"

"Yes."

"These are all his photographs?"

"Yes."

"Why are there no pictures of her clothed?"

"The cadaver was delivered to the morgue nude."

"By whom?"

"An old man in a van driven by Rizzo the innkeeper and a couple of carabiniere - so I am told. I was not there. I did not interview them."

"Who did?"

"My assistant."

"I see. Was it your assistant who supplied you her name and her age?"

"Yes. I mean no. He got them from the report made by the carabiniere."

"Which of these pictures were taken before your assistant washed the corpse?"

Silence.

"I have taken the liberty of having certain details in several of these photographs enlarged. I draw your attention to this picture. How do you explain the grab marks and bruising on the inner surface of the victim's upper arms?"

Silence.

"In this picture of the victim's right hand how do you explain the torn fingernails?"

Silence.

"This is a picture of the victim's anus. How do you explain the tearing of the fascia and sphincter and the perianal skin?"

Silence..

"This is a picture of the victim's vagina. How do you explain the torn vulva?"

Silence.

"Why is there no mention made in your otherwise exceptionally detailed report of any one of these injuries?"

Silence.

"Did you or your assistant examine the vaginal tract of the victim all of whose internal organs you say were ruptured by hitting a granite ledge at 112 kilometres an hour?"

Silence.

"If you did not, how can you ascertain there was no sign of menstruation?"
Silence.

"Or state she was a virgin?"

Silence.

The Magistrate made a note, looked up at the coroner, said, "I am waiting?"

Silence.

The Magistrate made another note. "Who concluded she committed suicide, you or your assistant?"

Silence.

The Magistrate sat back, steepled his fingers, and looked at the coroner. "One way or the other you will answer my questions. In the privacy of this room or in open court. Your choice?"

Silence. A long drawn out silence. Finally . . .

"If I were you," the Magistrate said, "as I've told you before, I would be fearful. Angelo Lividiani, as I am sure you know, will find out you were here being questioned by me. He will realise the implications and understand the consequence of your silence. Good day to you, Signore. Thank you for coming."

+

While she read her husband circled her in his wheelchair, the only noise the whisper the wheels made on the polished stone floor. When she had finished reading, Serafina was trembling. She looked up.

Her husband smiled. "You see, I take you into my confidence so that there are no secrets between us. You will invite the coroner, Dr. Mazzini, and his assistant to our Easter party, yes. I have some words of advice for them. Bene." He unbuttoned his trousers, took it out.

"Vieni qui," he said. "Down on your knees. Ora leccalo - now lick it."

+

"Thank you for coming. I know how unpleasant this must be for you." Standing next to the dried up spring in the shadow of the outbuilding on what had once been Batistero's farm the Magistrate greeted the old man as he came walking around the corner. "No problem with the fence?"

"Who cut the wire?"

"They did." With his chin Bombelli indicated two armed men standing ten metres away. "More of Lividiani's sicari."

"You're not scared? Where are your carabiniere?"

Bombelli spat on the ground. "This is official. Nothing is going to happen in broad daylight. Lividiani, l'uomo d'affari, was here personally to give orders, make sure we had everything we needed. Bastard even invited me to his Easter party. He was smiling when he drove off. Okay, Let's get on with it."

"They're over there," the old man said and pointed to two slight mounds each with a small cairn of stones at one end. "I see you've brought some help." He nodded greeting to a crew of four men with pickaxes and shovels. "The bodies are buried about two metres down."

The men got to work. The ground was hard and the day hot. Bombelli and the old man stood side by side in silence, watching as the hole grew deeper.

Eventually Bombelli said, "The bodyguard's wife gave us the lupara he used. Ballistics think they will be able to match whatever we find after an autopsy."

"After twelve years? What do you expect to find? They'll just be skeletons," the old man said. And remembered.

Another grave. Another place. Another day.

The priest who had come to the olive grove on the hill.

Said a few words as the coffin was lowered into the ground.

'Terra alla terra, cenere alla cenere, polvere alla polvere.'

Stood back as each of them in turn took up a shovel.

Rizzo, the schoolteacher, Paoli, his wife, his daughter. Matteo the son, weeping.

And finally himself.

Earth to earth, ashes to ashes, dust to dust. As tradition demanded, to say goodbye, each dropped a shovel load of freshly dug dirt on the coffin in which lay the broken body of his daughter, Sofia. How impossibly long ago it seemed. She had been alive. He looked up at the blue sky. It was so unjust. He bowed his head. And felt Bombelli put his arm around his shoulders. "Coraggio, amico mio," Bombelli said.

An hour later, from the bottom of the hole they had dug, the foreman of the crew wiped the sweat from his brow, stopped his men, looked up at the two men watching and said, "There's nothing here. If this was a grave it's empty now."

✝

INVESTIGATING MAGISTRATE: Devious bastard, no wonder he was smiling.

WITNESS: Robbing graves? What will you do?

I.M.: No. Stealing evidence you mean. There's not much I can do. Goes to show how thorough they are. I know I have told you this before, but please be very careful. Watch yourself out there.

W: With your car shot to pieces I could say the same to you. Could it be part of the coup you mentioned?

I.M.: We got a call. Same voice who tipped us off to Lividiani. He said they were freelancers, trying to show up old timers like himself, that if it had been their hit - arrivederci!

W: Still, your men must be asleep. You want some advice? Swap out your team, maybe they're stale.

I.M.: Despite what I told you, I plan to go ahead and summon Lividiani. I know what he did and how he did it. He will react in one of two ways - deny everything and go to ground or whistle up one of his high-powered lawyers who will claim he can't be reached, perhaps the matter can be discussed. They will do this as a way of testing my patience and continue stalling ad infinitum. Business as usual for him. Which is when I will summon his wife. She can't testify against her husband but it will make him wonder what it is I think she knows. It's the way this game is played.

W: There's a third way - they try to knock you off again.

I.M.: That too. But as long as my stick is stirring up their antheap it's no longer business as usual -" he shrugged, which the stenographer recorded with a little glyph she used to designate gestures.

W: I need to head for the mainland soon. Are we through?

I.M.: Yes, more or less. Leave an address where you can be reached, please.

When - if - we go to trial you will be the prize witness. In the meantime I will miss you. I have enjoyed your stories.

W: As I have our discussions. Watch your back, Magistrato. When I return maybe we will find the time to finish . . .

I.M.: Off the record. Permit me to walk you to the door.

+

Out in the street, the Magistrate took the old man's elbow and steered him away from the schoolhouse. In silence they walked fifty metres. Then, nodding back to the school, the old man said,

"You suspect her?"

"Certo! She's more reliable than the Post Office." He laughed. "I hope what I just said confuses them, but even if they suspect that I know she is the leak, they are left with the problem of what I say and don't say in those documents. I didn't mean to interrupt you just now, but one thing I must stress, we will not talk about your past. If they found out about all the aliases, and what shall we call it - the autobiographical aspect perhaps? - they'd have a field day. Take your lead from me. Like I said, it's all a game. You'll be in Paris, right? Stay in touch. Ciao."

He left the old man there, in the street, and walked back to work. Neither imagined they would never see each other again.

+

It was a small paragraph in the European News section of the Tribune:
THE MAFIA STRIKES BACK - Reuters reports
Naples, December 23, 1973

A senior Sicilian Magistrate, Judge Bombelli, and his wife, on their way home to Rome for the holidays, were severely wounded and are in critical condition when their car exploded on the Autostrada del Sol leaving Naples. It is known Justice Bombelli had been investigating the criminal activities of the Mafia in eastern Sicily. He is the fifth Magistrate to be attacked in the past three years; two have been killed.

The old man finished his breakfast, asked at the reception desk for his bill to be made ready, booked, with the help of the concierge, an Alitalia flight out of Orly to Rome with an onward connection to Naples, checked out of the Hotel Crillon and disappeared.

+

"That old man has been waiting for two days," the nurse said to the supervising surgeon of the Nuovo Ospedale Moderno di Napoli, Cardarelli.

204

"He says he is a friend of the Judge and his wife. He has a message for the Judge."

"Have you told him they are out of danger but due to the severity of their injuries they are being kept in an induced coma to aid their recovery and cannot be visited?"

"Yes, sir. He said, 'Tell the Judge when you wake him up . . . "

"What was the message?"

"He said to say 'Tocca a me.'"

"That's all?"

"Yes, sir. Just those three words - 'it's my turn'. He said the Judge would understand."

CHAPTER TWENTY-SEVEN

For a while it was all we could talk about in Rizzo's. Every sentence seemed to start with 'Remember when . . . '. Days after the attack on Bombelli the schoolhouse burned down. I lived a couple of doors away and smelled the smoke, saw the flames from my window and yelled for my neighbours to help. Somebody called the fire-brigade. We got a bucket chain going to stop the fire spreading, but apart from a few files, everything inside went up. Of course it was arson. The school was never rebuilt; like the ache of a rotten tooth, the burnt shell was there as a reminder that history is written by winners, with Don Angelo riding around as if nothing had happened to make the point.

Given the narrative history of Sicily, invaded successively by the Phoenicians, Carthaginians, Greeks, Romans, Arabs, Byzantines, Spaniards, Normans, the German House of Hohenstaufen, the Holy Roman Emperors, Angevins, Aragonese, Austrians and the Spanish Bourbons, who united Sicily with Naples as the Kingdom of the Two Sicilies, why grumble now if the Mafia ruled? In every case the losers, the conquered, perished in anonymity, their loss, agony and suffering obliterated by the successive monuments built by the victors on the ruins of what went before. I developed this line of reasoning in Rizzo's to the numbed indifference of the gathered intelligentsia until slowly the dull routine of everyday life re-established itself and I went back to making soup with the niggling thought - what monument would the Mafia leave to glorify their regime?

Helping Rizzo lock up one evening I was late getting home. There are no street lamps where I live but I could walk home blindfolded if I had to, the darkness familiar to me. Past the church, where the street turns left, there is a narrow alley the entrance to which is twenty metres from my front door and as I walked past an arm went around my neck and I was dragged into it.

"Don't struggle. I am not going to hurt you. Tell Matteo to meet me where the seats are two thousand years old. He must bring a backpack. Not a word to his father."

My assailant vanished. But not the memory of that voice, the voice of the old storyteller.

+

The appointment was kept. Instructions given. The shepherd's son began a discreet surveillance while supposedly herding his father's flock of sheep and goats, as anonymous in the surrounding landscape as the withered olive trees. Occasionally he would put down his backpack behind a stone wall and retrieve it the following day. It was always heavier. He never looked inside to see why and would carry it to another location where again he would leave it overnight. It would be empty the following morning. In his mind he was doing it for Sofia. His father never questioned why his son had abandoned the police academy, secretly pleased that the boy would follow in his footsteps, but he questioned why the lad thought there was better grazing to be found around Nicolazzo.

One day Serafina Lividiani and her children on their way home by car found the street blocked by a flock of sheep and goats. The children were delighted and wound the window down to get a closer look while their two bodyguards shouted at the embarrassed young shepherd. "Scuzi, Signora, scuzi," he apologised, "perdonami." And through the open window gave Serafina a gift of a round of goat cheese carefully wrapped with paper and twine. "Per i bambini," he said. "Un regalo del vecchio."

The last words said so quietly only she heard them. A present from the old man?

As they drove forward she distinctly saw the boy mouth the word 'leggere'. Leggere? Read. What? And felt the paper wrapping the cheese.

+

From where he lay motionless in his ghillie suit 150 metres behind the mafia compound the old man watched the caterers coming and going. Earlier he had seen the wives and children driving out in a cavalcade of cars, ostensibly to be with their grandparents for the Easter festivities, but in fact to clear the way for Lividiani's party for his men and those other men who owed him fealty or were in debt to him. A reward for the faithful, a show of magnanimity to the others, a demonstration of benevolence, disdain for danger and a useful reminder of power. His power. None who had received his invitation would fail to come. It would be a feast to remember, complete with fine food, rare wine and enough hookers to sate the libido of the most priapic guest.

It was hot in the ghillie suit, over 40°, and he had to constantly wipe perspiration from his binoculars. He was in a field, slightly elevated above the compound, surrounded by goats and sheep, some of which nearly stepped on him thinking his camouflage grass woven into the burlap of his suit was something they could eat. They occasionally got into his line of sight but never for long, as they munched their way from tuft to tuft their bells tinkling. Away out on the horizon he could see the boy. Only his dogs knew a man was lying there. They sniffed at him, recognised the smell, and left to go back to chivvying the herd. Left him watching the first guests arrive. Never showing out.

It had taken a few weeks to set up the surveillance, work out the logistics, comprehend the layout of the compound and its security - such as it was. Which was very little, Lividiani evidently feeling safe in his fife as evidenced by the unattentive appearance of a single chain-smoking guard slouched at the gated entrance, an old hunting rifle propped against the wall next to him, whiling away his 8-hour shift by chatting to passersby when he wasn't off taking a piss.

At the centre of the compound was a large fortified manor house built in the style of a late 18th century mansion, with two smaller buildings at right angles to it enclosing a motor court, the whole forming the southern boundary of a small square on the edge of town. At night a few feeble streetlamps came on in the four corners of the square leaving the compound in shadow apart from a single bare bulb at the entrance and such lights as might be seen in those rooms that were occupied. Most nights by midnight all the lights were out, the place asleep, and it had been relatively easy to come across the fields behind the compound, climb over a low perimeter wall and gain entrance to the property. Apart from the guard dozing at the gate there was not even a dog on duty.

Everything the Havildar taught came back to him - Be Calm, Practise, Coordinate, Execute. Carrying the explosives he repeated the mantra again and again. 'Learn this properly, let it be as natural as breathing, and you will be safe," the Havildar had said. He was right. Like riding a bicycle.

+

At 4.16 am, the day before Good Friday, April 11th, 1974, the explosions, at a distance of 44 kilometres, registered on the seismographs used to measure the Richter Scale for volcanic activity by the University of Catania, founded in 1434, the 29th oldest university in the world. The army was called in to cordon off the square in Nicolazzo and identify, if that were possible, what had caused the devastation which razed the fortified compound of Angelo Lividiani and the houses occupied by him and his men. The initial conclusion was that old ordnance, bombs, mines, dynamite, munitions illegally stored in hidden basement areas since the 2nd World War, had decomposed, self-combusted and detonated with such shattering power as to render a search for human life a waste of time.

Observing the scene from behind the tinted windows of a dilapidated Alfa Romeo Giulia Berlina parked 65 metres down the Via Garibaldi, the small grey man in the shabby grey suit, his unshaven face partially concealed by dark glasses, said, "Do you believe it?"

"That there are no survivors? Absolutely," said Dr. Mazzini, the coroner, with some relief not to say satisfaction, seated in the back of the car next to him. "We have positively identified the body parts of twenty-three different individuals but the pieces are so small we cannot say who they are or even if they are male or female. We also have another three possibilities, numerous animal parts . . . "

"Yes, yes. No Lividiani, no Easter party, you're safe now. That's not what I meant. Do you think it was accidental?"

"What else could it be?"

"I'm bothered by the precision. Do you see how each building has collapsed on itself? There's hardly any rubble outside their perimeter. Normally an explosion would go outwards from the epicentre. But look at those buildings across the square, they're hardly touched apart from a few broken windows, caused by concussion no doubt." The small grey man nodded to himself. "Fatto professionalmente - the work of an expert, bank on it." Who it could be he kept to himself. "Andiamo," he said to his driver.

+

Standing in the shadows behind the Pope, while from the window of the Apostolic Palace the Pontiff addressed the multitude assembled below in Piazza San Pietro, the Cardinal re-read the note from the Archbishop and debated whether or not he should attend the funeral. That it would be a grand affair was certain, attended by all the bosses of all the Families bearing elaborate floral tributes (and satchels stuffed full of cash for the Church), as a favourite son was laid to rest. Funny that Lividiani would be more useful dead than alive. If his schedule would allow it, he decided, he would go.

+

We were at once stunned by the news and intoxicated by the whiff of freedom that came from an obscure notion a yolk had been lifted off the bent back of the village. The euphoria lasted less than a week, during which time those in debt to the now departed Zu Angelo could not believe their good fortune. Then Rizzo reported the visit of a young thug called Salvatore accompanied by an accountant and a lawyer from Palermo. Apparently they held 'rights of succession' to Lividiani's estate and had the books and details of all outstanding loans to prove their claim. Plus the guns and muscle to back them up if needed. In short order the yolk was firmly back in place, if anything more demanding and less tolerant than before. In retrospect it was inevitable, Lividiani having never been anywhere near the top of the tree and if we were in thrall to him he in turn was paying 'up the ladder'. So it goes. The seasons change but remain the same.

Stirring the soup, there is one curious detail I forgot to mention, a glimpse caught by Mirella Guglielmo at night, as she disembarked from the evening ferryboat which linked Naples to Messina, of a family of four getting on board for the return trip to the mainland. She was burdened with the various purchases she had made at the monthly Napolitano farmer's market, and the family were moving away from her, but she swore it was the old man with his hair cut short, no bandana, wearing a black shirt, black pants and a black hat pulled down on his brow. It all happened quickly and she could not say who the woman was, but the children were a girl and a small boy.

ACKNOWLEDGMENTS

To the memory of the late Christopher Little, for his insight and tough demands.

To my daughter Pascale, and sons Erik and Alexander, for their support and encouragement - Merci !

To Walt (polarbear19325 @ Fiverr) for the interior design and layout, thank you for your skill and patience in making this book.

A PITCH TO MY READERS

The Murder at Midnight

The theory of the murder at midnight is as follows: M. DuPont, a man out for a late walk with his dog, finds a body in a field, a dagger in its back. Within a minute he rushes home to tell his wife. Within a minute this alarmed lady calls the neighbours, Monsieur and Madame Durand, to warn them.

'Did you call the cops?' Durand says.

'No,' she says.

'Don't worry, I'll do it. I know the Inspector,' he says. And in that same minute his wife is calling her ancient mother in the nursing home where they have placed her to tell her. 'Lock the door to your bedroom.'

Within the next minute the policeman, Inspector Petit, none to pleased at being woken up so late, nevertheless calls the station to tell the duty officer, Sergeant Dubois, to organise an investigation, and Dubois within a minute duly informs the gendarme on the late shift at the gendarmerie, Adjudant Leroy, who, on receiving the call, feels obliged, within the minute, to inform his superior, Adjutant-Chef Moreau, who is in bed with his mistress.

She asks why the fuss? But within the minute it takes her lover to tell her not to worry her pretty head, the old lady in the nursing home has already called the two elderly women either side of her room to tell them to lock their doors.

'There's a murderer outside.'

Within a minute, one of them, Madame Bonpoint, calls the Superintendent, Monsieur Langlois, to complain about the threat and he in turn tells his colleague, Monsieur Ségor, seated next to him at the booking desk, what a pain the old ladies are banging on about murderers next door, which conversation Ségor repeats a minute later to his mother, three times zones away in St.Barth, when he has her on the phone.

Within a minute of hanging up with her son, this worthy calls her daughter, Mathilde, a student at USC Los Angeles, another four time zones away, to tell her to be careful with all these murderers going around, and the two girls who share a dorm in the University with Mathilde, Lucy Lee, from Singapore, and Amy Miyako, from Osaka, overhear the conversation and call their families back home to say there was a murder at midnight and to be careful.

By simple multiplication, with each recipient of this information informing two others within a minute, within 20 minutes 5242 people knew, within 25 minutes 167,772 people knew, within 30 minutes 5,368,709 knew, and a minute later 10,737,418, and 3 minutes later, only 34 minutes after Dupont first saw the body, the entire population of France, all 66 million people, knew there had been a murder at midnight. By 1am all of Europe knew, and by 2am the entire world. The last to know was a tribal chief in New Guinea who heard on the bush telegraph that a man in France had eaten his wife in his own backyard.

The moral of the story is that tiny numbers become very big when multiplied by themselves. So if any one of you has enjoyed reading my novel, told two friends - go buy this book, you will enjoy it - and they in turn told two friends...etc, etc,...we could be cooking up a literary storm by tomorrow morning:)